MIDSUMMER MYSTERIES

ALSO BY AGATHA CHRISTIE

Mysteries
The Man in the Brown Suit
The Secret of Chimneys
The Seven Dials Mystery
The Mysterious Mr Quin
The Sittaford Mystery
The Hound of Death
The Listerdale Mystery
Why Didn't They Ask Evans?
Parker Pyne Investigates
Murder Is Easy
And Then There Were None
Towards Zero
Death Comes as the End
Sparkling Cyanide
Crooked House
They Came to Baghdad
Destination Unknown
Spider's Web *
The Unexpected Guest *
Ordeal by Innocence
The Pale Horse
Endless Night
Passenger To Frankfurt
Problem at Pollensa Bay
While the Light Lasts

Poirot
The Mysterious Affair at Styles
The Murder on the Links
Poirot Investigates
The Murder of Roger Ackroyd
The Big Four
The Mystery of the Blue Train
Black Coffee *
Peril at End House
Lord Edgware Dies
Murder on the Orient Express
Three-Act Tragedy
Death in the Clouds
The ABC Murders
Murder in Mesopotamia
Cards on the Table
Murder in the Mews
Dumb Witness
Death on the Nile
Appointment with Death
Hercule Poirot's Christmas
Sad Cypress
One, Two, Buckle My Shoe
Evil Under the Sun
Five Little Pigs
The Hollow
The Labours of Hercules
Taken at the Flood
Mrs McGinty's Dead
After the Funeral
Hickory Dickory Dock
Dead Man's Folly
Cat Among the Pigeons
The Adventure of the Christmas Pudding
The Clocks
Third Girl
Hallowe'en Party
Elephants Can Remember
Poirot's Early Cases
Curtain: Poirot's Last Case

Marple
The Murder at the Vicarage
The Thirteen Problems
The Body in the Library
The Moving Finger
A Murder Is Announced
They Do It with Mirrors
A Pocket Full of Rye
4.50 from Paddington
The Mirror Crack'd from Side to Side
A Caribbean Mystery
At Bertram's Hotel
Nemesis
Sleeping Murder
Miss Marple's Final Cases

Tommy & Tuppence
The Secret Adversary
Partners in Crime
N or M?
By the Pricking of My Thumbs
Postern of Fate

Published as Mary Westmacott
Giant's Bread
Unfinished Portrait
Absent in the Spring
The Rose and the Yew Tree
A Daughter's a Daughter
The Burden

Memoirs
An Autobiography
Come, Tell Me How You Live
The Grand Tour

Plays and Stories
Akhnaton
The Floating Admiral (contributor)
Hercule Poirot and the Greenshore Folly
Star Over Bethlehem

* novelized by Charles Osborne

AGATHA CHRISTIE

MIDSUMMER MYSTERIES

TALES FROM THE QUEEN OF MYSTERY

WILLIAM MORROW
An Imprint of HarperCollins*Publishers*

For information, address HarperCollins Publishers, 195 Broadway, New York, NY 10007.

HarperCollins books may be purchased for educational, business, or sales promotional use. For information, please email the Special Markets Department at SPsales@harpercollins.com.

FIRST US EDITION

Published in the United Kingdom in 2021 by HarperCollins UK.

First William Morrow paperback published 2023.

Library of Congress Cataloging-in-Publication Data has been applied for.

ISBN 978-0-06-331095-7

23 24 25 26 27 LBC 5 4 3 2 1

CONTENTS

INTRODUCTION

Summer in the Pyrenees

Father and Madge made a good many excursions on horseback, and in answer to my entreaties one day I was told that on the morrow I should be allowed to accompany them. I was thrilled. My mother had a few misgivings, but my father soon overruled them.

"We have a Guide with us," he said, "and he's quite used to children and will see to it that they don't fall off."

The next morning the three horses arrived, and off we went. We zigzagged along up the precipitous paths, and I enjoyed myself enormously perched on top of what seemed to me an immense horse. The Guide led it up, and occasionally picking little bunches of flowers, handed them to me to stick in my hatband. So far all was well, but when we arrived at the top and prepared to have lunch, the Guide excelled himself. He came running back to us bringing with him a magnificent butterfly he had trapped. "*Pour la petite mademoiselle*," he cried. Taking a pin from his lapel he transfixed the butterfly and stuck it in my hat! Oh the horror of that moment! The feeling of the poor butterfly fluttering, struggling against the pin. The agony I felt as the butterfly fluttered there. And of course I couldn't say anything. There were too many conflicting loyalties in my mind. This was a kindness on the part of the Guide. He had brought it to me. It was a special kind of present. How could I hurt his feelings by saying I didn't like it? How I wanted him to take it off! And all the time, there was the butterfly, fluttering, dying. That horrible flapping against my hat. There is only one thing a child can do in these circumstances. I cried.

The more anyone asked me questions the more I was unable to reply. "What's the matter?" demanded my father. "Have you got a pain?"

My sister said, "Perhaps she's frightened at riding on the horse."

I said No and No. I wasn't frightened and I hadn't got a pain.

"Tired," said my father.

"No," I said.

"Well, then, what *is* the matter?"

But I couldn't say. Of course I couldn't say. The Guide was standing there, watching me with an attentive and puzzled face. My father said rather crossly:

"She's too young a child. We shouldn't have brought her on this expedition."

I redoubled my weeping. I must have ruined the day for both him and my sister, and I knew I was doing so, but I couldn't stop. All I hoped and prayed was that presently he, or even my sister, would *guess* what was the matter. Surely they would look at that butterfly, they would see it, they would say, "Perhaps she doesn't like the butterfly on her hat." If *they* said it, it would be all right. But I couldn't tell them. It was a terrible day. I refused to eat any lunch. I sat there and cried, and the butterfly flapped. It stopped flapping in the end. That ought to have made me feel better. But by that time I had got into such a state of misery that nothing *could* have made me feel better.

We rode down again, my father definitely out of temper, my sister annoyed, the Guide still sweet, kindly and puzzled. Fortunately, he did not think of getting me a second butterfly to cheer me up. We arrived back, a most woeful party, and went into our sitting-room where mother was.

"Oh dear," she said, "what's the matter? Has Agatha hurt herself?"

"I don't know," said my father crossly. "I don't know what's the matter with the child. I suppose she's got a pain or something. She's been crying ever since lunch-time, and she wouldn't eat a thing."

"What is the matter, Agatha?" asked my mother.

I couldn't tell her. I only looked at her dumbly while tears still rolled down my cheeks. She looked at me thoughtfully for some minutes, then said, "Who put that butterfly in her hat?"

My sister explained that it had been the Guide.

"I see," said mother. Then she said to me, "You didn't like it, did you? It was alive and you thought it was being hurt?"

Oh, the glorious relief, the wonderful relief when somebody knows what's in your mind and tells it to you so that you are at last released from that long bondage of silence. I flung myself at her in a kind of frenzy, thrust my arms round her neck and said, "Yes, yes, yes. It's been flapping. It's been *flapping.* But he was so kind and he meant to be kind. I couldn't *say.*"

She understood it all and patted me gently. Suddenly the whole thing seemed to recede in the distance.

"I quite see what you felt," she said. "I know. But it's over now, and so we won't talk about it any more."

MIDSUMMER MYSTERIES

The Blood-Stained Pavement

"It's curious," said Joyce Lemprière, "but I hardly like telling you my story. It happened a long time ago—five years ago to be exact—but it's sort of haunted me ever since. The smiling, bright, top part of it—and the hidden gruesomeness underneath. And the queer thing is that the sketch I painted at the time has become tinged with the same atmosphere. When you look at it first it is just a rough sketch of a little steep Cornish street with the sunlight on it. But if you look long enough at it something sinister creeps in. I have never sold it but I never look at it. It lives in the studio in a corner with its face to the wall.

"The name of the place was Rathole. It is a queer little Cornish fishing village, very picturesque—too picturesque perhaps. There is rather too much of the atmosphere of 'Ye Olde Cornish Tea House' about it. It has shops with bobbed-headed girls in smocks doing hand-illuminated mottoes on parchment. It is pretty and it is quaint, but it is very self-consciously so."

"Don't I know," said Raymond West, groaning. "The curse of the charabanc, I suppose. No matter how narrow the lanes leading down to them, no picturesque village is safe."

Joyce nodded.

"They are narrow lanes that lead down to Rathole and very steep, like the side of a house. Well, to get on with my story. I had come down to Cornwall for a fortnight, to sketch. There is an old inn in Rathole, The Polharwith Arms. It was supposed to be the only house left standing by the Spaniards when they shelled the place in fifteen hundred and something."

"Not shelled," said Raymond West, frowning. "Do try to be historically accurate, Joyce."

"Well, at all events they landed guns somewhere along the coast and they fired them and the houses fell down. Anyway that is not the point. The inn was a wonderful old place with a kind of porch in front built on four pillars. I got a very good pitch and was just settling down to work when a car came creeping and twisting down the hill. Of course, it *would* stop before the inn—just where it was most awkward for me. The people got out—a man and a woman—I didn't notice them particularly. She had a kind of mauve linen dress on and a mauve hat.

"Presently the man came out again and to my great thankfulness drove the car down to the quay and left it there. He strolled back past me towards the inn. Just at that moment another beastly car came twisting down, and a woman got out of it dressed in the brightest chintz frock I have ever seen, scarlet poinsettias, I think they were, and she had on one of those big native straw hats—Cuban, aren't they?—in very bright scarlet.

"This woman didn't stop in front of the inn but drove the car farther down the street towards the other one. Then she got out and the man seeing her gave an astonished shout. 'Carol,' he cried, 'in the name of all that is wonderful. Fancy meeting you in this out-of-the-way spot. I haven't seen you for years. Hello, there's Margery—my wife, you know. You must come and meet her.'

"They went up the street towards the inn side by side,

and I saw the other woman had just come out of the door and was moving down towards them. I had had just a glimpse of the woman called Carol as she passed by me. Just enough to see a very white powdered chin and a flaming scarlet mouth and I wondered—I just wondered—if Margery would be so very pleased to meet her. I hadn't seen Margery near to, but in the distance she looked dowdy and extra prim and proper.

"Well, of course, it was not any of my business but you get very queer little glimpses of life sometimes, and you can't help speculating about them. From where they were standing I could just catch fragments of their conversation that floated down to me. They were talking about bathing. The husband, whose name seemed to be Denis, wanted to take a boat and row round the coast. There was a famous cave well worth seeing, so he said, about a mile along. Carol wanted to see the cave too but suggested walking along the cliffs and seeing it from the land side. She said she hated boats. In the end they fixed it that way. Carol was to go along the cliff path and meet them at the cave, and Denis and Margery would take a boat and row round.

"Hearing them talk about bathing made me want to bathe too. It was a very hot morning and I wasn't doing particularly good work. Also, I fancied that the afternoon sunlight would be far more attractive in effect. So I packed up my things and went off to a little beach that I knew of—it was quite the opposite direction from the cave, and was rather a discovery of mine. I had a ripping bathe there and I lunched off a tinned tongue and two tomatoes, and I came back in the afternoon full of confidence and enthusiasm to get on with my sketch.

"The whole of Rathole seemed to be asleep. I had been right about the afternoon sunlight, the shadows were far more telling. The Polharwith Arms was the principal note of my sketch. A ray of sunlight came slanting obliquely down and hit the ground in front of it and had rather a curious effect. I gathered that the bathing party had returned safely, because two bathing dresses, a scarlet one and a dark blue one, were hanging from the balcony, drying in the sun.

"Something had gone a bit wrong with one corner of my sketch and I bent over it for some moments doing something to put it right. When I looked up again there was a figure leaning against one of the pillars of The Polharwith Arms, who seemed to have appeared there by magic. He was dressed in seafaring clothes and was, I suppose, a fisherman. But he had a long dark beard, and if I had been looking for a model for a wicked Spanish captain I couldn't have imagined anyone better. I got to work with feverish haste before he should move away, though from his attitude he looked as though he was pefectly prepared to prop up the pillars through all eternity.

"He did move, however, but luckily not until I had got what I wanted. He came over to me and he began to talk. Oh, how that man talked.

" 'Rathole,' he said, 'was a very interesting place.'

"I knew that already but although I said so that didn't save me. I had the whole history of the shelling—I mean the destroying—of the village, and how the landlord of The Polharwith Arms was the last man to be killed. Run through on his own threshold by a Spanish captain's sword, and of how his blood spurted out on the pavement and no one could wash out the stain for a hundred years.

"It all fitted in very well with the languorous drowsy feeling of the afternoon. The man's voice was very suave and yet at the same time there was an undercurrent in it of something rather frightening. He was very obsequious in his manner, yet I felt underneath he was cruel. He made me understand the Inquisition and the terrors of all the things the Spaniards did better than I have ever done before.

"All the time he was talking to me I went on painting, and suddenly I realized that in the excitement of listening to his story I had painted in something that was not there. On that white square of pavement where the sun fell before the door of The Polharwith Arms, I had painted in bloodstains. It seemed extraordinary that the mind could play such tricks with the hand, but as I looked over towards the inn again I got a second shock. My hand had only painted what my eyes saw—drops of blood on the white pavement.

"I stared for a minute or two. Then I shut my eyes, said to myself, 'Don't be so stupid, there's nothing there, really,' then I opened them again, but the bloodstains were still there.

"I suddenly felt I couldn't stand it. I interrupted the fisherman's flood of language.

"'Tell me,' I said, 'my eyesight is not very good. Are those bloodstains on that pavement over there?'

"He looked at me indulgently and kindly.

"'No bloodstains in these days, lady. What I am telling you about is nearly five hundred years ago.'

"'Yes,' I said, 'but now—on the pavement'—the words died away in my throat. I *knew—I knew* that he wouldn't see what I was seeing. I got up and with shaking hands began to put my things together. As I did so the young man who had come in the car that morning came out of the inn door. He looked up and down the street perplexedly. On the balcony above his wife came out and collected the bathing things. He walked down towards the car but suddenly swerved and came across the road towards the fisherman.

"'Tell me, my man,' he said. 'You don't know whether the lady who came in that second car there has got back yet?'

"'Lady in a dress with flowers all over it? No, sir, I haven't seen her. She went along the cliff towards the cave this morning.'

"'I know, I know. We all bathed there together, and then she left us to walk home and I have not seen her since. It can't have taken her all this time. The cliffs round here are not dangerous, are they?'

"'It depends, sir, on the way you go. The best way is to take a man what knows the place with you.'

"He very clearly meant himself and was beginning to enlarge on the theme, but the young man cut him short unceremoniously and ran back towards the inn calling up to his wife on the balcony.

"'I say, Margery, Carol hasn't come back yet. Odd, isn't it?'

"I didn't hear Margery's reply, but her husband went on. 'Well, we can't wait any longer. We have got to push on to Penrithar. Are you ready? I will turn the car.'

"He did as he had said, and presently the two of them drove off together. Meanwhile I had deliberately been nerving myself to prove how ridiculous my fancies were. When the car had gone I went over to the inn and examined the pavement closely. Of course there were no bloodstains there. No, all along it had been the result of my distorted imagination. Yet, somehow, it seemed to make the thing more frightening. It was while I was standing there that I heard the fisherman's voice.

"He was looking at me curiously. 'You thought you saw bloodstains here, eh, lady?'

"I nodded.

"'That is very curious, that is very curious. We have

got a superstition here, lady. If anyone sees those bloodstains—'

"He paused.

"'Well?' I said.

"He went on in his soft voice, Cornish in intonation, but unconsciously smooth and well-bred in its pronunciation, and completely free from Cornish turns of speech.

"'They do say, lady, that if anyone sees those bloodstains that there will be a death within twenty-four hours.'

"Creepy! It gave me a nasty feeling all down my spine.

"He went on persuasively. 'There is a very interesting tablet in the church, lady, about a death—'

"'No thanks,' I said decisively, and I turned sharply on my heel and walked up the street towards the cottage where I was lodging. Just as I got there I saw in the distance the woman called Carol coming along the cliff path. She was hurrying. Against the grey of the rocks she looked like some poisonous scarlet flower. Her hat was the colour of blood . . .

"I shook myself. Really, I had blood on the brain.

"Later I heard the sound of her car. I wondered whether she too was going to Penrithar; but she took the road to the left in the opposite direction. I watched the car crawl up the hill and disappear, and I breathed somehow more easily. Rathole seemed its quiet sleepy self once more."

"If that is all," said Raymond West as Joyce came to a stop, "I will give my verdict at once. Indigestion, spots before the eyes after meals."

"It isn't all," said Joyce. "You have got to hear the sequel. I read it in the paper two days later under the heading of 'Sea Bathing Fatality.' It told how Mrs Dacre, the wife of Captain Denis Dacre, was unfortunately drowned at Landeer Cove, just a little farther along the coast. She and her husband were staying at the time at the hotel there, and had declared their intention of bathing, but a cold wind sprang up. Captain Dacre had declared it was too cold, so he and some other people in the hotel had gone off to the golf links near by. Mrs Dacre, however, had said it was not too cold for her and she went off alone down to the cove. As she didn't return her husband became alarmed, and in company with his friends went down to the beach. They found her clothes lying beside a rock, but no trace of the unfortunate lady. Her body was not found until nearly a week later when it was washed ashore at a point some distance down the coast. There was a bad blow on her head which had occurred before death, and the theory was that she must have dived into the sea and hit her head on a rock. As far as I could make out her death would have occurred just twenty-four hours after the time I saw the bloodstains."

"I protest," said Sir Henry. "This is not a problem—this is a ghost story. Miss Lemprière is evidently a medium."

Mr Petherick gave his usual cough.

"One point strikes me—" he said, "that blow on the head. We must not, I think, exclude the possibility of foul play. But I do not see that we have any data to go upon. Miss Lemprière's hallucination, or vision, is interesting certainly, but I do not see clearly the point on which she wishes us to pronounce."

"Indigestion and coincidence," said Raymond, "and anyway you can't be sure that they were the same people. Besides, the curse, or whatever it was, would only apply to the actual inhabitants of Rathole."

"I feel," said Sir Henry, "that the sinister seafaring man has something to do with this tale. But I agree with Mr Petherick, Miss Lemprière has given us very little data."

Joyce turned to Dr Pender who smilingly shook his head.

"It is a most interesting story," he said, "but I am afraid I agree with Sir Henry and Mr Petherick that there is very little data to go upon."

Joyce then looked curiously at Miss Marple, who smiled back at her. "I, too, think you are just a little unfair, Joyce dear," she said. "Of course, it is different for me. I mean, we, being women, appreciate the point about clothes. I don't think it is a fair problem to put to a man. It must have meant a lot of rapid changing. What a wicked woman! And a still more wicked man."

Joyce stared at her.

"Aunt Jane," she said. "Miss Marple, I mean, I believe—I do really believe you know the truth."

"Well, dear," said Miss Marple, "it is much easier for me sitting here quietly than it was for you—and being an artist you are so susceptible to atmosphere, aren't you? Sitting here with one's knitting, one just sees the facts. Bloodstains dropped on the pavement from the bathing dress hanging above, and being a red bathing dress, of course, the criminals themselves did not realize it was bloodstained. Poor thing, poor young thing!"

"Excuse me, Miss Marple," said Sir Henry, "but you do know that I am entirely in the dark still. You and Miss Lemprière seem to know what you are talking about, but we men are still in utter darkness."

"I will tell you the end of the story now," said Joyce. "It was a year later. I was at a little east coast seaside resort, and I was sketching, when suddenly I had that queer feeling one has of something having happened before. There were two people, a man and a woman, on the pavement in front of me, and they were greeting a third person, a woman dressed in a scarlet poinsettia chintz dress. 'Carol, by all that is wonderful! Fancy meeting you after all these years. You don't know my wife? Joan, this is an old friend of mine, Miss Harding.'

"I recognized the man at once. It was the same Denis I had seen at Rathole. The wife was different—that is, she was a Joan instead of a Margery; but she was the same type, young and rather dowdy and very inconspicuous. I thought for a minute I was going mad. They began to talk of going bathing. I will tell you what I did. I marched straight then and there to the police station. I thought they would probably think I was off my head, but I didn't care. And as it happened everything was quite all right. There was a man from Scotland Yard there, and he had come down just about this very thing. It seems—oh, it's horrible to talk about that the police had got suspicions of Denis Dacre. That wasn't his real name—he took different names on different occasions. He got to know girls, usually quiet inconspicuous girls without many relatives or friends, he married them and insured their lives for large sums and then—oh, it's horrible! The woman called Carol was his real wife, and they always carried out the same plan. That is really how they came to catch him. The insurance companies became suspicious. He would come to some quiet seaside place with his new wife, then the other woman would turn up and they would all go bathing together. Then the wife would be murdered and Carol would put on her clothes and go back in the boat with him. Then they would leave the place, wherever it was, after inquiring for the supposed Carol and when they got outside the village Carol would hastily change back into her own flamboyant clothes and her vivid make-up and would go back there and drive off in her own car. They would find out which way the current was flowing and the supposed death would take place at the next bathing place along the coast that way. Carol would play the part of the wife and would go down to some lonely beach and would leave the wife's clothes there by a rock and depart in her flowery chintz dress to wait quietly until her husband could rejoin her.

"I suppose when they killed poor Margery some of the blood must have spurted over Carol's bathing suit, and being a red one they didn't notice it, as Miss Marple says. But when they hung it over the balcony it dripped. Ugh!" she gave a shiver. "I can see it still."

"Of course," said Sir Henry, "I remember very well now. Davis was the man's real name. It had quite slipped my memory that one of his many aliases was Dacre. They were an extraordinarily cunning pair. It always seemed so amazing to me that no one spotted the change of identity. I suppose, as Miss Marple says, clothes are more easily identified than faces; but it was a very clever scheme, for although we suspected Davis it was not easy to bring the crime home to him as he always seemed to have an unimpeachable alibi."

"Aunt Jane," said Raymond, looking at her curiously, "how do you do it? You have lived such a peaceful life and yet nothing seems to surprise you."

"I always find one thing very like another in this world," said Miss Marple. "There was Mrs Green, you know, she buried five children—and every one of them insured. Well, naturally, one began to get suspicious."

She shook her head.

"There is a great deal of wickedness in village life. I hope you dear young people will never realize how very wicked the world is."

The Double Clue

"But above everything—no publicity," said Mr Marcus Hardman for perhaps the fourteenth time.

The word *publicity* occurred throughout his conversation with the regularity of a leitmotif. Mr Hardman was a small man, delicately plump, with exquisitely manicured hands and a plaintive tenor voice. In his way, he was somewhat of a celebrity and the fashionable life was his profession. He was rich, but not remarkably so, and he spent his money zealously in the pursuit of social pleasure. His hobby was collecting. He had the collector's soul. Old lace, old fans, antique jewellery—nothing crude or modern for Marcus Hardman.

Poirot and I, obeying an urgent summons, had arrived to find the little man writhing in an agony of indecision. Under the circumstances, to call in the police was abhorrent to him. On the other hand, not to call them in was to acquiesce in the loss of some of the gems of his collection. He hit upon Poirot as a compromise.

"My rubies, Monsieur Poirot, and the emerald necklace said to have belonged to Catherine de' Medici. Oh, the emerald necklace!"

"If you will recount to me the circumstances of their disappearance?" suggested Poirot gently.

"I am endeavouring to do so. Yesterday afternoon I had a little tea party—quite an informal affair, some half a dozen people or so. I have given one or two of them during the season, and though perhaps I should not say so, they have been quite a success. Some good music—Nacora, the pianist, and Katherine Bird, the Australian contralto—in the big studio. Well, early in the afternoon, I was showing my guests my collection of medieval jewels. I keep them in the small wall safe over there. It is arranged like a cabinet inside, with coloured velvet background, to display the stones. Afterwards we inspected the fans—in the case on the wall. Then we all went to the studio for music. It was not until after everyone had gone that I discovered the safe rifled! I must have failed to shut it properly, and someone had seized the opportunity to denude it of its contents. The rubies, Monsieur Poirot, the emerald necklace—the collection of a lifetime! What would I not give to recover them! But there must be no publicity! You fully understand that, do you not, Monsieur Poirot? My own guests, my personal friends! It would be a horrible scandal!"

"Who was the last person to leave this room when you went to the studio?"

"Mr Johnston. You may know him? The South African millionaire. He has just rented the Abbotburys' house in Park Lane. He lingered behind a few moments, I remember. But surely, oh, surely it could not be he!"

"Did any of your guests return to this room during the afternoon on any pretext?"

"I was prepared for that question, Monsieur Poirot. Three of them did so. Countess Vera Rossakoff, Mr Bernard Parker, and Lady Runcorn."

"Let us hear about them."

"The Countess Rossakoff is a very charming Russian lady, a member of the old régime. She has recently come to this country. She had bade me goodbye, and I was therefore somewhat surprised to find her in this room apparently gazing in rapture at my cabinet of fans. You know, Monsieur Poirot, the more I think of it, the more suspicious it seems to me. Don't you agree?"

"Extremely suspicious; but let us hear about the others."

"Well, Parker simply came here to fetch a case of miniatures that I was anxious to show to Lady Runcorn."

"And Lady Runcorn herself?"

"As I dare say you know, Lady Runcorn is a middle-aged woman of considerable force of character who devotes most of her time to various charitable committees. She simply returned to fetch a handbag she had laid down somewhere."

"*Bien*, monsieur. So we have four possible suspects. The Russian countess, the English *grande dame*, the South African millionaire, and Mr Bernard Parker. Who *is* Mr Parker, by the way?"

The question appeared to embarrass Mr Hardman considerably.

"He is—er—he is a young fellow. Well, in fact, a young fellow I know."

"I had already deduced as much," replied Poirot gravely. "What does he do, this Mr Parker?"

"He is a young man about town—not, perhaps, quite in the swim, if I may so express myself."

"How did he come to be a friend of yours, may I ask?"

"Well—er—on one or two occasions he has—performed certain little commissions for me."

"Continue, monsieur," said Poirot.

Hardman looked piteously at him. Evidently the last thing he wanted to do was to continue. But as Poirot maintained an inexorable silence, he capitulated.

"You see, Monsieur Poirot—it is well known that I am interested in antique jewels. Sometimes there is a family heirloom to be disposed of—which, mind you, would never be sold in the open market or to a dealer. But a private sale to me is a very different matter. Parker arranges the details of such things, he is in touch with both sides, and thus any little embarrassment is avoided. He brings anything of that kind to my notice. For instance, the Countess Rossakoff has brought some family jewels with her from Russia. She is anxious to sell them. Bernard Parker was to have arranged the transaction."

"I see," said Poirot thoughtfully. "And you trust him implicitly?"

"I have had no reason to do otherwise."

"Mr Hardman, of these four people, which do you yourself suspect?"

"Oh, Monsieur Poirot, what a question! They are my friends, as I told you. I suspect none of them—or all of them, whichever way you like to put it."

"I do not agree. You suspect one of those four. It is not Countess Rossakoff. It is not Mr Parker. Is it Lady Runcorn or Mr Johnston?"

"You drive me into a corner, Monsieur Poirot, you do indeed. I am most anxious to have no scandal. Lady Runcorn belongs to one of the oldest families in England; but it is true, it is most unfortunately true, that her aunt, Lady Caroline, suffered from a most melancholy affliction. It was understood, of course, by all her friends, and her maid returned the teaspoons, or whatever it was, as promptly as possible. You see my predicament!"

"So Lady Runcorn had an aunt who was a kleptomaniac? Very interesting. You permit that I examine the safe?"

Mr Hardman assenting, Poirot pushed back the door of the safe and examined the interior. The empty velvet-lined shelves gaped at us.

"Even now the door does not shut properly," murmured Poirot, as he swung it to and fro. "I wonder why? Ah, what have we here? A glove, caught in the hinge. A man's glove."

He held it out to Mr Hardman.

"That's not one of my gloves," the latter declared.

"Aha! Something more!" Poirot bent deftly and picked up a small object from the floor of the safe. It was a flat cigarette case made of black moiré.

"My cigarette case!" cried Mr Hardman.

"Yours? Surely not, monsieur. Those are not your—initials."

He pointed to an entwined monogram of two letters executed in platinum.

Hardman took it in his hand.

"You are right," he declared. "It is very like mine, but the initials are different. A '*B*' and a '*P*.' Good heavens—Parker!"

"It would seem so," said Poirot. "A somewhat careless young man—especially if the glove is his also. That would be a double clue, would it not?"

"Bernard Parker!" murmured Hardman. "What a relief! Well, Monsieur Poirot, I leave it to you to recover the jewels. Place the matter in the hands of the police if you think fit—that is, if you are quite sure that it is he who is guilty."

"See you, my friend," said Poirot to me, as we left the house together, "he has one law for the titled, and another law for the plain, this Mr Hardman. Me, I have not yet been ennobled, so I am on the side of the plain. I have sympathy for this young man. The whole thing was a little curious, was it not? There was Hardman suspecting Lady Runcorn; there was I, suspecting the Countess and Johnston; and all the time, the obscure Mr Parker was our man."

"Why did you suspect the other two?"

"*Parbleu!* It is such a simple thing to be a Russian refugee or a South African millionaire. Any woman can call herself a Russian countess; anyone can buy a house in Park Lane and call himself a South African millionaire. Who is going to contradict them? But I observe that we are passing through Bury Street. Our careless young friend lives here. Let us, as you say, strike while the iron is in the fire."

Mr Bernard Parker was at home. We found him reclining on some cushions, clad in an amazing dressing-gown of purple and orange. I have seldom taken a greater dislike to anyone than I did to this particular young man with his white, effeminate face and affected lisping speech.

"Good morning, monsieur," said Poirot briskly. "I come from Mr Hardman. Yesterday, at the party, somebody has stolen all his jewels. Permit me to ask you, monsieur—is this your glove?"

Mr Parker's mental processes did not seem very rapid. He stared at the glove, as though gathering his wits together.

"Where did you find it?" he asked at last.

"Is it your glove, monsieur?"

Mr Parker appeared to make up his mind.

"No, it isn't," he declared.

"And this cigarette case, is that yours?"

"Certainly not. I always carry a silver one."

"Very well, monsieur. I go to put matters in the hands of the police."

"Oh, I say, I wouldn't do that if I were you," cried Mr Parker in some concern. "Beastly unsympathetic people, the police. Wait a bit. I'll go round and see old Hardman. Look here—oh, stop a minute."

But Poirot beat a determined retreat.

"We have given him something to think about, have

we not?" he chuckled. "Tomorrow we will observe what has occurred."

But we were destined to have a reminder of the Hardman case that afternoon. Without the least warning the door flew open, and a whirlwind in human form invaded our privacy, bringing with her a swirl of sables (it was as cold as only an English June day can be) and a hat rampant with slaughtered ospreys. Countess Vera Rossakoff was a somewhat disturbing personality.

"You are Monsieur Poirot? What is this that you have done? You accuse that poor boy! It is infamous. It is scandalous. I know him. He is a chicken, a lamb—never would he steal. He has done everything for me. Will I stand by and see him martyred and butchered?"

"Tell me, madame, is this his cigarette case?" Poirot held out the black moiré case.

The Countess paused for a moment while she inspected it.

"Yes, it is his. I know it well. What of it? Did you find it in the room? We were all there; he dropped it then, I suppose. Ah, you policemen, you are worse than the Red Guards—"

"And is this his glove?"

"How should I know? One glove is like another. Do not try to stop me he must be set free. His character must be cleared. You shall do it. I will sell my jewels and give you much money."

"Madame—"

"It is agreed, then? No, no, do not argue. The poor boy! He came to me, the tears in his eyes. 'I will save you,' I said. 'I will go to this man, this ogre, this monster! Leave it to Vera.' Now it is settled, I go."

With as little ceremony as she had come, she swept from the room, leaving an overpowering perfume of an exotic nature behind her.

"What a woman!" I exclaimed. "And what furs!"

"Ah, yes, *they* were genuine enough. Could a spurious countess have real furs? My little joke, Hastings . . . No, she is truly Russian, I fancy. Well, well, so Master Bernard went bleating to her."

"The cigarette case is his. I wonder if the glove is also—"

With a smile Poirot drew from his pocket a second glove and placed it by the first. There was no doubt of their being a pair.

"Where did you get the second one, Poirot?"

"It was thrown down with a stick on the table in the hall in Bury Street. Truly, a very careless young man, Monsieur Parker. Well, well, *mon ami*, we must be thorough. Just for the form of the thing, I will make a little visit to Park Lane."

Needless to say, I accompanied my friend. Johnston was out, but we saw his private secretary. It transpired that Johnston had only recently arrived from South Africa. He had never been in England before.

"He is interested in precious stones, is he not?" hazarded Poirot.

"Gold mining is nearer the mark," laughed the secretary.

Poirot came away from the interview thoughtful. Late that evening, to my utter surprise, I found him earnestly studying a Russian grammar.

"Good heavens, Poirot!" I cried. "Are you learning Russian in order to converse with the Countess in her own language?"

"She certainly would not listen to my English, my friend!"

"But surely, Poirot, well-born Russians invariably speak French?"

"You are a mine of information, Hastings! I will cease puzzling over the intricacies of the Russian alphabet."

He threw the book from him with a dramatic gesture. I was not entirely satisfied. There was a twinkle in his eye which I knew of old. It was an invariable sign that Hercule Poirot was pleased with himself.

"Perhaps," I said sapiently, "you doubt her being really a Russian. You are going to test her?"

"Ah, no, no, she is Russian all right."

"Well, then—"

"If you really want to distinguish yourself over this case, Hastings, I recommend *First Steps in Russian* as an invaluable aid."

Then he laughed and would say no more. I picked up the book from the floor and dipped into it curiously, but could make neither head nor tail of Poirot's remarks.

The following morning brought us no news of any kind, but that did not seem to worry my little friend. At breakfast, he announced his intention of calling upon Mr Hardman early in the day. We found the elderly social butterfly at home, and seemingly a little calmer than on the previous day.

"Well, Monsieur Poirot, any news?" he demanded eagerly.

Poirot handed him a slip of paper.

"That is the person who took the jewels, monsieur. Shall I put matters in the hands of the police? Or would you prefer me to recover the jewels without bringing the police into the matter?"

Mr Hardman was staring at the paper. At last he found his voice.

"Most astonishing. I should infinitely prefer to have no scandal in the matter. I give you *carte blanche*, Monsieur Poirot. I am sure you will be discreet."

Our next procedure was to hail a taxi, which Poirot ordered to drive to the Carlton. There he inquired for Countess Rossakoff. In a few minutes we were ushered up into the lady's suite. She came to meet us with outstretched hands, arrayed in a marvellous negligée of barbaric design.

"Monsieur Poirot!" she cried. "You have succeeded? You have cleared that poor infant?"

"Madame la Comtesse, your friend Mr Parker is perfectly safe from arrest."

"Ah, but you are the clever little man! Superb! And so quickly too."

"On the other hand, I have promised Mr Hardman that the jewels shall be returned to him today."

"So?"

"Therefore, madame, I should be extremely obliged if you would place them in my hands without delay. I am sorry to hurry you, but I am keeping a taxi—in case it should be necessary for me to go on to Scotland Yard; and we Belgians, madame, we practise the thrift."

The Countess had lighted a cigarette. For some seconds she sat perfectly still, blowing smoke rings, and gazing steadily at Poirot. Then she burst into a laugh, and rose. She went across to the bureau, opened a drawer, and took out a black silk handbag. She tossed it lightly to Poirot. Her tone, when she spoke, was perfectly light and unmoved.

"We Russians, on the contrary, practise prodigality," she said. "And to do that, unfortunately, one must have money. You need not look inside. They are all there."

Poirot arose.

"I congratulate you, madame, on your quick intelligence and your promptitude."

"Ah! But since you were keeping your taxi waiting, what else could I do?"

"You are too amiable, madame. You are remaining long in London?"

"I am afraid no—owing to you."

"Accept my apologies."

"We shall meet again elsewhere, perhaps."

"I hope so."

"And I—do not!" exclaimed the Countess with a laugh. "It is a great compliment that I pay you there—there are very few men in the world whom I fear. Goodbye, Monsieur Poirot."

"Goodbye, Madame la Comtesse. Ah—pardon me, I forgot! Allow me to return you your cigarette case."

And with a bow he handed to her the little black moiré case we had found in the safe. She accepted it without any change of expression—just a lifted eyebrow and a murmured: "I see!"

"What a woman!" cried Poirot enthusiastically as we descended the stairs. "*Mon Dieu, quelle femme!* Not a word of argument—of protestation, of bluff! One quick glance, and she had sized up the position correctly. I tell you, Hastings, a woman who can accept defeat like that—with a careless smile—will go far! She is dangerous, she has the nerves of steel; she—" He tripped heavily.

"If you can manage to moderate your transports and look where you're going, it might be as well," I suggested. "When did you first suspect the Countess?"

"*Mon ami*, it was the glove *and* the cigarette case—the double clue, shall we say—that worried me. Bernard Parker might easily have dropped one or the other—but hardly both. Ah, no, that would have been *too* careless! In the same way, if someone else had placed them there to incriminate Parker, one would have been sufficient—the cigarette case *or* the glove again not both. So I was forced to the conclusion that one of the two things did *not* belong to Parker. I imagined at first that the case was his, and that the glove was not. But when I discovered the fellow to the glove, I saw that it was the other way about. Whose, then, was the cigarette case? Clearly, it could not belong to Lady Runcorn. The initials were wrong. Mr Johnston? Only if he were here under a false name. I interviewed his secretary, and it was apparent at once that everything was clear and above board. There was no reticence about Mr Johnston's past. The Countess, then? She was supposed to have brought jewels with her from Russia; she had only to take the stones from their settings, and it was extremely doubtful if they could ever be identified. What could be easier for her than to pick up one of Parker's gloves from the hall that day and thrust it into the safe? But, *bien sûr*, she did not intend to drop her own cigarette case."

"But if the case was hers, why did it have '*B.P.*' on it? The Countess's initials are *V.R.*"

Poirot smiled gently upon me.

"Exactly, *mon ami*; but in the Russian alphabet, *B* is *V* and *P* is *R*."

"Well, you couldn't expect me to guess that. I don't know Russian."

"Neither do I, Hastings. That is why I bought my little book—and urged it on your attention."

He sighed.

"A remarkable woman. I have a feeling, my friend—a very decided feeling—I shall meet her again. Where, I wonder?"

Death on the Nile

Lady Grayle was nervous. From the moment of coming on board the S.S. *Fayoum* she complained of everything. She did not like her cabin. She could bear the morning sun, but not the afternoon sun. Pamela Grayle, her niece, obligingly gave up her cabin on the other side. Lady Grayle accepted it grudgingly.

She snapped at Miss MacNaughton, her nurse, for having given her the wrong scarf and for having packed her little pillow instead of leaving it out. She snapped at her husband, Sir George, for having just bought her the wrong string of beads. It was lapis she wanted, not carnelian. George was a fool!

Sir George said anxiously, "Sorry, me dear, sorry. I'll go back and change 'em. Plenty of time."

She did not snap at Basil West, her husband's private secretary, because nobody ever snapped at Basil. His smile disarmed you before you began.

But the worst of it fell assuredly to the dragoman—an imposing and richly dressed personage whom nothing could disturb.

When Lady Grayle caught sight of a stranger in a basket chair and realized that he was a fellow passenger, the vials of her wrath were poured out like water.

"They told me distinctly at the office that we were the only passengers! It was the end of the season and there was no one else going!"

"That right, lady," said Mohammed calmly. "Just you and party and one gentleman, that's all."

"But I was told that there would be only ourselves."

"That quite right, lady."

"It's not all right! It was a lie! What is that man doing here?"

"He come later, lady. After you take tickets. He only decide to come this morning."

"It's an absolute swindle!"

"That's all right, lady; him very quiet gentleman, very nice, very quiet."

"You're a fool! You know nothing about it. Miss MacNaughton, where are you? Oh, there you are. I've repeatedly asked you to stay near me. I might feel faint. Help me to my cabin and give me an aspirin, and don't let Mohammed come near me. He keeps on saying 'That's right, lady,' till I feel I could scream."

Miss McNaughton proffered an arm without a word.

She was a tall woman of about thirty-five, handsome in a quiet, dark way. She settled Lady Grayle in the cabin, propped her up with cushions, administered an aspirin and listened to the thin flow of complaint.

Lady Grayle was forty-eight. She had suffered since she was sixteen from the complaint of having too much money. She had married that impoverished baronet, Sir George Grayle, ten years before.

She was a big woman, not bad-looking as regarded features, but her face was fretful and lined, and the lavish make-up she applied only accentuated the blemishes of time and temper. Her hair had been in turn platinum-blonde and henna-red, and was looking tired in consequence. She was overdressed and wore too much jewellery.

"Tell Sir George," she finished, while the silent Miss MacNaughton waited with an expressionless face—"tell

Sir George that he *must* get that man off the boat! I *must* have privacy. All I've gone through lately—" She shut her eyes.

"Yes, Lady Grayle," said Miss MacNaughton, and left the cabin.

The offending last-minute passenger was still sitting in the deck-chair. He had his back to Luxor and was staring out across the Nile to where the distant hills showed golden above a line of dark green.

Miss MacNaughton gave him a swift, appraising glance as she passed.

She found Sir George in the lounge. He was holding a string of beads in his hand and looking at it doubtfully.

"Tell me, Miss MacNaughton, do you think these will be all right?"

Miss MacNaughton gave a swift glance at the lapis.

"Very nice indeed," she said.

"You think Lady Grayle will be pleased—eh?"

"Oh no, I shouldn't say that, Sir George. You see, nothing *would* please her. That's the real truth of it. By the way, she sent me with a message to you. She wants you to get rid of this extra passenger."

Sir George's jaw dropped. "How can I? What could I say to the fellow?"

"Of course you can't." Elsie MacNaughton's voice was brisk and kindly. "Just say there was nothing to be done."

She added encouragingly, "It will be all right."

"You think it will, eh?" His face was ludicrously pathetic.

Elsie MacNaughton's voice was still kinder as she said: "You really must not take these things to heart, Sir George. It's just health, you know. Don't take it seriously."

"You think she's really bad, nurse?"

A shadow crossed the nurse's face. There was something odd in her voice as she answered: "Yes, I—I don't quite like her condition. But please don't worry, Sir

George. You mustn't. You really mustn't." She gave him a friendly smile and went out.

Pamela came in, very languid and cool in her white.

"Hallo, Nunks."

"Hallo, Pam, my dear."

"What have you got there? Oh, nice!"

"Well, I'm so glad you think so. Do you think your aunt will think so, too?"

"She's incapable of liking anything. I can't think why you married the woman, Nunks."

Sir George was silent. A confused panorama of unsuccessful racing, pressing creditors and a handsome if domineering woman rose before his mental vision.

"Poor old dear," said Pamela. "I suppose you had to do it. But she does give us both rather hell, doesn't she?"

"Since she's been ill—" began Sir George.

Pamela interrupted him.

"She's not ill! Not really. She can always do anything she wants to. Why, while you were up at Assouan she was as merry as a—a cricket. I bet you Miss MacNaughton knows she's a fraud."

"I don't know what we'd do without Miss MacNaughton," said Sir George with a sigh.

"She's an efficient creature," admitted Pamela. "I don't exactly dote on her as you do, though, Nunks. Oh, you do! Don't contradict. You think she's wonderful. So she is, in a way. But she's a dark horse. I never know what she's thinking. Still, she manages the old cat quite well."

"Look here, Pam, you mustn't speak of your aunt like that. Dash it all, she's very good to you."

"Yes, she pays all our bills, doesn't she? It's a hell of a life, though."

Sir George passed on to a less painful subject. "What are we to do about this fellow who's coming on the trip? Your aunt wants the boat to herself."

"Well, she can't have it," said Pamela coolly. "The man's quite presentable. His name's Parker Pyne. I should think he was a civil servant out of the Records Department—if there is such a thing. Funny thing is, I seem to have heard the name somewhere. Basil!" The secretary had just entered. "Where have I seen the name Parker Pyne?"

"Front page of *The Times* Agony column," replied the young man promptly. " 'Are you happy? If not, consult Mr Parker Pyne.' "

"Never! How frightfully amusing! Let's tell him all our troubles all the way to Cairo."

"I haven't any," said Basil West simply. "We're going to glide down the golden Nile, and see temples"—he looked quickly at Sir George, who had picked up a paper—"together."

The last word was only just breathed, but Pamela caught it. Her eyes met his.

"You're right, Basil," she said lightly. "It's good to be alive."

Sir George got up and went out. Pamela's face clouded over.

"What's the matter, my sweet?"

"My detested aunt by marriage—"

"Don't worry," said Basil quickly. "What does it matter what she gets into her head? Don't contradict her. You see," he laughed, "it's good camouflage."

The benevolent figure of Mr Parker Pyne entered the lounge. Behind him came the picturesque figure of Mohammed, prepared to say his piece.

"Lady, gentlemans, we start now. In a few minutes we pass temples of Karnak right-hand side. I tell you story now about little boy who went to buy a roasted lamb for his father . . ."

⋆ ⋆ ⋆

Mr Parker Pyne mopped his forehead. He had just returned from a visit to the Temple of Dendera. Riding on a donkey was, he felt, an exercise ill suited to his figure. He was proceeding to remove his collar when a note propped up on the dressing table caught his attention. He opened it. It ran as follows:

> *Dear Sir,—I should be obliged if you should not visit the Temple of Abydos, but would remain on the boat, as I wish to consult you.*
>
> *Yours truly,*
> *Ariadne Grayle*

A smile creased Mr Parker Pyne's large, bland face. He reached for a sheet of paper and unscrewed his fountain pen.

> *Dear Lady Grayle* (he wrote), *I am sorry to disappoint you, but I am at present on holiday and am not doing any professional business.*

He signed his name and dispatched the letter by a steward. As he completed his change of toilet, another note was brought to him.

> *Dear Mr Parker Pyne,—I appreciate the fact that you are on holiday, but I am prepared to pay a fee of a hundred pounds for a consultation.*
>
> *Yours truly,*
> *Ariadne Grayle*

Mr Parker Pyne's eyebrows rose. He tapped his teeth thoughtfully with his fountain pen. He wanted to see Abydos, but a hundred pounds was a hundred pounds.

And Egypt had been even more wickedly expensive than he had imagined.

Dear Lady Grayle (he wrote),*—I shall not visit the Temple of Abydos.*
Yours faithfully,
J. Parker Pyne

Mr Parker Pyne's refusal to leave the boat was a source of great grief to Mohammed.

"Very nice temple. All my gentlemans like see that temple. I get you carriage. I get you chair and sailors carry you."

Mr Parker Pyne refused all these tempting offers.

The others set off.

Mr Parker Pyne waited on deck. Presently the door of Lady Grayle's cabin opened and the lady herself trailed out on deck.

"Such a hot afternoon," she observed graciously. "I see you have stayed behind, Mr Pyne. Very wise of you. Shall we have some tea together in the lounge?"

Mr Parker Pyne rose promptly and followed her. It cannot be denied that he was curious.

It seemed as though Lady Grayle felt some difficulty in coming to the point. She fluttered from this subject to that. But finally she spoke in an altered voice.

"Mr Pyne, what I am about to tell you is in the strictest confidence! You do understand that, don't you?"

"Naturally."

She paused, took a deep breath. Mr Parker Pyne waited.

"I want to know whether or not my husband is poisoning me."

Whatever Mr Parker Pyne had expected, it was not this. He showed his astonishment plainly. "That is a very serious accusation to make, Lady Grayle."

"Well, I'm not a fool and I wasn't born yesterday. I've had my suspicions for some time. Whenever George goes away I get better. My food doesn't disagree with me and I feel a different woman. There must be some reason for that."

"What you say is very serious, Lady Grayle. You must remember I am not a detective. I am, if you like to put it that way, a heart specialist—"

She interrupted him. "Eh—and don't you think it worries me, all this? It's not a policeman I want—I can look after myself, thank you—it's certainty I want. I've got to *know.* I'm not a wicked woman, Mr Pyne. I act fairly by those who act fairly by me. A bargain's a bargain. I've kept my side of it. I've paid my husband's debts and I've not stinted him in money."

Mr Parker Pyne had a fleeting pang of pity for Sir George. "And as for the girl she's had clothes and parties and this, that and the other. Common gratitude is all I ask."

"Gratitude is not a thing that can be produced to order, Lady Grayle."

"Nonsense!" said Lady Grayle. She went on: "Well, there it is! Find out the truth for me! Once I *know*—"

He looked at her curiously. "Once you know, what then, Lady Grayle?"

"That's my business." Her lips closed sharply.

Mr Parker Pyne hesitated a minute, then he said: "You will excuse me, Lady Grayle, but I have the impression that you are not being entirely frank with me."

"That's absurd. I've told you exactly what I want you to find out."

"Yes, but not the reason *why*?"

Their eyes met. Hers fell first.

"I should think the reason was self-evident," she said.

"No, because I am in doubt upon one point."

"What is that?"

"Do you want your suspicions proved right or wrong?"

"Really, Mr Pyne!" The lady rose to her feet, quivering with indignation.

Mr Parker Pyne nodded his head gently. "Yes, yes," he said. "But that doesn't answer my question, you know."

"Oh!" Words seemed to fail her. She swept out of the room.

Left alone, Mr Parker Pyne became very thoughtful. He was so deep in his own thoughts that he started perceptibly when someone came in and sat down opposite him. It was Miss MacNaughton.

"Surely you're all back very soon," said Mr Parker Pyne.

"The others aren't back. I said I had a headache and came back alone." She hesitated. "Where is Lady Grayle?"

"I should imagine lying down in her cabin."

"Oh, then that's all right. I don't want her to know I've come back."

"You didn't come on her account then?"

Miss MacNaughton shook her head. "No, I came back to see you."

Mr Parker Pyne was surprised. He would have said off-hand that Miss MacNaughton was eminently capable of looking after troubles herself without seeking outside advice. It seemed that he was wrong.

"I've watched you since we all came on board. I think you're a person of wide experience and good judgement. And I want advice very badly."

"And yet—excuse me, Miss MacNaughton—but you're not the type that usually seeks advice. I should say that you were a person who was quite content to rely on her own judgement."

"Normally, yes. But I am in a very peculiar position."

She hesitated a moment. "I do not usually talk about

my cases. But in this instance I think it is necessary. Mr Pyne, when I left England with Lady Grayle, she was a straightforward case. In plain language, there was nothing the matter with her. That's not quite true, perhaps. Too much leisure and too much money do produce a definite pathological condition. Having a few floors to scrub every day and five or six children to look after would have made Lady Grayle a perfectly healthy and a much happier woman."

Mr Parker Pyne nodded.

"As a hospital nurse, one sees a lot of these nervous cases. Lady Grayle *enjoyed* her bad health. It was my part not to minimize her sufferings, to be as tactful as I could—and to enjoy the trip myself as much as possible."

"Very sensible," said Mr Parker Pyne.

"But Mr Pyne, things are not as they were. The suffering that Lady Grayle complains of now is real and not imagined."

"You mean?"

"I have come to suspect that Lady Grayle is being poisoned."

"Since when have you suspected this?"

"For the past three weeks."

"Do you suspect—any particular person?"

Her eyes dropped. For the first time her voice lacked sincerity. "No."

"I put it to you, Miss MacNaughton, that you do suspect one particular person, and that that person is Sir George Grayle."

"Oh, no, no, I can't believe it of him! He is so pathetic, so child-like. He couldn't be a cold-blooded poisoner." Her voice had an anguished note in it.

"And yet you have noticed that whenever Sir George is absent his wife is better and that her periods of illness correspond with his return."

She did not answer.

"What poison do you suspect? Arsenic?"

"Something of that kind. Arsenic or antimony."

"And what steps have you taken?"

"I have done my utmost to supervise what Lady Grayle eats and drinks."

Mr Parker Pyne nodded. "Do you think Lady Grayle has any suspicion herself?" he asked casually.

"Oh, no, I'm sure she hasn't."

"There you are wrong," said Mr Parker Pyne. "Lady Grayle *does* suspect."

Miss MacNaughton showed her astonishment.

"Lady Grayle is more capable of keeping a secret than you imagine," said Mr Parker Pyne. "She is a woman who knows how to keep her own counsel very well."

"That surprises me very much," said Miss MacNaughton slowly.

"I should like to ask you one more question, Miss MacNaughton. Do you think Lady Grayle likes you?"

"I've never thought about it."

They were interrupted. Mohammed came in, his face beaming, his robes flowing behind him.

"Lady, she hear you come back; she ask for you. She say why you not come to her?"

Elsie MacNaughton rose hurriedly. Mr Parker Pyne rose also.

"Would a consultation early tomorrow morning suit you?" he asked.

"Yes, that would be the best time. Lady Grayle sleeps late. In the meantime, I shall be very careful."

"I think Lady Grayle will be careful too."

Miss MacNaughton disappeared.

Mr Parker Pyne did not see Lady Grayle till just before dinner. She was sitting smoking a cigarette and burning what seemed to be a letter. She took no notice at all of him, by which he gathered that she was still offended.

After dinner he played bridge with Sir George, Pamela and Basil. Everyone seemed a little distrait, and the bridge game broke up early.

It was some hours later when Mr Parker Pyne was roused. It was Mohammed who came to him.

"Old lady, she very ill. Nurse, she very frightened. I try to get doctor."

Mr Parker Pyne hurried on some clothes. He arrived at the doorway of Lady Grayle's cabin at the same time as Basil West. Sir George and Pamela were inside. Elsie MacNaughton was working desperately over her patient. As Mr Parker Pyne arrived, a final convulsion seized the poor lady. Her arched body writhed and stiffened. Then she fell back on her pillows.

Mr Parker Pyne drew Pamela gently outside.

"How awful!" the girl was half-sobbing. "How awful! Is she, is she—?"

"Dead? Yes, I am afraid it is all over."

He put her into Basil's keeping. Sir George came out of the cabin, looking dazed.

"I never thought she was really ill," he was muttering. "Never thought it for a moment."

Mr Parker Pyne pushed past him and entered the cabin.

Elsie MacNaughton's face was white and drawn. "They have sent for a doctor?" she asked.

"Yes." Then he said: "Strychnine?"

"Yes. Those convulsions are unmistakable. Oh, I can't believe it!" She sank into a chair, weeping. He patted her shoulder.

Then an idea seemed to strike him. He left the cabin hurriedly and went to the lounge. There was a little scrap of paper left unburnt in an ash-tray. Just a few words were distinguishable:

"Now, that's interesting," said Mr Parker Pyne.

Mr Parker Pyne sat in the room of a prominent Cairo official. "So that's the evidence," he said thoughtfully.

"Yes, pretty complete. Man must have been a damned fool."

"I shouldn't call Sir George a brainy man."

"All the same!" The other recapitulated: "Lady Grayle wants a cup of Bovril. The nurse makes it for her. Then she must have sherry in it. Sir George produces the sherry. Two hours later, Lady Grayle dies with unmistakable signs of strychnine poisoning. A packet of strychnine is found in Sir George's cabin and another packet actually in the pocket of his dinner jacket."

"Very thorough," said Mr Parker Pyne. "Where did the strychnine come from, by the way?"

"There's a little doubt over that. The nurse had some—in case Lady Grayle's heart troubled her—but she's contradicted herself once or twice. First she said her supply was intact, and now she says it isn't."

"Very unlike her not to be sure," was Mr Parker Pyne's comment. "They were in it together, in my opinion. They've got a weakness for each other, those two."

"Possibly; but if Miss MacNaughton had been planning murder, she'd have done it a good deal better. She's an efficient young woman."

"Well, there it is. In my opinion, Sir George is in for it. He hasn't a dog's chance."

"Well, well," said Mr Parker Pyne, "I must see what I can do."

He sought out the pretty niece.

Pamela was white and indignant. "Nunks never did such a thing—never—never—never!"

"Then who did?" said Mr Parker Pyne placidly.

Pamela came nearer. "Do you know what I think? *She did it herself.* She's been frightfully queer lately. She used to imagine things."

"What things?"

"Queer things. Basil, for instance. She was always hinting that Basil was in love with her. And Basil and I are—we are—"

"I realize that," said Mr Parker Pyne, smiling.

"All that about Basil was pure imagination. I think she had a down on poor little Nunks, and I think she made up that story and told it to you, and then put the strychnine in his cabin and in his pocket and poisoned herself. People have done things like that, haven't they?"

"They have," admitted Mr Parker Pyne. "But I don't think that Lady Grayle did. She wasn't, if you'll allow me to say so, the type."

"But the delusions?"

"Yes, I'd like to ask Mr West about that."

He found the young man in his room. Basil answered his questions readily enough.

"I don't want to sound fatuous, but she took a fancy to me. That's why I daren't let her know about me and Pamela. She'd have had Sir George fire me."

"You think Miss Grayle's theory a likely one?"

"Well, it's possible, I suppose." The young man was doubtful.

"But not good enough," said Mr Parker Pyne quietly.

"No, we must find something better." He became lost in meditation for a minute or two. "A confession would be best," he said briskly. He unscrewed his fountain pen and produced a sheet of paper. "Just write it out, will you?"

Basil West stared at him in amazement. "Me? What on earth do you mean?"

"My dear young man"—Mr Parker Pyne sounded almost paternal—"I know all about it. How you made love to the good lady. How she had scruples. How you fell in love with the pretty, penniless niece. How you arranged your plot. Slow poisoning. It might pass for natural death from gastroenteritis—if not, it would be laid to Sir George's doing, since you were careful to let the attacks coincide with his presence.

"Then your discovery that the lady was suspicious and had talked to me about the matter. Quick action! You abstracted some strychnine from Miss MacNaughton's store. Planted some of it in Sir George's cabin, and some in his pocket, and put sufficient into a cachet which you enclosed with a note to the lady, telling her it was a 'cachet of dreams.'

"A romantic idea. She'd take it as soon as the nurse had left her, and no one would know anything about it. But you made one mistake, my young man. It is useless asking a lady to burn letters. They never do. I've got all that pretty correspondence, including the one about the cachet."

Basil West had turned green. All his good looks had vanished. He looked like a trapped rat.

"Damn you," he snarled. "So you know all about it. You damned interfering Nosey Parker."

Mr Parker Pyne was saved from physical violence by the appearance of the witnesses he had thoughtfully arranged to have listening outside the half-closed door.

* * *

Mr Parker Pyne was again discussing the case with his friend the high official.

"And I hadn't a shred of evidence! Only an almost indecipherable fragment, with "*Burn this!*" on it. I deduced the whole story and tried it on him. It worked. I'd stumbled on the truth. The letters did it. Lady Grayle had burned every scrap he wrote, but *he didn't know that.*

"She was really a very unusual woman. I was puzzled when she came to me. What she wanted was for me to tell her that her husband was poisoning her. In that case, she meant to go off with young West. But she wanted to act fairly. Curious character."

"That poor little girl is going to suffer," said the other.

"She'll get over it," said Mr Parker Pyne callously. "She's young. I'm anxious that Sir George should get a little enjoyment before it's too late. He's been treated like a worm for ten years. Now, Elsie MacNaughton will be very kind to him."

He beamed. Then he sighed. "I am thinking of going incognito to Greece. I really *must* have a holiday!"

Harlequin's Lane

Mr Satterthwaite was never quite sure what took him to stay with the Denmans. They were not of his kind—that is to say, they belonged neither to the great world, nor to the more interesting artistic circles. They were Philistines, and dull Philistines at that. Mr Satterthwaite had met them first at Biarritz, had accepted an invitation to stay with them, had come, had been bored, and yet strangely enough had come again and yet again.

Why? He was asking himself that question on this twenty-first of June, as he sped out of London in his Rolls Royce.

John Denman was a man of forty, a solid well-established figure respected in the business world. His friends were not Mr Satterthwaite's friends, his ideas even less so. He was a man clever in his own line but devoid of imagination outside it.

Why am I doing this thing? Mr Satterthwaite asked himself once more—and the only answer that came seemed to him so vague and so inherently preposterous that he almost put it aside. For the only reason that presented itself was the fact that one of the rooms in the house (a comfortable well-appointed house) stirred his curiosity. That room was Mrs Denman's own sitting-room.

It was hardly an expression of her personality because, so far as Mr Satterthwaite could judge, she had no personality. He had never met a woman so completely expressionless. She was, he knew, a Russian by birth. John Denman had been in Russia at the outbreak of the European war, he had fought with the Russian troops, had narrowly escaped with his life on the outbreak of the Revolution, and had brought this Russian girl with him, a penniless refugee. In face of strong disapproval from his parents he had married her.

Mrs Denman's room was in no way remarkable. It was well and solidly furnished with good Hepplewhite furniture—a trifle more masculine than feminine in atmosphere. But in it there was one incongruous item: a Chinese lacquer screen—a thing of creamy yellow and pale rose. Any museum might have been glad to own it. It was a collector's piece, rare and beautiful.

It was out of place against that solid English background. It should have been the keynote of the room with everything arranged to harmonize subtly with it. And yet Mr Satterthwaite could not accuse the Denmans of lack of taste. Everything else in the house was in perfectly blended accord.

He shook his head. The thing—trivial though it was—puzzled him. Because of it, so he verily believed, he had come again and again to the house. It was, perhaps, a woman's fantasy—but that solution did not satisfy him as he thought of Mrs Denman—a quiet, hard-featured woman, speaking English so correctly that no one would ever have guessed her a foreigner.

The car drew up at his destination and he got out, his mind still dwelling on the problem of the Chinese screen. The name of the Denman's house was "Ashmead," and it occupied some five acres of Melton Heath, which is thirty miles from London, stands five hundred feet above sea level and is, for the most part, inhabited by those who have ample incomes.

The butler received Mr Satterthwaite suavely. Mr and Mrs Denman were both out—at a rehearsal—they hoped Mr Satterthwaite would make himself at home until they returned.

Mr Satterthwaite nodded and proceeded to carry out these injunctions by stepping into the garden. After a cursory examination of the flower beds, he strolled down a shady walk and presently came to a door in the wall. It was unlocked and he passed through it and came out into a narrow lane.

Mr Satterthwaite looked to left and right. A very charming lane, shady and green, with high hedges—a rural lane that twisted and turned in good old-fashioned style. He remembered the stamped address: ASHMEAD, HARLEQUIN'S LANE—remembered too, a local name for it that Mrs Denman had once told him.

"Harlequin's Lane," he murmured to himself softly. "I wonder—"

He turned a corner.

Not at the time, but afterwards, he wondered why this time he felt no surprise at meeting that elusive friend of his: Mr Harley Quin. The two men clasped hands.

"So *you're* down here," said Mr Satterthwaite.

"Yes," said Mr Quin. "I'm staying in the same house as you are."

"Staying there?"

"Yes. Does it surprise you?"

"No," said Mr Satterthwaite slowly. "Only—well, you never stay anywhere for long, do you?"

"Only as long as is necessary," said Mr Quin gravely.

"I see," said Mr Satterthwaite.

They walked on in silence for some minutes.

"This lane," began Mr Satterthwaite, and stopped.

"Belongs to me," said Mr Quin.

"I thought it did," said Mr Satterthwaite. "Somehow,

I thought it must. There's the other name for it, too, the local name. They call it the 'Lovers' Lane.' You know that?"

Mr Quin nodded.

"But surely," he said gently, "there is a 'Lovers' Lane' in every village?"

"I suppose so," said Mr Satterthwaite, and he sighed a little.

He felt suddenly rather old and out of things, a little dried-up wizened old fogey of a man. Each side of him were the hedges, very green and alive.

"Where does this lane end, I wonder?" he asked suddenly.

"It ends—*here*," said Mr Quin.

They came round the last bend. The lane ended in a piece of waste ground, and almost at their feet a great pit opened. In it were tin cans gleaming in the sun, and other cans that were too red with rust to gleam, old boots, fragments of newspapers, a hundred and one odds and ends that were no longer of account to anybody.

"A rubbish heap," exclaimed Mr Satterthwaite, and breathed deeply and indignantly.

"Sometimes there are very wonderful things on a rubbish heap," said Mr Quin.

"I know, I know," cried Mr Satterthwaite, and quoted with just a trace of self-consciousness: "*Bring me the two most beautiful things in the city, said God.* You know how it goes, eh?"

Mr Quin nodded.

Mr Satterthwaite looked up at the ruins of a small cottage perched on the brink of the wall of the cliff.

"Hardly a pretty view for a house," he remarked.

"I fancy this wasn't a rubbish heap in those days," said Mr Quin. "I believe the Denmans lived there when they were first married. They moved into the big house when the old people died. The cottage was pulled down when they began to quarry the rock here—but nothing much was done, as you can see."

They turned and began retracing their steps.

"I suppose," said Mr Satterthwaite, smiling, "that many couples come wandering down this lane on these warm summer evenings."

"Probably."

"Lovers," said Mr Satterthwaite. He repeated the word thoughtfully and quite without the normal embarrassment of the Englishman. Mr Quin had that effect upon him. "Lovers . . . You have done a lot for lovers, Mr Quin."

The other bowed his head without replying.

"You have saved them from sorrow—from worse than sorrow, from death. You have been an advocate for the dead themselves."

"You are speaking of yourself—of what *you* have done—not of me."

"It is the same thing," said Mr Satterthwaite. "You know it is," he urged, as the other did not speak. "You have acted—through me. For some reason or other you do not act directly—yourself."

"Sometimes I do," said Mr Quin.

His voice held a new note. In spite of himself Mr Satterthwaite shivered a little. The afternoon, he thought, must be growing chilly. And yet the sun seemed as bright as ever.

At that moment a girl turned the corner ahead of them and came into sight. She was a very pretty girl, fair-haired and blue-eyed, wearing a pink cotton frock. Mr Satterthwaite recognized her as Molly Stanwell, whom he had met down here before.

She waved a hand to welcome him.

"John and Anna have just gone back," she cried. "They thought you must have come, but they simply had to be at the rehearsal."

"Rehearsal of what?" inquired Mr Satterthwaite.

"This masquerade thing—I don't quite know what you'll call it. There is singing and dancing and all sorts of things in it. Mr Manly, do you remember him down here? He had quite a good tenor voice, is to be Pierrot, and I am Pierrette. Two professionals are coming down for the dancing—Harlequin and Columbine, you know. And then there is a big chorus of girls. Lady Roscheimer is so keen on training village girls to sing. She's really getting the thing up for that. The music is rather lovely—but very modern—next to no tune anywhere. Claude Wickam. Perhaps you know him?"

Mr Satterthwaite nodded, for, as has been mentioned before, it was his *métier* to know everybody. He knew all about that aspiring genius Claude Wickam, and about Lady Roscheimer, who was a fat Jewish woman with a *penchant* for young men of the artistic persuasion. And he knew all about Sir Leopold Roscheimer, who liked his wife to be happy and, most rare among husbands, did not mind her being happy in her own way.

They found Claude Wickam at tea with the Denmans, cramming his mouth indiscriminately with anything handy, talking rapidly, and waving long white hands that had a double-jointed appearance. His short-sighted eyes peered through large hornrimmed spectacles.

John Denman, upright, slightly florid, with the faintest possible tendency to sleekness, listened with an air of bored attention. On the appearance of Mr Satterthwaite, the musician transferred his remarks to him. Anna Denman sat behind the tea things, quiet and expressionless as usual.

Mr Satterthwaite stole a covert glance at her. Tall, gaunt, very thin, with the skin tightly stretched over high cheek bones, black hair parted in the middle, a skin that was weather-beaten. An out of door woman who cared nothing for the use of cosmetics. A Dutch Doll of a woman, wooden, lifeless—and yet . . .

He thought: "There *should* be meaning behind that face, and yet there isn't. That's what's all wrong. Yes, all wrong." And to Claude Wickam he said: "I beg your pardon? You were saying?"

Claude Wickam, who liked the sound of his own voice, began all over again. "Russia," he said, "that was the only country in the world worth being interested in. They experimented. With lives, if you like, but still they experimented. Magnificent!" He crammed a sandwich into his mouth with one hand, and added a bite of the chocolate éclair he was waving about in the other. "Take," he said (with his mouth full), "the Russian Ballet." Remembering his hostess, he turned to her. What did *she* think of the Russian Ballet?

The question was obviously only a prelude to the important point—what Claude Wickam thought of the Russian Ballet, but her answer was unexpected and threw him completely out of his stride.

"I have never seen it."

"What?" He gazed at her open-mouthed. "But—surely—"

Her voice went on, level and emotionless.

"Before my marriage, I was a dancer. So now—"

"A busman's holiday," said her husband.

"Dancing." She shrugged her shoulders. "I know all the tricks of it. It does not interest me."

"Oh!"

It took but a moment for Claude to recover his aplomb. His voice went on.

"Talking of lives," said Mr Satterthwaite, "and experimenting in them. The Russian nation made one costly experiment."

Claude Wickam swung round on him.

"I know what you are going to say," he cried. "Kharsanova! The immortal, the only Kharsanova! You saw her dance?"

"Three times," said Mr Satterthwaite. "Twice in Paris, once in London. I shall—not forget it."

He spoke in an almost reverent voice.

"I saw her, too," said Claude Wickam. "I was ten years old. An uncle took me. God! I shall never forget it."

He threw a piece of bun fiercely into a flower bed.

"There is a statuette of her in a museum in Berlin," said Mr Satterthwaite. "It is marvellous. That impression of fragility—as though you could break her with a flip of the thumb nail. I have seen her as Columbine, in the Swan, as the dying Nymph." He paused, shaking his head. "There was genius. It will be long years before such another is born. She was young too. Destroyed ignorantly and wantonly in the first days of the Revolution."

"Fools! Madmen! Apes!" said Claude Wickam. He choked with a mouthful of tea.

"I studied with Kharsanova," said Mrs Denman. "I remember her well."

"She was wonderful?" said Mr Satterthwaite.

"Yes," said Mrs Denman quietly. "She was wonderful."

Claude Wickam departed and John Denman drew a deep sigh of relief at which his wife laughed.

Mr Satterthwaite nodded. "I know what you think. But in spite of everything, the music that that boy writes *is* music."

"I suppose it is," said Denman.

"Oh, undoubtedly. How long it will be—well, that is different."

John Denman looked at him curiously.

"You mean?"

"I mean that success has come early. And that is dangerous. Always dangerous." He looked across at Mr Quin. "You agree with me?"

"You are always right," said Mr Quin.

"We will come upstairs to my room," said Mrs Denman. "It is pleasant there."

She led the way, and they followed her. Mr Satterthwaite drew a deep breath as he caught sight of the Chinese screen. He looked up to find Mrs Denman watching him.

"You are the man who is always right," she said, nodding her head slowly at him. "What do you make of my screen?"

He felt that in some way the words were a challenge to him, and he answered almost haltingly, stumbling over the words a little.

"Why, it's—it's beautiful. More, it's unique."

"You're right." Denman had come up behind him. "We bought it early in our married life. Got it for about a tenth of its value, but even then—well, it crippled us for over a year. You remember, Anna?"

"Yes," said Mrs Denman, "I remember."

"In fact, we'd no business to buy it at all—not then. Now, of course, it's different. There was some very good lacquer going at Christie's the other day. Just what we need to make this room perfect. All Chinese together. Clear out the other stuff. Would you believe it, Satterthwaite, my wife wouldn't hear of it?"

"I like this room as it is," said Mrs Denman.

There was a curious look on her face. Again Mr Satterthwaite felt challenged and defeated. He looked round him, and for the first time he noticed the absence of all personal touch. There were no photographs, no flowers, no knick-knacks. It was not like a woman's room at all. Save for that one incongruous factor of the Chinese screen, it might have been a sample room shown at some big furnishing house.

He found her smiling at him.

"Listen," she said. She bent forward, and for a moment she seemed less English, more definitely foreign. "I speak to you for you will understand. We bought that screen with more than money—with love. For love of it, because it was beautiful and unique, we went without other things, things we needed and missed. These other Chinese pieces my husband speaks of, those we should buy with money only, we should not pay away anything of ourselves."

Her husband laughed.

"Oh, have it your own way," he said, but with a trace of irritation in his voice. "But it's all wrong against this English background. This other stuff, it's good enough of its kind, genuine solid, no fake about it—but mediocre. Good plain late Hepplewhite."

She nodded.

"Good, solid, genuine English," she murmured softly.

Mr Satterthwaite stared at her. He caught a meaning behind these words. The English room—the flaming beauty of the Chinese screen ... No, it was gone again.

"I met Miss Stanwell in the lane," he said conversationally. "She tells me she is going to be Pierrette in this show tonight."

"Yes," said Denman. "And she's awfully good, too."

"She has clumsy feet," said Anna.

"Nonsense," said her husband. "All women are alike, Satterthwaite. Can't bear to hear another woman praised. Molly is a very good-looking girl, and so of course every woman has to have their knife into her."

"I spoke of dancing," said Anna Denman. She sounded faintly surprised. "She is very pretty, yes, but her feet move clumsily. You cannot tell me anything else because I know about dancing."

Mr Satterthwaite intervened tactfully.

"You have two professional dancers coming down, I understand?"

"Yes. For the ballet proper. Prince Oranoff is bringing them down in his car."

"Sergius Oranoff?"

The question came from Anna Denman. Her husband turned and looked at her.

"You know him?"

"I used to know him—in Russia."

Mr Satterthwaite thought that John Denman looked disturbed.

"Will he know you?"

"Yes. He will know me."

She laughed—a low, almost triumphant laugh. There was nothing of the Dutch Doll about her face now. She nodded reassuringly at her husband.

"Sergius. So he is bringing down the two dancers. He was always interested in dancing."

"I remember."

John Denman spoke abruptly, then turned and left the room. Mr Quin followed him. Anna Denman crossed to the telephone and asked for a number. She arrested Mr Satterthwaite with a gesture as he was about to follow the example of the other two men.

"Can I speak to Lady Roscheimer. Oh! it is you. This is Anna Denman speaking. Has Prince Oranoff arrived yet? What? *What?* Oh, my dear! But how ghastly."

She listened for a few moments longer, then replaced the receiver. She turned to Mr Satterthwaite.

"There has been an accident. There would be with Sergius Ivanovitch driving. Oh, he has not altered in all these years. The girl was not badly hurt, but bruised and shaken, too much to dance tonight. The man's arm is broken. Sergius Ivanovitch himself is unhurt. The devil looks after his own, perhaps."

"And what about tonight's performance?"

"Exactly, my friend. Something must be done about it."

She sat thinking. Presently she looked at him.

"I am a bad hostess, Mr Satterthwaite. I do not entertain you."

"I assure you that it is not necessary. There's one thing though, Mrs Denman, that I would very much like to know."

"Yes?"

"How did you come across Mr Quin?"

"He is often down here," she said slowly. "I think he owns land in this part of the world."

"He does, he does. He told me so this afternoon," said Mr Satterthwaite.

"He is—" She paused. Her eyes met Mr Satterthwaite's. "I think you know what he is better than I do," she finished.

"I?"

"Is it not so?"

He was troubled. His neat little soul found her disturbing. He felt that she wished to force him further than he was prepared to go, that she wanted him to put into words that which he was not prepared to admit to himself.

"*You* know!" she said. "I think you know most things, Mr Satterthwaite."

Here was incense, yet for once it failed to intoxicate him. He shook his head in unwonted humility.

"What can anyone know?" he asked. "So little—so very little."

She nodded in assent. Presently she spoke again, in a queer brooding voice, without looking at him.

"Supposing I were to tell you something—you would not laugh? No, I do not think you would laugh. Supposing, then, that to carry on one's"—she paused—"one's trade, one's profession, one were to make use of a fantasy—one were to pretend to oneself something that did not exist—that one were to imagine a certain person . . . It is a pretence, you understand, a make believe—nothing more. But one day—"

"Yes?" said Mr Satterthwaite.

He was keenly interested.

"The fantasy came true! The thing one imagined—the impossible thing, the thing that could not be—was real! Is that madness? Tell me, Mr Satterthwaite. Is that madness—or do you believe it too?"

"I—" Queer how he could not get the words out. How they seemed to stick somewhere at the back of his throat.

"Folly," said Anna Denman. "Folly."

She swept out of the room and left Mr Satterthwaite with his confession of faith unspoken.

He came down to dinner to find Mrs Denman entertaining a guest, a tall dark man approaching middle age.

"Prince Oranoff—Mr Satterthwaite."

The two men bowed. Mr Satterthwaite had the feeling that some conversation had been broken off on his entry which would not be resumed. But there was no sense of strain. The Russian conversed easily and naturally on those objects which were nearest to Mr Satterthwaite's heart. He was a man of very fine artistic taste, and they soon found that they had many friends in common. John Denman joined them, and the talk became localized. Oranoff expressed regret for the accident.

"It was not my fault. I like to drive fast—yes, but I am a good driver. It was Fate—chance"—he shrugged his shoulders—"the masters of all of us."

"There speaks the Russian in you, Sergius Ivanovitch," said Mrs Denman.

"And finds an echo in you, Anna Mikalovna," he threw back quickly.

Mr Satterthwaite looked from one to the other of the three of them. John Denman, fair, aloof, English, and the other two, dark, thin, strangely alike. Something rose in his mind—what was it? Ah! he had it now. The first Act of the Walküre. Siegmund and Sieglinde—so alike—and the alien Hunding. Conjectures began to stir in his brain. Was this the meaning of the presence of Mr Quin? One thing he believed in firmly—wherever Mr Quin showed himself—there lay drama. Was this it here—the old hackneyed three-cornered tragedy?

He was vaguely disappointed. He had hoped for better things.

"What has been arranged, Anna?" asked Denman. "The thing will have to be put off, I suppose. I heard you ringing the Roscheimers up."

She shook her head.

"No—there is no need to put it off."

"But you can't do it without the ballet?"

"You certainly couldn't have a Harlequinade without Harlequin and Columbine," agreed Anna Denman drily. "I'm going to be Columbine, John."

"You?" He was astonished—disturbed, Mr Satterthwaite thought.

She nodded composedly.

"You need not be afraid, John. I shall not disgrace you. You forget—it was my profession once."

Mr Satterthwaite thought: "What an extraordinary thing a voice is. The things it says—and the things it leaves unsaid and means! I wish I knew . . ."

"Well," said John Denman grudgingly, "that solves

one half of the problem. What about the other? Where will you find Harlequin?"

"I *have* found him—there!"

She gestured towards the open doorway where Mr Quin had just appeared. He smiled back at her.

"Good lord, Quin," said John Denman. "Do you know anything of this game? I should never have imagined it."

"Mr Quin is vouched for by an expert," said his wife. "Mr Satterthwaite will answer for him."

She smiled at Mr Satterthwaite, and the little man found himself murmuring:

"Oh, yes—I answer for Mr Quin."

Denman turned his attention elsewhere.

"You know there's to be a fancy dress dance business afterwards. Great nuisance. We'll have to rig you up, Satterthwaite."

Mr Satterthwaite shook his head very decidedly.

"My years will excuse me." A brilliant idea struck him. A table napkin under his arm. "There I am, an elderly waiter who has seen better days."

He laughed.

"An interesting profession," said Mr Quin. "One sees so much."

"I've got to put on some fool pierrot thing," said Denman gloomily. "It's cool anyway, that's one thing. What about you?" He looked at Oranoff.

"I have a Harlequin costume," said the Russian. His eyes wandered for a minute to his hostess's face.

Mr Satterthwaite wondered if he was mistaken in fancying that there was just a moment of constraint.

"There might have been three of us," said Denman, with a laugh. "I've got an old Harlequin costume my wife made me when we were first married for some show or other." He paused, looking down on his broad shirt front. "I don't suppose I could get into it now."

"No," said his wife. "You couldn't get into it now."

And again her voice said something more than mere words.

She glanced up at the clock.

"If Molly doesn't turn up soon, we won't wait for her."

But at that moment the girl was announced. She was already wearing her Pierrette dress of white and green, and very charming she looked in it, so Mr Satterthwaite reflected.

She was full of excitement and enthusiasm over the forthcoming performance.

"I'm getting awfully nervous, though," she announced, as they drank coffee after dinner. "I know my voice will wobble, and I shall forget the words."

"Your voice is very charming," said Anna. "I should not worry about it if I were you."

"Oh, but I do. The other I don't mind about—the dancing, I mean. That's sure to go all right. I mean, you can't go very far wrong with your feet, can you?"

She appealed to Anna, but the older woman did not respond. Instead she said:

"Sing something now to Mr Satterthwaite. You will find that he will reassure you."

Molly went over to the piano. Her voice rang out, fresh and tuneful, in an old Irish ballad.

"Shiela, dark Shiela, what is it that you're seeing?
What is it that you're seeing, that you're seeing in the fire?"
"I see a lad that loves me—and I see a lad that leaves me,
And a third lad, a Shadow Lad—and he's the lad that grieves me."

The song went on. At the end, Mr Satterthwaite nodded vigorous approval.

"Mrs Denman is right. Your voice is charming. Not,

perhaps, very fully trained, but delightfully natural, and with that unstudied quality of youth in it."

"That's right," agreed John Denman. "You go ahead, Molly, and don't be downed by stage fright. We'd better be getting over to the Roscheimers now."

The party separated to don cloaks. It was a glorious night and they proposed to walk over, the house being only a few hundred yards down the road.

Mr Satterthwaite found himself by his friend.

"It's an odd thing," he said, "but that song made me think of you. *A third lad—a Shadow Lad*—there's mystery there, and wherever there's mystery I—well, think of you."

"Am I so mysterious?" smiled Mr Quin.

Mr Satterthwaite nodded vigorously.

"Yes, indeed. Do you know, until tonight, I had no idea that you were a professional dancer."

"Really?" said Mr Quin.

"Listen," said Mr Satterthwaite. He hummed the love motif from the Walküre. "That is what has been ringing in my head all through dinner as I looked at those two."

"Which two?"

"Prince Oranoff and Mrs Denman. Don't you see the difference in her tonight? It's as though—as though a shutter had suddenly been opened and you see the glow within."

"Yes," said Mr Quin. "Perhaps so."

"The same old drama," said Mr Satterthwaite. "I am right, am I not? Those two belong together. They are of the same world, think the same thoughts, dream the same dreams . . . One sees how it has come about. Ten years ago Denman must have been very good-looking, young, dashing, a figure of romance. And he saved her life. All quite natural. But now—what is he, after all? A good fellow—prosperous, successful—but—well, mediocre, good honest English stuff—very much like that Hepplewhite furniture upstairs. As English—and as ordinary—as that pretty English girl with her fresh untrained voice. Oh, you may smile, Mr Quin, but you cannot deny what I am saying."

"I deny nothing. In what you see you are always right. And yet—"

"Yet what?"

Mr Quin leaned forward. His dark melancholy eyes searched for those of Mr Satterthwaite.

"Have you learned so little of life?" he breathed.

He left Mr Satterthwaite vaguely disquieted, such a prey to meditation that he found the others had started without him owing to his delay in selecting a scarf for his neck. He went out by the garden, and through the same door as in the afternoon. The lane was bathed in moonlight, and even as he stood in the doorway he saw a couple enlaced in each other's arms.

For a moment he thought—

And then he saw. *John Denman and Molly Stanwell.* Denman's voice came to him, hoarse and anguished.

"I can't live without you. What are we to do?"

Mr Satterthwaite turned to go back the way he had come, but a hand stayed him. Someone else stood in the doorway beside him, someone else whose eyes had also seen.

Mr Satterthwaite had only to catch one glimpse of her face to know how wildly astray all his conclusions had been.

Her anguished hand held him there until those other two had passed up the lane and disappeared from sight. He heard himself speaking to her, saying foolish little things meant to be comforting, and ludicrously inadequate to the agony he had divined. She only spoke once.

"Please," she said, "don't leave me."

He found that oddly touching. He was, then, of use to someone. And he went on saying those things that meant nothing at all, but which were, somehow, better than silence. They went that way to the Roscheimers. Now and then her hand tightened on his shoulder, and he understood that she was glad of his company. She only took it away when they finally came to their destination. She stood very erect, her head held high.

"Now," she said, "I shall dance! Do not be afraid for me, my friend. I shall dance."

She left him abruptly. He was seized upon by Lady Roscheimer, much bediamonded and very full of lamentations. By her he was passed on to Claude Wickam.

"Ruined! Completely ruined. The sort of thing that always happens to me. All these country bumpkins think they can dance. I was never even consulted—" His voice went on—went on interminably. He had found a sympathetic listener, a man who *knew*. He gave himself up to an orgy of self-pity. It only ended when the first strains of music began.

Mr Satterthwaite came out of his dreams. He was alert, once more the critic. Wickam was an unutterable ass, but he could write music—delicate gossamer stuff, intangible as a fairy web—yet with nothing of the pretty pretty about it.

The scenery was good. Lady Roscheimer never spared expense when aiding her protégés. A glade of Arcady with lighting effects that gave it the proper atmosphere of unreality.

Two figures dancing as they had danced through time immemorial. A slender Harlequin flashing spangles in the moonlight with magic wand and masked face . . . A white Columbine pirouetting like some immortal dream . . .

Mr Satterthwaite sat up. He had lived through this before. Yes, surely . . .

Now his body was far away from Lady Roscheimer's drawing room. It was in a Berlin museum at a statuette of an immortal Columbine.

Harlequin and Columbine danced on. The wide world was theirs to dance in . . .

Moonlight—and a human figure. Pierrot wandering through the wood, singing to the moon. Pierrot who has seen Columbine and knows no rest. The Immortal two vanish, but Columbine looks back. She has heard the song of a human heart.

Pierrot wandering on through the wood . . . darkness . . . his voice dies away in the distance . . .

The village green—dancing of village girls—pierrots and pierrettes. Molly as Pierrette. No dancer—Anna Denman was right there—but a fresh tuneful voice as she sings her song "Pierrette dancing on the Green."

A good tune—Mr Satterthwaite nodded approval. Wickham wasn't above writing a tune when there was a need for it. The majority of the village girls made him shudder, but he realized that Lady Roscheimer was determinedly philanthropical.

They press Pierrot to join the dance. He refuses. With white face he wanders on—the eternal lover seeking his ideal. Evening falls. Harlequin and Columbine, invisible, dance in and out of the unconscious throng. The place is deserted, only Pierrot, weary, falls asleep on a grassy bank. Harlequin and Columbine dance round him. He wakes and sees Columbine. He woos her in vain, pleads, beseeches . . .

She stands uncertain. Harlequin beckons to her to begone. But she sees him no longer. She is listening to Pierrot, to his song of love outpoured once more. She falls into his arms, and the curtain comes down.

The Second Act is Pierrot's cottage. Columbine sits on her hearth. She is pale, weary. She listens—for what? Pierrot sings to her—woos her back to thoughts of him once more. The evening darkens. Thunder is heard . . . Columbine puts aside her spinning wheel. She is eager, stirred . . . She listens no longer to Pierrot. It is her own music that is in the air, the music of Harlequin and Columbine . . . She is awake. She remembers.

A crash of thunder! Harlequin stands in the doorway. Pierrot cannot see him, but Columbine springs up with a glad laugh. Children come running, but she pushes them aside. With another crash of thunder the walls fall, and Columbine dances out into the wild night with Harlequin.

Darkness, and through it the tune that Pierrette has sung. Light comes slowly. The cottage once more. Pierrot and Pierrette grown old and grey sit in front of the fire in two armchairs. The music is happy, but subdued. Pierrette nods in her chair. Through the window comes a shaft of moonlight, and with it the motif of Pierrot's long-forgotten song. He stirs in his chair.

Faint music—fairy music . . . Harlequin and Columbine outside. The door swings open and Columbine dances in. She leans over the sleeping Pierrot, kisses him on the lips . . .

Crash! A peal of thunder. She is outside again. In the centre of the stage is the lighted window and through it are seen the two figures of Harlequin and Columbine dancing slowly away, growing fainter and fainter . . .

A log falls. Pierrette jumps up angrily, rushes across to the window and pulls the blind. So it ends, on a sudden discord . . .

Mr Satterthwaite sat very still among the applause and vociferations. At last he got up and made his way outside. He came upon Molly Stanwell, flushed and eager, receiving compliments. He saw John Denman, pushing and elbowing his way through the throng, his eyes alight with a new flame. Molly came towards him, but, almost unconsciously, he put her aside. It was not her he was seeking.

"My wife? Where is she?"

"I think she went out in the garden."

It was, however, Mr Satterthwaite who found her, sitting on a stone seat under a cypress tree. When he came up to her, he did an odd thing. He knelt down and raised her hand to his lips.

"Ah!" she said. "You think I danced well?"

"You danced—as you always danced, Madame Kharsanova."

She drew in her breath sharply.

"So—you have guessed."

"There is only one Kharsanova. No one could see you dance and forget. But why—why?"

"What else is possible?"

"You mean?"

She had spoken very simply. She was just as simple now. "Oh! but you understand. You are of the world. A great dancer—she can have lovers, yes—but a husband, that is different. And he—he did not want the other. He wanted me to belong to him as—as Kharsanova could never have belonged."

"I see," said Mr Satterthwaite. "I see. So you gave it up?"

She nodded.

"You must have loved him very much," said Mr Satterthwaite gently.

"To make such a sacrifice?" She laughed.

"Not quite that. To make it so light-heartedly."

"Ah, yes—perhaps—you are right."

"And now?" asked Mr Satterthwaite.

Her face grew grave.

"Now?" She paused, then raised her voice and spoke into the shadows.

"Is that you, Sergius Ivanovitch?"

Prince Oranoff came out into the moonlight. He took her hand and smiled at Mr Satterthwaite without self-consciousness.

"Ten years ago I mourned the death of Anna Kharsanova," he said simply. "She was to me as my other self. Today I have found her again. We shall part no more."

"At the end of the lane in ten minutes," said Anna. "I shall not fail you."

Oranoff nodded and went off again. The dancer turned to Mr Satterthwaite. A smile played about her lips.

"Well—you are not satisfied, my friend?"

"Do you know," said Mr Satterthwaite abruptly, "that your husband is looking for you?"

He saw the tremor that passed over her face, but her voice was steady enough.

"Yes," she said gravely. "That may well be."

"I saw his eyes. They—" he stopped abruptly.

She was still calm.

"Yes, perhaps. For an hour. An hour's magic, born of past memories, of music, of moonlight—That is all."

"Then there is nothing that I can say?" He felt old, dispirited.

"For ten years I have lived with the man I love," said Anna Kharsanova. "Now I am going to the man who for ten years has loved me."

Mr Satterthwaite said nothing. He had no arguments left. Besides it really seemed the simplest solution. Only—only, somehow, it was not the solution he wanted. He felt her hand on his shoulder.

"I know, my friend, I know. But there is no third way. Always one looks for one thing—the lover, the perfect, the eternal lover ... It is the music of Harlequin one hears. No lover ever satisfies one, for all lovers are mortal. And Harlequin is only a myth, an invisible presence ... unless—"

"Yes," said Mr Satterthwaite. "Yes?"

"Unless—his name is—Death!"

Mr Satterthwaite shivered. She moved away from him, was swallowed up in the shadows ...

He never knew quite how long he sat on there, but suddenly he started up with the feeling that he had been wasting valuable time. He hurried away, impelled in a certain direction almost in spite of himself.

As he came out into the lane he had a strange feeling of unreality. Magic—magic and moonlight! And two figures coming towards him ...

Oranoff in his Harlequin dress. So he thought at first. Then, as they passed him, he knew his mistake. That lithe swaying figure belonged to one person only—Mr Quin ...

They went on down the lane—their feet light as though they were treading on air. Mr Quin turned his head and looked back, and Mr Satterthwaite had a shock, for it was not the face of Mr Quin as he had ever seen it before. It was the face of a stranger—no, not quite a stranger. Ah! he had it now, it was the face of John Denman as it might have looked before life went too well with him. Eager, adventurous, the face at once of a boy and a lover ...

Her laugh floated down to him, clear and happy ... He looked after them and saw in the distance the lights of a little cottage. He gazed after them like a man in a dream.

He was rudely awakened by a hand that fell on his shoulder and he was jerked round to face Sergius Oranoff. The man looked white and distracted.

"Where is she? Where is she? She promised—and she has not come."

"Madam has just gone up the lane—alone."

It was Mrs Denman's maid who spoke from the shadow of the door behind them. She had been waiting with her mistress's wraps.

"I was standing here and saw her pass," she added.

Mr Satterthwaite threw one harsh word at her.

"Alone? Alone, did you say?"

The maid's eyes widened in surprise.

"Yes, sir. Didn't you see her off?"

Mr Satterthwaite clutched at Oranoff.

"Quickly," he muttered. "I'm—I'm afraid."

They hurried down the lane together, the Russian talking in quick disjointed sentences.

"She is a wonderful creature. Ah! how she danced to-night. And that friend of yours. Who is he? Ah! but he is wonderful—unique. In the old days, when she danced the Columbine of Rimsky Korsakoff, she never found the perfect Harlequin. Mordoff, Kassnine—none of them were quite perfect. She had her own little fancy. She told me of it once. Always she danced with a dream Harlequin—a man who was not really there. It was Harlequin himself, she said, who came to dance with her. It was that fancy of hers that made her Columbine so wonderful."

Mr Satterthwaite nodded. There was only one thought in his head.

"Hurry," he said. "We must be in time. Oh! we must be in time."

They came round the last corner—came to the deep pit and to something lying in it that had not been there before, the body of a woman lying in a wonderful pose, arms flung wide and head thrown back. A dead face and body that were triumphant and beautiful in the moonlight.

Words came back to Mr Satterthwaite dimly—Mr Quin's words: "*wonderful things on a rubbish heap*' . . . He understood them now.

Oranoff was murmuring broken phrases. The tears were streaming down his face.

"I loved her. Always I loved her." He used almost the same words that had occurred to Mr Satterthwaite earlier in the day. "We were of the same world, she and I. We had the same thoughts, the same dreams. I would have loved her always . . ."

"How do you know?"

The Russian stared at him—at the fretful peevishness of the tone.

"How do you know?" went on Mr Satterthwaite. "It is what all lovers think—what all lovers say . . . There is only one lover—"

He turned and almost ran into Mr Quin. In an agitated manner, Mr Satterthwaite caught him by the arm and drew him aside.

"It was *you*," he said. "It was *you* who were with her just now?"

Mr Quin waited a minute and then said gently:

"You can put it that way, if you like."

"And the maid didn't see you?"

"The maid didn't see me."

"But *I* did. Why was that?"

"Perhaps, as a result of the price you have paid, you see things that other people—do not."

Mr Satterthwaite looked at him uncomprehendingly for a minute or two. Then he began suddenly to quiver all over like an aspen leaf.

"What is this place?" he whispered. "What is this place?"

"I told you earlier today. It is *My* lane."

"A Lovers' Lane," murmured Mr Satterthwaite. "And people pass along it."

"Most people, sooner or later."

"And at the end of it—what do they find?"

Mr Quin smiled. His voice was very gentle. He pointed at the ruined cottage above them.

"The house of their dreams—or a rubbish heap—who shall say?"

Mr Satterthwaite looked up at him suddenly. A wild rebellion surged over him. He felt cheated, defrauded.

"But *I*—" His voice shook. "*I* have never passed down your lane . . ."

"And do you regret?"

Mr Satterthwaite quailed. Mr Quin seemed to have loomed to enormous proportions . . . Mr Satterthwaite had a vista of something at once menacing and terrifying . . . Joy, Sorrow, Despair.

And his comfortable little soul shrank back appalled.

"Do you regret?" Mr Quin repeated his question. There was something terrible about him.

"No," Mr Satterthwaite stammered. "N-no."

And then suddenly he rallied.

"But I see things," he cried. "I may have been only a looker-on at Life—but I see things that other people do not. You said so yourself, Mr Quin . . ."

But Mr Quin had vanished.

The Adventure of the Italian Nobleman

Poirot and I had many friends and acquaintances of an informal nature. Amongst these was to be numbered Dr Hawker, a near neighbour of ours, and a member of the medical profession. It was the genial doctor's habit to drop in sometimes of an evening and have a chat with Poirot, of whose genius he was an ardent admirer. The doctor himself, frank and unsuspicious to the last degree, admired the talents so far removed from his own.

On one particular evening in early June, he arrived about half past eight and settled down to a comfortable discussion on the cheery topic of the prevalence of arsenical poisoning in crimes. It must have been about a quarter of an hour later when the door of our sitting room flew open, and a distracted female precipitated herself into the room.

"Oh, doctor, you're wanted! Such a terrible voice. It gave me a turn, it did indeed."

I recognized in our new visitor Dr Hawker's housekeeper, Miss Rider. The doctor was a bachelor, and lived in a gloomy old house a few streets away. The usually placid Miss Rider was now in a state bordering on incoherence.

"What terrible voice? Who is it, and what's the trouble?"

"It was the telephone, doctor. I answered it—and a

voice spoke. 'Help,' it said. 'Doctor—help. They've killed me!' Then it sort of tailed away. 'Who's speaking?' I said. 'Who's speaking?' Then I got a reply, just a whisper, it seemed, 'Foscatine'—something like that—'Regent's Court.'"

The doctor uttered an exclamation.

"Count Foscatini. He has a flat in Regent's Court. I must go at once. What can have happened?"

"A patient of yours?" asked Poirot.

"I attended him for some slight ailment a few weeks ago. An Italian, but he speaks English perfectly. Well, I must wish you good night, Monsieur Poirot, unless—" He hesitated.

"I perceive the thought in your mind," said Poirot, smiling. "I shall be delighted to accompany you. Hastings, run down and get hold of a taxi."

Taxis always make themselves sought for when one is particularly pressed for time, but I captured one at last, and we were soon bowling along in the direction of Regent's Park. Regent's Court was a new block of flats, situated just off St John's Wood Road. They had only recently been built, and contained the latest service devices.

There was no one in the hall. The doctor pressed the lift-bell impatiently, and when the lift arrived questioned the uniformed attendant sharply.

"Flat 11. Count Foscatini. There's been an accident there, I understand."

The man stared at him.

"First I've heard of it. Mr Graves—that's Count Foscatini's man—went out about half an hour ago, and he said nothing."

"Is the Count alone in the flat?"

"No, sir, he's got two gentlemen dining with him."

"What are they like?" I asked eagerly.

We were in the lift now, ascending rapidly to the second floor, on which Flat 11 was situated.

"I didn't see them myself, sir, but I understand that they were foreign gentlemen."

He pulled back the iron door, and we stepped out on the landing. No. 11 was opposite to us. The doctor rang the bell. There was no reply, and we could hear no sound from within. The doctor rang again and again; we could hear the bell trilling within, but no sign of life rewarded us.

"This is getting serious," muttered the doctor. He turned to the lift attendant.

"Is there any pass-key to this door?"

"There is one in the porter's office downstairs."

"Get it, then, and, look here, I think you'd better send for the police."

Poirot approved with a nod of the head.

The man returned shortly; with him came the manager.

"Will you tell me, gentlemen, what is the meaning of all this?"

"Certainly. I received a telephone message from Count Foscatini stating that he had been attacked and was dying. You can understand that we must lose no time—if we are not already too late."

The manager produced the key without more ado, and we all entered the flat.

We passed first into the small square lounge hall. A door on the right of it was half open. The manager indicated it with a nod.

"The dining room."

Dr Hawker led the way. We followed close on his heels. As we entered the room I gave a gasp. The round table in the centre bore the remains of a meal; three chairs were pushed back, as though their occupants had just risen. In the corner, to the right of the fireplace, was a big writing-table, and sitting at it was a man—or what had been a man. His right hand still grasped the base of the telephone, but he had fallen forward, struck down by a terrific blow on the head from behind. The weapon was not far to seek. A marble statue stood where it had been hurriedly put down, the base of it stained with blood.

The doctor's examination did not take a minute. "Stone dead. Must have been almost instantaneous. I wonder he even managed to telephone. It will be better not to move him until the police arrive."

On the manager's suggestion we searched the flat, but the result was a foregone conclusion. It was not likely that the murderers would be concealed there when all they had to do was to walk out.

We came back to the dining room. Poirot had not accompanied us in our tour. I found him studying the centre table with close attention. I joined him. It was a well-polished round mahogany table. A bowl of roses decorated the centre, and white lace mats reposed on the gleaming surface. There was a dish of fruit, but the three dessert plates were untouched. There were three coffee-cups with remains of coffee in them—two black, one with milk. All three men had taken port, and the decanter, half-full, stood before the centre plate. One of the men had smoked a cigar, the other two cigarettes. A tortoiseshell-and-silver box, holding cigars and cigarettes, stood open upon the table.

I enumerated all these facts to myself, but I was forced to admit that they did not shed any brilliant light on the situation. I wondered what Poirot saw in them to make him so intent. I asked him.

"*Mon ami*," he replied, "you miss the point. I am looking for something that I do *not* see."

"What is that?"

"A mistake—even a little mistake—on the part of the murderer."

He stepped swiftly to the small adjoining kitchen, looked in, and shook his head.

"Monsieur," he said to the manager, "explain to me, I pray, your system of serving meals here."

The manager stepped to a small hatch in the wall.

"This is the service lift," he explained. "It runs to the kitchens at the top of the building. You order through this telephone, and the dishes are sent down in the lift, one course at a time. The dirty plates and dishes are sent up in the same manner. No domestic worries, you understand, and at the same time you avoid the wearying publicity of always dining in a restaurant."

Poirot nodded.

"Then the plates and dishes that were used tonight are on high in the kitchen. You permit that I mount there?"

"Oh, certainly, if you like! Roberts, the lift man, will take you up and introduce you; but I'm afraid you won't find anything that's of any use. They're handling hundreds of plates and dishes, and they'll be all lumped together."

Poirot remained firm, however, and together we visited the kitchens and questioned the man who had taken the order from Flat 11.

"The order was given from the à la carte menu—for three," he explained. "Soup julienne, filet de sole normande, tournedos of beef, and a rice soufflé. What time? Just about eight o'clock, I should say. No, I'm afraid the plates and dishes have been all washed up by now. Unfortunate. You were thinking of fingerprints, I suppose?"

"Not exactly," said Poirot, with an enigmatical smile.

"I am more interested in Count Foscatini's appetite. Did he partake of every dish?"

"Yes; but of course I can't say how much of each he ate. The plates were all soiled, and the dishes empty—that is to say, with the exception of the rice soufflé. There was a fair amount of that left."

"Ah!" said Poirot, and seemed satisfied with the fact.

As we descended to the flat again he remarked in a low tone:

"We have decidedly to do with a man of method."

"Do you mean the murderer, or Count Foscatini?"

"The latter was undoubtedly an orderly gentleman. After imploring help and announcing his approaching demise, he carefully hung up the telephone receiver."

I stared at Poirot. His words now and his recent inquiries gave me the glimmering of an idea.

"You suspect poison?" I breathed. "The blow on the head was a blind."

Poirot merely smiled.

We re-entered the flat to find the local inspector of police had arrived with two constables. He was inclined to resent our appearance, but Poirot calmed him with the mention of our Scotland Yard friend, Inspector Japp, and we were accorded a grudging permission to remain. It was a lucky thing we were, for we had not been back five minutes before an agitated middle-aged man came rushing into the room with every appearance of grief and agitation.

This was Graves, valet-butler to the late Count Foscatini. The story he had to tell was a sensational one.

On the previous morning, two gentlemen had called to see his master. They were Italians, and the elder of the two, a man of about forty, gave his name as Signor Ascanio. The younger was a well-dressed lad of about twenty-four.

Count Foscatini was evidently prepared for their visit and immediately sent Graves out upon some trivial errand. Here the man paused and hesitated in his story. In the end, however, he admitted that, curious as to the purport of the interview, he had not obeyed immediately, but had lingered about endeavouring to hear something of what was going on.

The conversation was carried on in so low a tone that he was not as successful as he had hoped; but he gathered enough to make it clear that some kind of monetary proposition was being discussed, and that the basis of it was a threat. The discussion was anything but amicable. In the end, Count Foscatini raised his voice slightly, and the listener heard these words clearly:

> "I have no time to argue further now, gentlemen. If you will dine with me tomorrow night at eight o'clock, we will resume the discussion."

Afraid of being discovered listening, Graves had then hurried out to do his master's errand. This evening the two men had arrived punctually at eight. During dinner they had talked of indifferent matters—politics, the weather, and the theatrical world. When Graves had placed the port upon the table and brought in the coffee his master told him that he might have the evening off.

"Was that a usual proceeding of his when he had guests?" asked the inspector.

"No, sir; it wasn't. That's what made me think it must be some business of a very unusual kind that he was going to discuss with these gentlemen."

That finished Graves's story. He had gone out about 8.30, and meeting a friend, had accompanied him to the Metropolitan Music Hall in Edgware Road.

Nobody had seen the two men leave, but the time

of the murder was fixed clearly enough at 8.47. A small clock on the writing-table had been swept off by Foscatini's arm, and had stopped at that hour, which agreed with Miss Rider's telephone summons.

The police surgeon had made his examination of the body, and it was now lying on the couch. I saw the face for the first time—the olive complexion, the long nose, the luxuriant black moustache, and the full red lips drawn back from the dazzlingly white teeth. Not altogether a pleasant face.

"Well," said the inspector, refastening his notebook. "The case seems clear enough. The only difficulty will be to lay our hands on this Signor Ascanio. I suppose his address is not in the dead man's pocket-book by any chance?"

As Poirot had said, the late Foscatini was an orderly man. Neatly written in small, precise handwriting was the inscription, "Signor Paolo Ascanio, Grosvenor Hotel."

The inspector busied himself with the telephone, then turned to us with a grin.

"Just in time. Our fine gentleman was off to catch the boat train to the Continent. Well, gentlemen, that's about all we can do here. It's a bad business, but straightforward enough. One of these Italian vendetta things, as likely as not."

Thus airily dismissed, we found our way downstairs. Dr Hawker was full of excitement.

"Like the beginning of a novel, eh? Real exciting stuff. Wouldn't believe it if you read about it."

Poirot did not speak. He was very thoughtful. All the evening he had hardly opened his lips.

"What says the master detective, eh?" asked Hawker, clapping him on the back. "Nothing to work your grey cells over this time."

"You think not?"

"What could there be?"

"Well, for example, there is the window."

"The window? But it was fastened. Nobody could have got out or in that way. I noticed it specially."

"And why were you able to notice it?"

The doctor looked puzzled. Poirot hastened to explain.

"It is to the curtains that I refer. They were not drawn. A little odd, that. And then there was the coffee. It was very black coffee."

"Well, what of it?"

"Very black," repeated Poirot. "In conjunction with that let us remember that very little of the rice soufflé was eaten, and we get—what?"

"Moonshine," laughed the doctor. "You're pulling my leg."

"Never do I pull the leg. Hastings here knows that I am perfectly serious."

"I don't know what you are getting at, all the same," I confessed. "You don't suspect the manservant, do you? He might have been in with the gang, and put some dope in the coffee. I suppose they'll test his alibi?"

"Without doubt, my friend; but it is the alibi of Signor Ascanio that interests me."

"You think he has an alibi?"

"That is just what worries me. I have no doubt that we shall soon be enlightened on that point."

The *Daily Newsmonger* enabled us to become conversant with succeeding events.

Signor Ascanio was arrested and charged with the murder of Count Foscatini. When arrested, he denied knowing the Count, and declared he had never been near Regent's Court either on the evening of the crime or on the previous morning. The younger man had disappeared entirely. Signor Ascanio had arrived alone at the Grosvenor Hotel from the Continent two days before the murder. All efforts to trace the second man failed.

Ascanio, however, was not sent for trial. No less a personage than the Italian Ambassador himself came forward and testified at the police-court proceedings that Ascanio had been with him at the Embassy from eight till nine that evening. The prisoner was discharged. Naturally, a lot of people thought that the crime was a political one, and was being deliberately hushed up.

Poirot had taken a keen interest in all these points. Nevertheless, I was somewhat surprised when he suddenly informed me one morning that he was expecting a visitor at eleven o'clock, and that the visitor was none other than Ascanio himself.

"He wishes to consult you?"

"*Du tout*, Hastings, I wish to consult him."

"What about?"

"The Regent's Court murder."

"You are going to prove that he did it?"

"A man cannot be tried twice for murder, Hastings. Endeavour to have the common sense. Ah, that is our friend's ring."

A few minutes later Signor Ascanio was ushered in—a small, thin man with a secretive and furtive glance in his eyes. He remained standing, darting suspicious glances from one to the other of us.

"Monsieur Poirot?"

My little friend tapped himself gently on the chest.

"Be seated, signor. You received my note. I am determined to get to the bottom of this mystery. In some small measure you can aid me. Let us commence. You—in company with a friend—visited the late Count Foscatini on the morning of Tuesday the 9th—"

The Italian made an angry gesture.

"I did nothing of the sort. I have sworn in court—"

"*Précisément*—and I have a little idea that you have sworn falsely."

"You threaten me? Bah! I have nothing to fear from you. I have been acquitted."

"Exactly; and as I am not an imbecile, it is not with the gallows I threaten you—but with publicity. Publicity! I see that you do not like the word. I had an idea that you would not. My little ideas, you know, they are very valuable to me. Come, signor, your only chance is to be frank with me. I do not ask to know whose indiscretions brought you to England. I know this much, you came for the special purpose of seeing Count Foscatini."

"He was not a count," growled the Italian.

"I have already noted the fact that his name does not appear in the *Almanach de Gotha*. Never mind, the title of count is often useful in the profession of blackmailing."

"I suppose I might as well be frank. You seem to know a good deal."

"I have employed my grey cells to some advantage. Come, Signor Ascanio, you visited the dead man on the Tuesday morning—that is so, is it not?"

"Yes; but I never went there on the following evening. There was no need. I will tell you all. Certain information concerning a man of great position in Italy had come into this scoundrel's possession. He demanded a big sum of money in return for the papers. I came over to England to arrange the matter. I called upon him by appointment that morning. One of the young secretaries of the Embassy was with me. The Count was more reasonable than I had hoped, although even then the sum of money I paid him was a huge one."

"Pardon, how was it paid?"

"In Italian notes of comparatively small denomination. I paid over the money then and there. He handed me the incriminating papers. I never saw him again."

"Why did you not say all this when you were arrested?"

"In my delicate position I was forced to deny any association with the man."

"And how do you account for the events of the evening then?"

"I can only think that someone must have deliberately impersonated me. I understand that no money was found in the flat."

Poirot looked at him and shook his head.

"Strange," he murmured. "We all have the little grey cells. And so few of us know how to use them. Good morning, Signor Ascanio. I believe your story. It is very much as I had imagined. But I had to make sure."

After bowing his guest out, Poirot returned to his armchair and smiled at me.

"Let us hear M. le Capitaine Hastings on the case."

"Well, I suppose Ascanio is right—somebody impersonated him."

"Never, never will you use the brains the good God has given you. Recall to yourself some words I uttered after leaving the flat that night. I referred to the window-curtains not being drawn. We are in the month of June. It is still light at eight o'clock. The light is failing by half-past. *Ça vous dit quelque chose?* I perceive a struggling impression that you will arrive some day. Now let us continue. The coffee was, as I said, very black. Count Foscatini's teeth were magnificently white. Coffee stains the teeth. We reason from that that Count Foscatini did not drink any coffee. Yet there was coffee in all three cups. Why should anyone pretend Count Foscatini had drunk coffee when he had not done so?"

I shook my head, utterly bewildered.

"Come, I will help you. What evidence have we that Ascanio and his friend, or two men posing as them, ever came to the flat that night? Nobody saw them go in; nobody saw them go out. We have the evidence of one man and of a host of inanimate objects."

"You mean?"

"I mean knives and forks and plates and empty dishes. Ah, but it was a clever idea! Graves is a thief and a scoundrel, but what a man of method! He overhears a portion of the conversation in the morning, enough to realize that Ascanio will be in an awkward position to defend himself. The following evening, about eight o'clock, he tells his master he is wanted at the telephone. Foscatini sits down, stretches out his hand to the telephone, and from behind Graves strikes him down with the marble figure. Then quickly to the service telephone—dinner for three! It comes, he lays the table, dirties the plates, knives, and forks, etc. But he has to get rid of the food too. Not only is he a man of brain; he has a resolute and capacious stomach! But after eating three tournedos, the rice soufflé is too much for him! He even smokes a cigar and two cigarettes to carry out the illusion. Ah, but it was magnificently thorough! Then, having moved on the hands of the clock to 8.47, he smashes it and stops it. The one thing he does not do is to draw the curtains. But if there had been a real dinner party the curtains would have been drawn as soon as the light began to fail. Then he hurries out, mentioning the guests to the lift man in passing. He hurries to a telephone box, and as near as possible to 8.47 rings up the doctor with his master's dying cry. So successful is his idea that no one ever inquires if a call was put through from Flat 11 at that time."

"Except Hercule Poirot, I suppose?" I said sarcastically.

"Not even Hercule Poirot," said my friend, with a

smile. "I am about to inquire now. I had to prove my point to you first. But you will see, I shall be right; and then Japp, to whom I have already given a hint, will be able to arrest the respectable Graves. I wonder how much of the money he has spent."

Poirot *was* right. He always is, confound him!

Jane in Search of a Job

Jane Cleveland rustled the pages of the *Daily Leader* and sighed. A deep sigh that came from the innermost recesses of her being. She looked with distaste at the marble-topped table, the poached egg on toast which reposed on it, and the small pot of tea. Not because she was not hungry. That was far from being the case. Jane was extremely hungry. At that moment she felt like consuming a pound and a half of well-cooked beefsteak, with chip potatoes, and possibly French beans. The whole washed down with some more exciting vintage than tea.

But young women whose exchequers are in a parlous condition cannot be choosers. Jane was lucky to be able to order a poached egg and a pot of tea. It seemed unlikely that she would be able to do so tomorrow. That is unless—

She turned once more to the advertisement columns of the *Daily Leader.* To put it plainly, Jane was out of a job, and the position was becoming acute. Already the genteel lady who presided over the shabby boarding-house was looking askance at this particular young woman.

"And yet," said Jane to herself, throwing up her chin indignantly, which was a habit of hers, "and yet I'm intelligent and good-looking and well educated. What more does anyone want?"

According to the *Daily Leader*, they seemed to want shorthand typists of vast experience, managers for business houses with a little capital to invest, ladies to share in the profits of poultry farming (here again a little capital was required), and innumerable cooks, housemaids and parlourmaids—particularly parlourmaids.

"I wouldn't mind being a parlourmaid," said Jane to herself. "But there again, no one would take me without experience. I could go somewhere, I dare say, as a Willing Young Girl—but they don't pay willing young girls anything to speak of."

She sighed again, propped the paper up in front of her, and attacked the poached egg with all the vigour of healthy youth.

When the last mouthful had been despatched, she turned the paper, and studied the Agony and Personal column whilst she drank her tea. The Agony column was always the last hope.

Had she but possessed a couple of thousand pounds, the thing would have been easy enough. There were at least seven unique opportunities—all yielding not less than three thousand a year. Jane's lip curled a little. "If I had two thousand pounds," she murmured, "it wouldn't be easy to separate me from it."

She cast her eyes rapidly down to the bottom of the column and ascended with the ease born of long practice.

There was the lady who gave such wonderful prices for cast-off clothing. "Ladies' wardrobes inspected at their own dwellings." There were gentlemen who bought anything—but principally teeth. There were ladies of title going abroad who would dispose of their furs at a ridiculous figure. There was the distressed clergyman and the hard-working widow, and the disabled officer, all needing sums varying from fifty pounds to two thousand. And then suddenly Jane came to an abrupt halt. She put down her teacup and read the advertisement through again.

"There's a catch in it, of course," she murmured. "There always is a catch in these sort of things. I shall have to be careful. But still—"

The advertisement which so intrigued Jane Cleveland ran as follows:

> *If a young lady of twenty-five to thirty years of age, eyes dark blue, very fair hair, black lashes and brows, straight nose, slim figure, height five feet seven inches, good mimic and able to speak French, will call at 7 Endersleigh Street, between 5 and 6 p.m., she will hear of something to her advantage.*

"Guileless Gwendolen, or why girls go wrong," murmured Jane. "I shall certainly have to be careful. But there are too many specifications, really, for that sort of thing. I wonder now . . . Let us overhaul the catalogue."

She proceeded to do so.

"Twenty-five to thirty—I'm twenty-six. Eyes dark blue, that's right. Hair very fair—black lashes and brows—all OK. Straight nose? Ye-es—straight enough, anyway. It doesn't hook or turn up. And I've got a slim figure—slim even for nowadays. I'm only five feet six inches—but I could wear high heels. I *am* a good mimic—nothing wonderful, but I can copy people's voices, and I speak French like an angel or a Frenchwoman. In fact, I'm absolutely the goods. They ought to tumble over themselves with delight when I turn up. Jane Cleveland, go in and win."

Resolutely Jane tore out the advertisement and placed it in her handbag. Then she demanded her bill, with a new briskness in her voice.

At ten minutes to five Jane was reconnoitring in

the neighbourhood of Endersleigh Street. Endersleigh Street itself is a small street sandwiched between two larger streets in the neighbourhood of Oxford Circus. It is drab, but respectable.

No. 7 seemed in no way different from the neighbouring houses. It was composed like they were of offices. But looking up at it, it dawned upon Jane for the first time that she was not the only blue-eyed, fair-haired, straight-nosed, slim-figured girl of between twenty-five and thirty years of age. London was evidently full of such girls, and forty or fifty of them at least were grouped outside No. 7 Endersleigh Street.

"Competition," said Jane. "I'd better join the queue quickly."

She did so, just as three more girls turned the corner of the street. Others followed them. Jane amused herself by taking stock of her immediate neighbours. In each case she managed to find something wrong—fair eyelashes instead of dark, eyes more grey than blue, fair hair that owed its fairness to art and not to Nature, interesting variations in noses, and figures that only an all-embracing charity could have described as slim. Jane's spirits rose.

"I believe I've got as good an all-round chance as anyone," she murmured to herself. "I wonder what it's all about? A beauty chorus, I hope."

The queue was moving slowly but steadily forward. Presently a second stream of girls began, issuing from inside the house. Some of them tossed their heads, some of them smirked.

"Rejected," said Jane, with glee. "I hope to goodness they won't be full up before I get in."

And still the queue of girls moved forwards. There were anxious glances in tiny mirrors, and a frenzied powdering of noses. Lipsticks were brandished freely.

"I wish I had a smarter hat," said Jane to herself sadly.

At last it was her turn. Inside the door of the house was a glass door at one side, with the legend, Messrs. Cuthbertsons, inscribed on it. It was through this glass door that the applicants were passing one by one. Jane's turn came. She drew a deep breath and entered.

Inside was an outer office, obviously intended for clerks. At the end was another glass door. Jane was directed to pass through this, and did so. She found herself in a smaller room. There was a big desk in it, and behind the desk was a keen-eyed man of middle age with a thick rather foreign-looking moustache. His glance swept over Jane, then he pointed to a door on the left.

"Wait in there, please," he said crisply.

Jane obeyed. The apartment she entered was already occupied. Five girls sat there, all very upright and all glaring at each other. It was clear to Jane that she had been included amongst the likely candidates, and her spirits rose. Nevertheless, she was forced to admit that these five girls were equally eligible with herself as far as the terms of the advertisement went.

The time passed. Streams of girls were evidently passing through the inner office. Most of them were dismissed through another door giving on the corridor, but every now and then a recruit arrived to swell the select assembly. At half-past six there were fourteen girls assembled there.

Jane heard a murmur of voices from the inner office, and then the foreign-looking gentleman, whom she had nicknamed in her mind "the Colonel' owing to the military character of his moustache, appeared in the doorway.

"I will see you ladies one at a time, if you please," he announced. "In the order in which you arrived, please."

Jane was, of course, the sixth on the list. Twenty minutes elapsed before she was called in. "The Colonel' was standing with his hands behind his back. He put her through a rapid catechism, tested her knowledge of French, and measured her height.

"It is possible, mademoiselle," he said in French, "that you may suit. I do not know. But it is possible."

"What is this post, if I may ask?" said Jane bluntly.

He shrugged his shoulders.

"That I cannot tell you as yet. If you are chosen—then you shall know."

"This seems very mysterious," objected Jane. "I couldn't possibly take up anything without knowing all about it. Is it connected with the stage, may I ask?"

"The stage? Indeed, no."

"Oh!" said Jane, rather taken aback.

He was looking at her keenly.

"You have intelligence, yes? And discretion?"

"I've quantities of intelligence and discretion," said Jane calmly. "What about the pay?"

"The pay will amount to two thousand pounds—for a fortnight's work."

"Oh!" said Jane faintly.

She was too taken aback by the munificence of the sum named to recover all at once.

The Colonel resumed speaking.

"One other young lady I have already selected. You and she are equally suitable. There may be others I have not yet seen. I will give you instruction as to your further proceedings. You know Harridge's Hotel?"

Jane gasped. Who in England did not know Harridge's Hotel? That famous hostelry situated modestly in a bystreet of Mayfair, where notabilities and royalties arrived and departed as a matter of course. Only this morning Jane had read of the arrival of the

Grand Duchess Pauline of Ostrova. She had come over to open a big bazaar in aid of Russian refugees, and was, of course, staying at Harridge's.

"Yes," said Jane, in answer to the Colonel's question.

"Very good. Go there. Ask for Count Streptitch. Send up your card—you have a card?"

Jane produced one. The Colonel took it from her and inscribed in the corner a minute P. He handed the card back to her.

"That ensures that the count will see you. He will understand that you come from me. The final decision lies with him—and another. If he considers you suitable, he will explain matters to you, and you can accept or decline his proposal. Is that satisfactory?"

"Perfectly satisfactory," said Jane.

"So far," she murmured to herself as she emerged into the street, "I can't see the catch. And yet, there must be one. There's no such thing as money for nothing. It must be crime! There's nothing else left."

Her spirits rose. In moderation Jane did not object to crime. The papers had been full lately of the exploits of various girl bandits. Jane had seriously thought of becoming one if all else failed.

She entered the exclusive portals of Harridge's with slight trepidation. More than ever, she wished that she had a new hat.

But she walked bravely up to the bureau and produced her card, and asked for Count Streptitch without a shade of hesitation in her manner. She fancied that the clerk looked at her rather curiously. He took the card, however, and gave it to a small page boy with some low-voiced instructions which Jane did not catch. Presently the page returned, and Jane was invited to accompany him. They went up in the lift and along a corridor to some big double doors where the page knocked. A moment later Jane found herself in a big room, facing a tall thin man with a fair beard, who was holding her card in a languid white hand.

"Miss Jane Cleveland," he read slowly. "I am Count Streptitch."

His lips parted suddenly in what was presumably intended to be a smile, disclosing two rows of white even teeth. But no effect of merriment was obtained.

"I understand that you applied in answer to our advertisement," continued the count. "The good Colonel Kranin sent you on here."

"He *was* a colonel," thought Jane, pleased with her perspicacity, but she merely bowed her head.

"You will pardon me if I ask you a few questions?"

He did not wait for a reply, but proceeded to put Jane through a catechism very similar to that of Colonel Kranin. Her replies seemed to satisfy him. He nodded his head once or twice.

"I will ask you now, mademoiselle, to walk to the door and back again slowly."

"Perhaps they want me to be a mannequin," thought Jane, as she complied. "But they wouldn't pay two thousand pounds to a mannequin. Still, I suppose I'd better not ask questions yet awhile."

Count Streptitch was frowning. He tapped on the table with his white fingers. Suddenly he rose, and opening the door of an adjoining room, he spoke to someone inside.

He returned to his seat, and a short middle-aged lady came through the door, closing it behind her. She was plump and extremely ugly, but had nevertheless the air of being a person of importance.

"Well, Anna Michaelovna," said the count. "What do you think of her?"

The lady looked Jane up and down much as though

the girl had been a wax-work at a show. She made no pretence of any greeting.

"She might do," she said at length. "Of actual likeness in the real sense of the word, there is very little. But the figure and the colouring are very good, better than any of the others. What do you think of it, Feodor Alexandrovitch?"

"I agree with you, Anna Michaelovna."

"Does she speak French?"

"Her French is excellent."

Jane felt more and more of a dummy. Neither of these strange people appeared to remember that she was a human being.

"But will she be discreet?" asked the lady, frowning heavily at the girl.

"This is the Princess Poporensky," said Count Streptitch to Jane in French. "She asks whether you can be discreet?"

Jane addressed her reply to the princess.

"Until I have had the position explained to me, I can hardly make promises."

"It is just what she says there, the little one," remarked the lady. "I think she is intelligent, Feodor Alexandrovitch—more intelligent than the others. Tell me, little one, have you also courage?"

"I don't know," said Jane, puzzled. "I don't particularly like being hurt, but I can bear it."

"Ah! that is not what I mean. You do not mind danger, no?"

"Oh!" said Jane. "Danger! That's all right. I like danger."

"And you are poor? You would like to earn much money?"

"Try me," said Jane with something approaching enthusiasm.

Count Streptitch and Princess Poporensky exchanged glances. Then, simultaneously, they nodded.

"Shall I explain matters, Anna Michaelovna?" the former asked.

The princess shook her head.

"Her Highness wishes to do that herself."

"It is unnecessary—and unwise."

"Nevertheless those are her commands. I was to bring the girl in as soon as you had done with her."

Streptitch shrugged his shoulders. Clearly he was not pleased. Equally clearly he had no intention of disobeying the edict. He turned to Jane.

"The Princess Poporensky will present you to Her Highness the Grand Duchess Pauline. Do not be alarmed."

Jane was not in the least alarmed. She was delighted at the idea of being presented to a real live grand duchess. There was nothing of the Socialist about Jane. For the moment she had even ceased to worry about her hat.

The Princess Poporensky led the way, waddling along with a gait that she managed to invest with a certain dignity in spite of adverse circumstances. They passed through the adjoining room, which was a kind of antechamber, and the princess knocked upon a door in the farther wall. A voice from inside replied and the princess opened the door and passed in, Jane close upon her heels.

"Let me present to you, madame," said the princess in a solemn voice, "Miss Jane Cleveland."

A young woman who had been sitting in a big armchair at the other end of the room jumped up and ran forward. She stared fixedly at Jane for a minute or two, and then laughed merrily.

"But this is splendid, Anna," she replied. "I never imagined we should succeed so well. Come, let us see ourselves side by side."

Taking Jane's arm, she drew the girl across the room, pausing before a full-length mirror which hung on the wall.

"You see?" she cried delightedly. "It is a perfect match!"

Already, with her first glance at the Grand Duchess Pauline, Jane had begun to understand. The Grand Duchess was a young woman perhaps a year or two older than Jane. She had the same shade of fair hair, and the same slim figure. She was, perhaps, a shade taller. Now that they stood side by side, the likeness was very apparent. Detail for detail, the colouring was almost exactly the same.

The Grand Duchess clapped her hands. She seemed an extremely cheerful young woman.

"Nothing could be better," she declared. "You must congratulate Feodor Alexandrovitch for me, Anna. He has indeed done well."

"As yet, madame," murmured the princess, in a low voice, "this young woman does not know what is required of her."

"True," said the Grand Duchess, becoming somewhat calmer in manner. "I forgot. Well, I will enlighten her. Leave us together, Anna Michaelovna."

"But, madame—"

"Leave us alone, I say."

She stamped her foot angrily. With considerable reluctance Anna Michaelovna left the room. The Grand Duchess sat down and motioned to Jane to do the same.

"They are tiresome, these old women," remarked Pauline. "But one has to have them. Anna Michaelovna is better than most. Now then, Miss—ah, yes, Miss Jane Cleveland. I like the name. I like you too. You are sympathetic. I can tell at once if people are sympathetic."

"That's very clever of you, ma'am," said Jane, speaking for the first time.

"I am clever," said Pauline calmly. "Come now, I will explain things to you. Not that there is much to explain. You know the history of Ostrova. Practically all of my family are dead—massacred by the Communists. I am, perhaps, the last of my line. I am a woman, I cannot sit upon the throne. You think they would let me be. But no, wherever I go attempts are made to assassinate me. Absurd, is it not? These vodka-soaked brutes never have any sense of proportion."

"I see," said Jane, feeling that something was required of her.

"For the most part I live in retirement—where I can take precautions, but now and then I have to take part in public ceremonies. While I am here, for instance, I have to attend several semi-public functions. Also in Paris on my way back. I have an estate in Hungary, you know. The sport there is magnificent."

"Is it really?" said Jane.

"Superb. I adore sport. Also—I ought not to tell you this, but I shall because your face is so sympathetic—there are plans being made there—very quietly, you understand. Altogether it is very important that I should not be assassinated during the next two weeks."

"But surely the police—" began Jane.

"The police? Oh, yes, they are very good, I believe. And we too—we have our spies. It is possible that I shall be forewarned when the attempt is to take place. But then, again, I might not."

She shrugged her shoulders.

"I begin to understand," said Jane slowly. "You want me to take your place?"

"Only on certain occasions," said the Grand Duchess eagerly. "You must be somewhere at hand, you understand? I may require you twice, three times, four times in the next fortnight. Each time it will be upon the occasion of some public function. Naturally in intimacy of any kind, you could not represent me."

"Of course not," agreed Jane.

"You will do very well indeed. It was clever of Feodor Alexandrovitch to think of an advertisement, was it not?"

"Supposing," said Jane, "that I get assassinated?"

The Grand Duchess shrugged her shoulders.

"There is the risk, of course, but according to our own secret information, they want to kidnap me, not kill me outright. But I will be quite honest—it is always possible that they might throw a bomb."

"I see," said Jane.

She tried to imitate the light-hearted manner of Pauline. She wanted very much to come to the question of money, but did not quite see how best to introduce the subject. But Pauline saved her the trouble.

"We will pay you well, of course," she said carelessly. "I cannot remember now exactly how much Feodor Alexandrovitch suggested. We were speaking in francs or kronen."

"Colonel Kranin," said Jane, "said something about two thousand pounds."

"That was it," said Pauline, brightening. "I remember now. It is enough, I hope? Or would you rather have three thousand?"

"Well," said Jane, "if it's all the same to you, I'd rather have three thousand."

"You are business-like, I see," said the Grand Duchess kindly. "I wish I was. But I have no idea of money at all. What I want I have to have, that is all."

It seemed to Jane a simple but admirable attitude of mind.

"And of course, as you say, there is danger," Pauline continued thoughtfully. "Although you do not look to me as though you minded danger. I do not myself.

I hope you do not think that it is because I am a coward that I want you to take my place? You see, it is most important for Ostrova that I should marry and have at least two sons. After that, it does not matter what happens to me."

"I see," said Jane.

"And you accept?"

"Yes," said Jane resolutely. "I accept."

Pauline clapped her hands vehemently several times. Princess Poporensky appeared immediately.

"I have told her all, Anna," announced the Grand Duchess. "She will do what we want, and she is to have three thousand pounds. Tell Feodor to make a note of it. She is really very like me, is she not? I think she is better looking, though."

The princess waddled out of the room, and returned with Count Streptitch.

"We have arranged everything, Feodor Alexandrovitch," the Grand Duchess said.

He bowed.

"Can she play her part, I wonder?" he queried, eyeing Jane doubtfully.

"I'll show you," said the girl suddenly. "You permit, ma'am?" she said to the Grand Duchess.

The latter nodded delightedly.

Jane stood up.

"But this is splendid, Anna," she said. "I never imagined we should succeed so well. Come, let us see ourselves, side by side."

And, as Pauline had done, she drew the other girl to the glass.

"You see? A perfect match!"

Words, manner and gesture, it was an excellent imitation of Pauline's greeting. The princess nodded her head, and uttered a grunt of approbation.

"It is good, that," she declared. "It would deceive most people."

"You are very clever," said Pauline appreciatively. "I could not imitate anyone else to save my life."

Jane believed her. It had already struck her that Pauline was a young woman who was very much herself.

"Anna will arrange details with you," said the Grand Duchess. "Take her into my bedroom, Anna, and try some of my clothes on her."

She nodded a gracious farewell, and Jane was convoyed away by the Princess Poporensky.

"This is what Her Highness will wear to open the bazaar," explained the old lady, holding up a daring creation of white and black. "This is in three days' time. It may be necessary for you to take her place there. We do not know. We have not yet received information."

At Anna's bidding, Jane slipped off her own shabby garments, and tried on the frock. It fitted her perfectly. The other nodded approvingly.

"It is almost perfect—just a shade long on you, because you are an inch or so shorter than Her Highness."

"That is easily remedied," said Jane quickly. "The Grand Duchess wears low-heeled shoes, I noticed. If I wear the same kind of shoes, but with high heels, it will adjust things nicely."

Anna Michaelovna showed her the shoes that the Grand Duchess usually wore with the dress. Lizard skin with a strap across. Jane memorized them, and arranged to get a pair just like them, but with different heels.

"It would be well," said Anna Michaelovna, "for you to have a dress of distinctive colour and material quite unlike Her Highness's. Then in case it becomes necessary for you to change places at a moment's notice, the substitution is less likely to be noticed."

Jane thought a minute.

"What about a flame-red marocain? And I might, perhaps, have plain glass pince-nez. That alters the appearance very much."

Both suggestions were approved, and they went into further details.

Jane left the hotel with bank-notes for a hundred pounds in her purse, and instructions to purchase the necessary outfit and engage rooms at the Blitz Hotel as Miss Montresor of New York.

On the second day after this, Count Streptitch called upon her there.

"A transformation indeed," he said, as he bowed.

Jane made him a mock bow in return. She was enjoying the new clothes and the luxury of her life very much.

"All this is very nice," she sighed. "But I suppose that your visit means I must get busy and earn my money."

"That is so. We have received information. It seems possible that an attempt will be made to kidnap Her Highness on the way home from the bazaar. That is to take place, as you know, at Orion House, which is about ten miles out of London. Her Highness will be forced to attend the bazaar in person, as the Countess of Anchester, who is promoting it, knows her personally. But the following is the plan I have concocted."

Jane listened attentively as he outlined it to her.

She asked a few questions, and finally declared that she understood perfectly the part that she had to play.

The next day dawned bright and clear—a perfect day for one of the great events of the London Season, the bazaar at Orion House, promoted by the Countess of Anchester in aid of Ostrovian refugees in this country.

Having regard to the uncertainty of the English climate, the bazaar itself took place within the spacious rooms of Orion House, which has been for five hundred years in the possession of the Earls of Anchester. Various collections had been loaned, and a charming idea was the gift by a hundred society women of one pearl each taken from their own necklaces, each pearl to be sold by auction on the second day. There were also numerous sideshows and attractions in the grounds.

Jane was there early in the rôle of Miss Montresor. She wore a dress of flame-coloured marocain, and a small red cloche hat. On her feet were high-heeled lizard-skin shoes.

The arrival of the Grand Duchess Pauline was a great event. She was escorted to the platform and duly presented with a bouquet of roses by a small child. She made a short but charming speech and declared the bazaar open. Count Streptitch and Princess Poporensky were in attendance upon her.

She wore the dress that Jane had seen, white with a bold design of black, and her hat was a small cloche of black with a profusion of white ospreys hanging over the brim and a tiny lace veil coming half-way down the face. Jane smiled to herself.

The Grand Duchess went round the bazaar, visiting every stall, making a few purchases, and being uniformly gracious. Then she prepared to depart.

Jane was prompt to take up her cue. She requested a word with the Princess Poporensky and asked to be presented to the Grand Duchess.

"Ah, yes!" said Pauline, in a clear voice. "Miss Montresor, I remember the name. She is an American journalist, I believe. She has done much for our cause. I should be glad to give her a short interview for her paper. Is there anywhere where we could be undisturbed?"

A small anteroom was immediately placed at the Grand Duchess's disposal, and Count Streptitch was despatched to bring in Miss Montresor. As soon as he had done so, and withdrawn again, the Princess Poporensky remaining in attendance, a rapid exchange of garments took place.

Three minutes later, the door opened and the Grand Duchess emerged, her bouquet of roses held up to her face.

Bowing graciously, and uttering a few words of farewell to Lady Anchester in French, she passed out and entered her car which was waiting. Princess Poporensky took her place beside her, and the car drove off.

"Well," said Jane, "that's that. I wonder how Miss Montresor's getting on."

"No one will notice her. She can slip out quietly."

"That's true," said Jane. "I did it nicely, didn't I?"

"You acted your part with great distinction."

"Why isn't the count with us?"

"He was forced to remain. Someone must watch over the safety of Her Highness."

"I hope nobody's going to throw bombs," said Jane apprehensively. "Hi! we're turning off the main road. Why's that?"

Gathering speed, the car was shooting down a side road.

Jane jumped up and put her head out of the window, remonstrating with the driver. He only laughed and increased his speed. Jane sank back into her seat again.

"Your spies were right," she said, with a laugh. "We're for it all right. I suppose the longer I keep it up, the safer it is for the Grand Duchess. At all events we must give her time to return to London safely."

At the prospect of danger, Jane's spirits rose. She had not relished the prospect of a bomb, but this type of adventure appealed to her sporting instincts.

Suddenly, with a grinding of brakes, the car pulled up in its own length. A man jumped on the step. In his hand was a revolver.

"Put your hands up," he snarled.

The Princess Poporensky's hands rose swiftly, but Jane merely looked at him disdainfully, and kept her hands on her lap.

"Ask him the meaning of this outrage," she said in French to her companion.

But before the latter had time to say a word, the man broke in. He poured out a torrent of words in some foreign language.

Not understanding a single thing, Jane merely shrugged her shoulders and said nothing. The chauffeur had got down from his seat and joined the other man.

"Will the illustrious lady be pleased to descend?" he asked, with a grin.

Raising the flowers to her face again, Jane stepped out of the car. The Princess Poporensky followed her.

"Will the illustrious lady come this way?"

Jane took no notice of the man's mock insolent manner, but of her own accord she walked towards a low-built, rambling house which stood about a hundred yards away from where the car had stopped. The road had been a *cul-de-sac* ending in the gateway and drive which led to this apparently untenanted building.

The man, still brandishing his pistol, came close behind the two women. As they passed up the steps, he brushed past them and flung open a door on the left. It was an empty room, into which a table and two chairs had evidently been brought.

Jane passed in and sat down. Anna Michaelovna followed her. The man banged the door and turned the key.

Jane walked to the window and looked out.

"I could jump out, of course," she remarked. "But I shouldn't get far. No, we'll just have to stay here for the present and make the best of it. I wonder if they'll bring us anything to eat?"

About half an hour later her question was answered. A big bowl of steaming soup was brought in and placed on the table in front of her. Also two pieces of dry bread.

"No luxury for aristocrats evidently," remarked Jane cheerily as the door was shut and locked again. "Will you start, or shall I?"

The Princess Poporensky waved the mere idea of food aside with horror.

"How could I eat? Who knows what danger my mistress might not be in?"

"She's all right," said Jane. "It's myself I'm worrying about. You know these people won't be at all pleased when they find they have got hold of the wrong person. In fact, they may be very unpleasant. I shall keep up the haughty Grand Duchess stunt as long as I can, and do a bunk if the opportunity offers."

The Princess Poporensky offered no reply.

Jane, who was hungry, drank up all the soup. It had a curious taste, but was hot and savoury.

Afterwards she felt rather sleepy. The Princess Poporensky seemed to be weeping quietly. Jane arranged herself on her uncomfortable chair in the least uncomfortable way, and allowed her head to droop.

She slept.

Jane awoke with a start. She had an idea that she had been a very long time asleep. Her head felt heavy and uncomfortable.

And then suddenly she saw something that jerked her faculties wide awake again.

She was wearing the flame-coloured marocain frock.

She sat up and looked around her. Yes, she was still in the room in the empty house. Everything was exactly as it had been when she went to sleep, except for two facts. The first was that the Princess Poporensky was no longer sitting on the other chair. The second was her own inexplicable change of costume.

"I can't have dreamt it," said Jane. "Because if I'd dreamt it, I shouldn't be here."

She looked across at the window and registered a second significant fact. When she had gone to sleep the sun had been pouring through the window. Now the house threw a sharp shadow on the sunlit drive.

"The house faces west," she reflected. "It was afternoon when I went to sleep. Therefore it must be tomorrow morning now. Therefore that soup was drugged. Therefore—oh, I don't know. It all seems mad."

She got up and went to the door. It was unlocked. She explored the house. It was silent and empty.

Jane put her hand to her aching head and tried to think.

And then she caught sight of a torn newspaper lying by the front door. It had glaring headlines which caught her eye.

"American Girl Bandit in England," she read. "The Girl in the Red Dress. Sensational hold-up at Orion House Bazaar."

Jane staggered out into the sunlight. Sitting on the steps she read, her eyes growing bigger and bigger. The facts were short and succinct.

Just after the departure of the Grand Duchess Pauline, three men and a girl in a red dress had produced revolvers and successfully held up the crowd. They had annexed the hundred pearls and made a getaway in a fast racing car. Up to now, they had not been traced.

In the stop press (it was a late evening paper) were a few words to the effect that the "girl bandit in the red dress' had been staying at the Blitz as a Miss Montresor of New York.

"I'm dished," said Jane. "Absolutely dished. I always knew there was a catch in it."

And then she started. A strange sound had smote the air. The voice of a man, uttering one word at frequent intervals.

"Damn," it said. "Damn." And yet again, "Damn!"

Jane thrilled to the sound. It expressed so exactly her own feelings. She ran down the steps. By the corner of them lay a young man. He was endeavouring to raise his head from the ground. His face struck Jane as one of the nicest faces she had ever seen. It was freckled and slightly quizzical in expression.

"Damn my head," said the young man. "Damn it. I—"

He broke off and stared at Jane.

"I must be dreaming," he said faintly.

"That's what I said," said Jane. "But we're not. What's the matter with your head?"

"Somebody hit me on it. Fortunately it's a thick one."

He pulled himself into a sitting position, and made a wry face.

"My brain will begin to function shortly, I expect. I'm still in the same old spot, I see."

"How did you get here?" asked Jane curiously.

"That's a long story. By the way, you're not the Grand Duchess What's-her-name, are you?"

"I'm not. I'm plain Jane Cleveland."

"You're not plain anyway," said the young man, looking at her with frank admiration.

Jane blushed.

"I ought to get you some water or something, oughtn't I?" she asked uncertainly.

"I believe it is customary," agreed the young man. "All the same, I'd rather have whisky if you can find it."

Jane was unable to find any whisky. The young man took a deep draught of water, and announced himself better.

"Shall I relate my adventures, or will you relate yours?" he asked.

"You first."

"There's nothing much to mine. I happened to notice that the Grand Duchess went into that room with low-heeled shoes on and came out with high-heeled ones. It struck me as rather odd. I don't like things to be odd.

"I followed the car on my motor bicycle, I saw you taken into the house. About ten minutes later a big racing car came tearing up. A girl in red got out and three men. She had low-heeled shoes on, all right. They went into the house. Presently low heels came out dressed in black and white, and went off in the first car, with an old pussy and a tall man with a fair beard. The others went off in the racing car. I thought they'd all gone, and was just trying to get in at that window and rescue you when someone hit me on the head from behind. That's all. Now for your turn."

Jane related her adventures.

"And it's awfully lucky for me that you did follow," she ended. "Do you see what an awful hole I should have been in otherwise? The Grand Duchess would have had a perfect alibi. She left the bazaar before the hold-up began, and arrived in London in her car. Would anybody ever have believed my fantastic improbable story?"

"Not on your life," said the young man with conviction.

They had been so absorbed in their respective narratives that they had been quite oblivious of their surroundings. They looked up now with a slight start to see a tall sad-faced man leaning against the house. He nodded at them.

"Very interesting," he commented.

"Who are you?" demanded Jane.

The sad-faced man's eyes twinkled a little.

"Detective-Inspector Farrell," he said gently. "I've been very interested in hearing your story and this young lady's. We might have found a little difficulty in believing hers, but for one or two things."

"For instance?"

"Well, you see, we heard this morning that the real Grand Duchess had eloped with a chauffeur in Paris."

Jane gasped.

"And then we knew that this American 'girl bandit' had come to this country, and we expected a coup of some kind. We'll have laid hands on them very soon, I can promise you that. Excuse me a minute, will you?"

He ran up the steps into the house.

"*Well!*" said Jane. She put a lot of force into the expression.

"I think it was awfully clever of you to notice those shoes," she said suddenly.

"Not at all," said the young man. "I was brought up in the boot trade. My father's a sort of boot king. He wanted me to go into the trade—marry and settle down. All that sort of thing. Nobody in particular—just the principle of the thing. But I wanted to be an artist." He sighed.

"I'm so sorry," said Jane kindly.

"I've been trying for six years. There's no blinking it. I'm a rotten painter. I've a good mind to chuck it and go home like the prodigal son. There's a good billet waiting for me."

"A job is the great thing," agreed Jane wistfully.

"Do you think you could get me one trying on boots somewhere?"

"I could give you a better one than that—if you'd take it."

"Oh, what?"

"Never mind now. I'll tell you later. You know, until yesterday I never saw a girl I felt I could marry."

"Yesterday?"

"At the bazaar. And then I saw her—the one and only Her!"

He looked very hard at Jane.

"How beautiful the delphiniums are," said Jane hurriedly, with very pink cheeks.

"They're lupins," said the young man.

"It doesn't matter," said Jane.

"Not a bit," he agreed. And he drew a little nearer.

The Disappearance of Mr Davenheim

Poirot and I were expecting our old friend Inspector Japp of Scotland Yard to tea. We were sitting round the tea-table awaiting his arrival. Poirot had just finished carefully straightening the cups and saucers which our landlady was in the habit of throwing, rather than placing, on the table. He had also breathed heavily on the metal teapot, and polished it with a silk handkerchief. The kettle was on the boil, and a small enamel saucepan beside it contained some thick, sweet chocolate which was more to Poirot's palate than what he described as "your English poison."

A sharp "rat-tat" sounded below, and a few minutes afterwards Japp entered briskly.

"Hope I'm not late," he said as he greeted us. "To tell the truth, I was yarning with Miller, the man who's in charge of the Davenheim case."

I pricked up my ears. For the last three days the papers had been full of the strange disappearance of Mr Davenheim, senior partner of Davenheim and Salmon, the well-known bankers and financiers. On Saturday last he had walked out of his house, and had never been seen since. I looked forward to extracting some interesting details from Japp.

"I should have thought," I remarked, "that it would be almost impossible for anyone to 'disappear' nowadays."

Poirot moved a plate of bread and butter the eighth of an inch, and said sharply:

"Be exact, my friend. What do you mean by 'disappear?' To which class of disappearance are you referring?"

"Are disappearances classified and labelled, then?" I laughed.

Japp smiled also. Poirot frowned at both of us.

"But certainly they are! They fall into three categories: First, and most common, the voluntary disappearance. Second, the much abused 'loss of memory' case—rare, but occasionally genuine. Third, murder, and a more or less successful disposal of the body. Do you refer to all three as impossible of execution?"

"Very nearly so, I should think. You might lose your own memory, but someone would be sure to recognize you—especially in the case of a well-known man like Davenheim. Then 'bodies' can't be made to vanish into thin air. Sooner or later they turn up, concealed in lonely places, or in trunks. Murder will out. In the same way, the absconding clerk, or the domestic defaulter, is bound to be run down in these days of wireless telegraphy. He can be headed off from foreign countries; ports and railway stations are watched; and as for concealment in this country, his features and appearance will be known to everyone who reads a daily newspaper. He's up against civilization."

"*Mon ami*," said Poirot, "you make one error. You do not allow for the fact that a man who had decided to make away with another man—or with himself in a figurative sense—might be that rare machine, a man of method. He might bring intelligence, talent, a careful calculation of detail to the task; and then I do not see why he should not be successful in baffling the police force."

"But not *you*, I suppose?" said Japp good-humouredly,

winking at me. "He couldn't baffle you, eh, Monsieur Poirot?"

Poirot endeavoured, with a marked lack of success, to look modest. "Me also! Why not? It is true that I approach such problems with an exact science, a mathematical precision, which seems, alas, only too rare in the new generation of detectives!"

Japp grinned more widely.

"I don't know," he said. "Miller, the man who's on this case, is a smart chap. You may be very sure he won't overlook a footprint, or a cigar-ash, or a crumb even. He's got eyes that see everything."

"So, *mon ami*," said Poirot, "has the London sparrow. But all the same, I should not ask the little brown bird to solve the problem of Mr Davenheim."

"Come now, monsieur, you're not going to run down the value of details as clues?"

"By no means. These things are all good in their way. The danger is they may assume undue importance. Most details are insignificant; one or two are vital. It is the brain, the little grey cells"—he tapped his forehead—"on which one must rely. The senses mislead. One must seek the truth within—not without."

"You don't mean to say, Monsieur Poirot, that you would undertake to solve a case without moving from your chair, do you?"

"That is exactly what I do mean—granted the facts were placed before me. I regard myself as a consulting specialist."

Japp slapped his knee. "Hanged if I don't take you at your word. Bet you a fiver that you can't lay your hand—or rather tell me where to lay my hand—on Mr Davenheim, dead or alive, before a week is out."

Poirot considered. "*Eh bien, mon ami*, I accept. *Le sport*, it is the passion of you English. Now—the facts."

"On Saturday last, as is his usual custom, Mr Davenheim took the 12.40 train from Victoria to Chingside, where his palatial country seat, The Cedars, is situated. After lunch, he strolled round the grounds, and gave various directions to the gardeners. Everybody agrees that his manner was absolutely normal and as usual. After tea he put his head into his wife's boudoir, saying that he was going to stroll down to the village and post some letters. He added that he was expecting a Mr Lowen, on business. If he should come before he himself returned, he was to be shown into the study and asked to wait. Mr Davenheim then left the house by the front door, passed leisurely down the drive, and out at the gate, and—was never seen again. From that hour, he vanished completely."

"Pretty—very pretty—altogether a charming little problem," murmured Poirot. "Proceed, my good friend."

"About a quarter of an hour later a tall, dark man with a thick black moustache rang the front door-bell, and explained that he had an appointment with Mr Davenheim. He gave the name of Lowen, and in accordance with the banker's instructions was shown into the study. Nearly an hour passed. Mr Davenheim did not return. Finally Mr Lowen rang the bell, and explained that he was unable to wait any longer, as he must catch his train back to town.

"Mrs Davenheim apologized for her husband's absence, which seemed unaccountable, as she knew him to have been expecting the visitor. Mr Lowen reiterated his regrets and took his departure.

"Well, as everyone knows, Mr Davenheim did *not* return. Early on Sunday morning the police were communicated with, but could make neither head nor tail of the matter. Mr Davenheim seemed literally to have vanished into thin air. He had not been to the post office; nor had he been seen passing through the village. At the station they were positive he had not departed by any train. His own motor had not left the garage. If he had hired a car to meet him in some lonely spot, it seems almost certain that by this time, in view of the large reward offered for information, the driver of it would have come forward to tell what he knew. True, there was a small race-meeting at Entfield, five miles away, and if he had walked to that station he might have passed unnoticed in the crowd. But since then his photograph and a full description of him have been circulated in every newspaper, and nobody has been able to give any news of him. We have, of course, received many letters from all over England, but each clue, so far, has ended in disappointment.

"On Monday morning a further sensational discovery came to light. Behind a *portière* in Mr Davenheim's study stands a safe, and that safe had been broken into and rifled. The windows were fastened securely on the inside, which seems to put an ordinary burglary out of court, unless, of course, an accomplice within the house fastened them again afterwards. On the other hand, Sunday having intervened, and the household being in a state of chaos, it is likely that the burglary was committed on the Saturday, and remained undetected until Monday."

"*Précisément*," said Poirot dryly. "Well, is he arrested, *ce pauvre M. Lowen?*"

Japp grinned. "Not yet. But he's under pretty close supervision."

Poirot nodded. "What was taken from the safe? Have you any idea?"

"We've been going into that with the junior partner of the firm and Mrs Davenheim. Apparently there was a considerable amount in bearer bonds, and a very large sum in notes, owing to some large transaction having been just carried through. There was also a small fortune in jewellery. All Mrs Davenheim's jewels were kept in the safe. The purchasing of them had become a passion with her husband of late years, and hardly a month passed that he did not make her a present of some rare and costly gem."

"Altogether a good haul," said Poirot thoughtfully. "Now, what about Lowen? Is it known what his business was with Davenheim that evening?"

"Well, the two men were apparently not on very good terms. Lowen is a speculator in quite a small way. Nevertheless, he has been able once or twice to score a coup off Davenheim in the market, though it seems they seldom or never actually met. It was a matter concerning some South American shares which led the banker to make his appointment."

"Had Davenheim interests in South America, then?"

"I believe so. Mrs Davenheim happened to mention that he spent all last autumn in Buenos Aires."

"Any trouble in his home life? Were the husband and wife on good terms?"

"I should say his domestic life was quite peaceful and uneventful. Mrs Davenheim is a pleasant, rather unintelligent woman. Quite a nonentity, I think."

"Then we must not look for the solution of the mystery there. Had he any enemies?"

"He had plenty of financial rivals, and no doubt there are many people whom he has got the better of who bear him no particular goodwill. But there was no one likely to make away with him—and, if they had, where is the body?"

"Exactly. As Hastings says, bodies have a habit of coming to light with fatal persistency."

"By the way, one of the gardeners says he saw a figure going round to the side of the house towards the rose-garden. The long french window of the study opens on to the rose-garden, and Mr Davenheim frequently entered and left the house that way. But the man was a good way off, at work on some cucumber frames, and cannot even say whether it was the figure of his master or not. Also, he cannot fix the time with any accuracy. It must have been before six, as the gardeners cease work at that time."

"And Mr Davenheim left the house?"

"About half-past five or thereabouts."

"What lies beyond the rose-garden?"

"A lake."

"With a boathouse?"

"Yes, a couple of punts are kept there. I suppose you're thinking of suicide, Monsieur Poirot? Well, I don't mind telling you that Miller's going down tomorrow expressly to see that piece of water dragged. That's the kind of man he is!"

Poirot smiled faintly, and turned to me. "Hastings, I pray you, hand me that copy of *Daily Megaphone*. If I remember rightly, there is an unusually clear photograph there of the missing man."

I rose, and found the sheet required. Poirot studied the features attentively.

"H'm!" he murmured. "Wears his hair rather long and wavy, full moustache and pointed beard, bushy eyebrows. Eyes dark?"

"Yes."

"Hair and beard turning grey?"

The detective nodded. "Well, Monsieur Poirot, what have you got to say to it all? Clear as daylight, eh?"

"On the contrary, most obscure."

The Scotland Yard man looked pleased.

"Which gives me great hopes of solving it," finished Poirot placidly.

"Eh?"

"I find it a good sign when a case is obscure. If a thing is clear as daylight—*eh bien*, mistrust it! Someone has made it so."

Japp shook his head almost pityingly. "Well, each to their fancy. But it's not a bad thing to see your way clear ahead."

"I do not see," murmured Poirot. "I shut my eyes—and think."

Japp sighed. "Well, you've got a clear week to think in."

"And you will bring me any fresh developments that arise—the result of the labours of the hard-working and lynx-eyed Inspector Miller, for instance?"

"Certainly. That's in the bargain."

"Seems a shame, doesn't it?" said Japp to me as I accompanied him to the door. "Like robbing a child!"

I could not help agreeing with a smile. I was still smiling as I re-entered the room.

"*Eh bien!*" said Poirot immediately. "You make fun of Papa Poirot, is it not so?" He shook his finger at me. "You do not trust his grey cells? Ah, do not be confused! Let us discuss this little problem—incomplete as yet, I admit, but already showing one or two points of interest."

"The lake!" I said significantly.

"And even more than the lake, the boathouse!"

I looked sidewise at Poirot. He was smiling in his most inscrutable fashion. I felt that, for the moment, it would be quite useless to question him further.

We heard nothing of Japp until the following evening, when he walked in about nine o'clock. I saw at once by his expression that he was bursting with news of some kind.

"*Eh bien*, my friend," remarked Poirot. "All goes well? But do not tell me that you have discovered the body of

Mr Davenheim in your lake, because I shall not believe you."

"We haven't found the body, but we did find his *clothes*—the identical clothes he was wearing that day. What do you say to that?"

"Any other clothes missing from the house?"

"No, his valet was quite positive on that point. The rest of his wardrobe is intact. There's more. We've arrested Lowen. One of the maids, whose business it is to fasten the bedroom windows, declares that she saw Lowen coming *towards* the study through the rose-garden about a quarter past six. That would be about ten minutes before he left the house."

"What does he himself say to that?"

"Denied first of all that he had ever left the study. But the maid was positive, and he pretended afterwards that he had forgotten just stepping out of the window to examine an unusual species of rose. Rather a weak story! And there's fresh evidence against him come to light. Mr Davenheim always wore a thick gold ring set with a solitaire diamond on the little finger of his right hand. Well, that ring was pawned in London on Saturday night by a man called Billy Kellett! He's already known to the police—did three months last autumn for lifting an old gentleman's watch. It seems he tried to pawn the ring at no less than five different places, succeeded at the last one, got gloriously drunk on the proceeds, assaulted a policeman, and was run in in consequence. I went to Bow Street with Miller and saw him. He's sober enough now, and I don't mind admitting we pretty well frightened the life out of him, hinting he might be charged with murder. This is his yarn, and a very queer one it is.

"He was at Entfield races on Saturday, though I dare say scarfpins was his line of business, rather than betting. Anyway, he had a bad day, and was down on his luck. He was tramping along the road to Chingside, and sat down in a ditch to rest just before he got into the village. A few minutes later he noticed a man coming along the road to the village, 'dark-complexioned gent, with a big moustache, one of them city toffs," is his description of the man.

"Kellett was half concealed from the road by a heap of stones. Just before he got abreast of him, the man looked quickly up and down the road, and seeing it apparently deserted he took a small object from his pocket and threw it over the hedge. Then he went on towards the station. Now, the object he had thrown over the hedge had fallen with a slight 'chink' which aroused the curiosity of the human derelict in the ditch. He investigated and, after a short search, discovered the ring! That is Kellett's story. It's only fair to say that Lowen denies it utterly, and of course the word of a man like Kellett can't be relied upon in the slightest. It's within the bounds of possibility that he met Davenheim in the lane and robbed and murdered him."

Poirot shook his head.

"Very improbable, *mon ami*. He had no means of disposing of the body. It would have been found by now. Secondly, the open way in which he pawned the ring makes it unlikely that he did murder to get it. Thirdly, your sneak-thief is rarely a murderer. Fourthly, as he has been in prison since Saturday, it would be too much of a coincidence that he is able to give so accurate a description of Lowen."

Japp nodded. "I don't say you're not right. But all the same, you won't get a jury to take much note of a jailbird's evidence. What seems odd to me is that Lowen couldn't find a cleverer way of disposing of the ring."

Poirot shrugged his shoulders. "Well, after all, if it were found in the neighbourhood, it might be argued that Davenheim himself had dropped it."

"But why remove it from the body at all?" I cried.

"There might be a reason for that," said Japp. "Do you know that just beyond the lake, a little gate leads out on to the hill, and not three minutes' walk brings you to—what do you think?—a *lime kiln.*"

"Good heavens!" I cried. "You mean that the lime which destroyed the body would be powerless to affect the metal of the ring?"

"Exactly."

"It seems to me," I said, "that that explains everything. What a horrible crime!"

By common consent we both turned and looked at Poirot. He seemed lost in reflection, his brow knitted, as though with some supreme mental effort. I felt at last his keen intellect was asserting itself. What would his first words be? We were not long left in doubt. With a sigh, the tension of his attitude relaxed and turning to Japp, he asked:

"Have you any idea, my friend, whether Mr and Mrs Davenheim occupied the same bedroom?"

The question seemed so ludicrously inappropriate that for a moment we both stared in silence. Then Japp burst into a laugh. "Good Lord, Monsieur Poirot, I thought you were coming out with something startling. As to your question, I'm sure I don't know."

"You could find out?" asked Poirot with curious persistence.

"Oh, certainly—if you *really* want to know."

"*Merci, mon ami.* I should be obliged if you would make a point of it." Japp stared at him a few minutes longer, but Poirot seemed to have forgotten us both. The detective shook his head sadly at me, and murmuring,

"Poor old fellow! War's been too much for him!" gently withdrew from the room.

As Poirot seemed sunk in a daydream, I took a sheet of paper, and amused myself by scribbling notes upon it. My friend's voice aroused me. He had come out of his reverie, and was looking brisk and alert.

"*Que faites-vous là, mon ami?*"

"I was jotting down what occurred to me as the main points of interest in this affair."

"You become methodical—at last!" said Poirot approvingly.

I concealed my pleasure. "Shall I read them to you?"

"By all means."

I cleared my throat.

"'One: All the evidence points to Lowen having been the man who forced the safe.

"'Two: He had a grudge against Davenheim.

"'Three: He lied in his first statement that he had never left the study.

"'Four: If you accept Billy Kellett's story as true, Lowen is unmistakably implicated.'"

I paused. "Well?" I asked, for I felt that I had put my finger on all the vital facts.

Poirot looked at me pityingly, shaking his head very gently. "*Mon pauvre ami!* But it is that you have not the gift! The important detail, you appreciate him never! Also, your reasoning is false."

"How?"

"Let me take your four points."

"One: Mr Lowen could not possibly know that he would have the chance to open the safe. He came for a business interview. He could not know beforehand that Mr Davenheim would be absent posting a letter, and that he would consequently be alone in the study!"

"He might have seized the opportunity," I suggested.

"And the tools? City gentlemen do not carry round housebreaker's tools on the off chance! And one could not cut into that safe with penknife, *bien entendu!*"

"Well, what about Number Two?"

"You say Lowen had a grudge against Mr Davenheim. What you mean is that he had once or twice got the better of him. And presumably those transactions were entered into with the view of benefiting himself. In any case you do not as a rule bear a grudge against a man you have got the better of—it is more likely to be the other way about. Whatever grudge there might have been would have been on Mr Davenheim's side."

"Well, you can't deny that he lied about never having left the study?"

"No. But he may have been frightened. Remember, the missing man's clothes had just been discovered in the lake. Of course, as usual, he would have done better to speak the truth."

"And the fourth point?"

"I grant you that. If Kellett's story is true, Lowen is undeniably implicated. That is what makes the affair so very interesting."

"Then I *did* appreciate one vital fact?"

"Perhaps—but you have entirely overlooked the two most important points, the ones which undoubtedly hold the clue to the whole matter."

"And pray, what are they?"

"One, the passion which has grown upon Mr Davenheim in the last few years for buying jewellery. Two, his trip to Buenos Aires last autumn."

"Poirot, you are joking?"

"I am serious. Ah, sacred thunder, but I hope Japp will not forget my little commission."

But the detective, entering into the spirit of the joke, had remembered it so well that a telegram was handed to Poirot about eleven o'clock the next day. At his request I opened it and read it out:

> "'Husband and wife have occupied separate rooms since last winter.'"

"Aha!" cried Poirot. "And now we are in mid June! All is solved!"

I stared at him.

"You have no moneys in the bank of Davenheim and Salmon, *mon ami?*"

"No," I said wondering. "Why?"

"Because I should advise you to withdraw it—before it is too late."

"Why, what do you expect?"

"I expect a big smash in a few days—perhaps sooner. Which reminds me, we will return the compliment of a *dépêche* to Japp. A pencil, I pray you, and a form. *Voilà!* 'Advise you to withdraw any money deposited with firm in question.' That will intrigue him, the good Japp! His eyes will open wide—wide! He will not comprehend in the slightest—until tomorrow, or the next day!"

I remained sceptical, but the morrow forced me to render tribute to my friend's remarkable powers. In every paper was a huge headline telling of the sensational failure of the Davenheim bank. The disappearance of the famous financier took on a totally different aspect in the light of the revelation of the financial affairs of the bank.

Before we were half-way through breakfast, the door flew open and Japp rushed in. In his left hand was a paper; in his right was Poirot's telegram, which he banged down on the table in front of my friend.

"How did you know, Monsieur Poirot? How the blazes could you know?"

Poirot smiled placidly at him. "Ah, *mon ami*, after your wire, it was a certainty! From the commencement, see you, it struck me that the safe burglary was somewhat remarkable. Jewels, ready money, bearer bonds all so conveniently arranged for—whom? Well, the good Monsieur Davenheim was of those who 'look after Number One' as your saying goes! It seemed almost certain that it was arranged for—himself! Then his passion of late years for buying jewellery! How simple! The funds he embezzled, he converted into jewels, very likely replacing them in turn with paste duplicates, and so he put away in a safe place, under another name, a considerable fortune to be enjoyed all in good time when everyone has been thrown off the track. His arrangements completed, he makes an appointment with Mr Lowen (who has been imprudent enough in the past to cross the great man once or twice), drills a hole in the safe, leaves orders that the guest is to be shown into the study, and walks out of the house—where?" Poirot stopped, and stretched out his hand for another boiled egg. He frowned. "It is really insupportable," he murmured, "that every hen lays an egg of a different size! What symmetry can there be on the breakfast table? At least they should sort them in dozens at the shop!"

"Never mind the eggs," said Japp impatiently. "Let 'em lay 'em square if they like. Tell us where our customer went to when he left The Cedars—that is, if you know!"

"*Eh bien*, he went to his hiding place. Ah, this Monsieur Davenheim, there may be some malformation in his grey cells, but they are of the first quality!"

"Do you know where he is hiding?"

"Certainly! It is most ingenious."

"For the Lord's sake, tell us, then!"

Poirot gently collected every fragment of shell from his plate, placed them in the egg-cup, and reversed the empty egg-shell on top of them. This little operation concluded, he smiled on the neat effect, and then beamed affectionately on us both.

"Come, my friends, you are men of intelligence. Ask yourself the question I asked myself. 'If I were this man, where should *I* hide?' Hastings, what do you say?"

"Well," I said, "I'm rather inclined to think I'd not do a bolt at all. I'd stay in London—in the heart of things, travel by tubes and buses; ten to one I'd never be recognized. There's safety in a crowd."

Poirot turned inquiringly to Japp.

"I don't agree. Get clear away at once—that's the only chance. I would have had plenty of time to prepare things beforehand. I'd have a yacht waiting, with steam up, and I'd be off to one of the most out-of-the-way corners of the world before the hue and cry began!"

We both looked at Poirot. "What do *you* say, monsieur?"

For a moment he remained silent. Then a very curious smile flitted across his face.

"My friends, if *I* were hiding from the police, do you know *where* I should hide? *In a prison!*"

"*What?*"

"You are seeking Monsieur Davenheim in order to put him in prison, so you never dream of looking to see if he may not be already there!"

"What do you mean?"

"You tell me Madame Davenheim is not a very intelligent woman. Nevertheless I think if you took her up to Bow Street and confronted her with the man Billy Kellett she would recognize him! In spite of the fact that he has shaved his beard and moustache and those bushy eyebrows, and has cropped his hair close.

A woman nearly always knows her husband, though the rest of the world may be deceived."

"Billy Kellett? But he's known to the police!"

"Did I not tell you Davenheim was a clever man? He prepared his alibi long beforehand. He was not in Buenos Aires last autumn—he was creating the character of Billy Kellett, 'doing three months,' so that the police should have no suspicions when the time came. He was playing, remember, for a large fortune, as well as liberty. It was worth while doing the thing thoroughly. Only—"

"Yes?"

"*Eh bien*, afterwards he had to wear a false beard and wig, had to *make up as himself again*, and to sleep with a false beard is not easy—it invites detection! He cannot risk continuing to share the chamber of madame his wife. You found out for me that for the last six months, or ever since his supposed return from Buenos Aires, he and Mrs Davenheim occupied separate rooms. Then I was sure! Everything fitted in. The gardener who fancied he saw his master going round to the side of the house was quite right. He went to the boathouse, donned his 'tramp' clothes, which you may be sure had been safely hidden from the eyes of his valet, dropped the others in the lake, and proceeded to carry out his plan by pawning the ring in an obvious manner, and then assaulting a policeman, getting himself safely into the haven of Bow Street, where nobody would ever dream of looking for him!"

"It's impossible," murmured Japp.

"Ask Madame," said my friend, smiling.

The next day a registered letter lay beside Poirot's plate. He opened it and a five-pound note fluttered out. My friend's brow puckered.

"*Ah, sacré!* But what shall I do with it? I have much

remorse! *Ce pauvre Japp?* Ah, an idea! We will have a little dinner, we three! That consoles me. It was really too easy. I am ashamed. I, who would not rob a child—*mille tonnerres! Mon ami*, what have you, that you laugh so heartily?"

The Idol House of Astarte

"And now, Dr Pender, what are you going to tell us?"

The old clergyman smiled gently.

"My life has been passed in quiet places," he said. "Very few eventful happenings have come my way. Yet once, when I was a young man, I had one very strange and tragic experience."

"Ah!" said Joyce Lemprière encouragingly.

"I have never forgotten it," continued the clergyman. "It made a profound impression on me at the time, and to this day by a slight effort of memory I can feel again the awe and horror of that terrible moment when I saw a man stricken to death by apparently no mortal agency."

"You make me feel quite creepy, Pender," complained Sir Henry.

"It made me feel creepy, as you call it," replied the other. "Since then I have never laughed at the people who use the word atmosphere. There is such a thing. There are certain places imbued and saturated with good or evil influences which can make their power felt."

"That house, The Larches, is a very unhappy one," remarked Miss Marple. "Old Mr Smithers lost all his money and had to leave it, then the Carslakes took it and Johnny Carslake fell downstairs and broke his leg and Mrs Carslake had to go away to the south of France for her health, and now the Burdens have got it and

I hear that poor Mr Burden has got to have an operation almost immediately."

"There is, I think, rather too much superstition about such matters," said Mr Petherick. "A lot of damage is done to property by foolish reports heedlessly circulated."

"I have known one or two 'ghosts' that have had a very robust personality," remarked Sir Henry with a chuckle.

"I think," said Raymond, "we should allow Dr Pender to go on with his story."

Joyce got up and switched off the two lamps, leaving the room lit only by the flickering firelight.

"Atmosphere," she said. "Now we can get along."

Dr Pender smiled at her, and leaning back in his chair and taking off his pince-nez, he began his story in a gentle reminiscent voice.

"I don't know whether any of you know Dartmoor at all. The place I am telling you about is situated on the borders of Dartmoor. It was a very charming property, though it had been on the market without finding a purchaser for several years. The situation was perhaps a little bleak in winter, but the views were magnificent and there were certain curious and original features about the property itself. It was bought by a man called Haydon—Sir Richard Haydon. I had known him in his college days, and though I had lost sight of him for some years, the old ties of friendship still held, and I accepted with pleasure his invitation to go down to Silent Grove, as his new purchase was called.

"The house party was not a very large one. There was Richard Haydon himself, and his cousin, Elliot Haydon. There was a Lady Mannering with a pale, rather inconspicuous daughter called Violet. There was a Captain Rogers and his wife, hard riding, weather-beaten people, who lived only for horses and hunting. There was also a young Dr Symonds and there was Miss Diana Ashley. I knew something about the last named. Her picture was very often in the Society papers and she was one of the notorious beauties of the Season. Her appearance was indeed very striking. She was dark and tall, with a beautiful skin of an even tint of pale cream, and her half closed dark eyes gave her a curiously piquant Asian appearance. She had, too, a wonderful speaking voice, deep-toned and bell-like.

"I saw at once that my friend Richard Haydon was very much attracted by her, and I guessed that the whole party was merely arranged as a setting for her. Of her own feelings I was not so sure. She was capricious in her favours. One day talking to Richard and excluding everyone else from her notice, and another day she would favour his cousin, Elliot, and appear hardly to notice that such a person as Richard existed, and then again she would bestow the most bewitching smiles upon the quiet and retiring Dr Symonds.

"On the morning after my arrival our host showed us all over the place. The house itself was unremarkable, a good solid house built of Devonshire granite. Built to withstand time and exposure. It was unromantic but very comfortable. From the windows of it one looked out over the panorama of the Moor, vast rolling hills crowned with weather-beaten Tors.

"On the slopes of the Tor nearest to us were various hut circles, relics of the bygone days of the late Stone Age. On another hill was a barrow which had recently been excavated, and in which certain bronze implements had been found. Haydon was by way of being interested in antiquarian matters and he talked to us with a great deal of energy and enthusiasm. This particular spot, he explained, was particularly rich in relics of the past.

"Neolithic hut dwellers, Druids, Romans, and even traces of the early Phoenicians were to be found.

"'But this place is the most interesting of all,' he said 'You know its name—Silent Grove. Well, it is easy enough to see what it takes its name from.'

"He pointed with his hand. That particular part of the country was bare enough—rocks, heather and bracken, but about a hundred yards from the house there was a densely planted grove of trees.

"'That is a relic of very early days,' said Haydon, 'The trees have died and been replanted, but on the whole it has been kept very much as it used to be—perhaps in the time of the Phoenician settlers. Come and look at it.'

"We all followed him. As we entered the grove of trees a curious oppression came over me. I think it was the silence. No birds seemed to nest in these trees. There was a feeling about it of desolation and horror. I saw Haydon looking at me with a curious smile.

"'Any feeling about this place, Pender?' he asked me. 'Antagonism now? Or uneasiness?'

"'I don't like it,' I said quietly.

"'You are within your rights. This was a stronghold of one of the ancient enemies of your faith. This is the Grove of Astarte.'

"'Astarte?'

"'Astarte, or Ishtar, or Ashtoreth, or whatever you choose to call her. I prefer the Phoenician name of Astarte. There is, I believe, one known Grove of Astarte in this country—in the North on the Wall. I have no evidence, but I like to believe that we have a true and authentic Grove of Astarte here. Here, within this dense circle of trees, sacred rites were performed.'

"'Sacred rites,' murmured Diana Ashley. Her eyes had a dreamy faraway look. 'What were they, I wonder?'

"'Not very reputable by all accounts,' said Captain Rogers with a loud unmeaning laugh. 'Rather hot stuff, I imagine.'

"Haydon paid no attention to him.

"'In the centre of the Grove there should be a Temple,' he said. 'I can't run to Temples, but I have indulged in a little fancy of my own.'

"We had at that moment stepped out into a little clearing in the centre of the trees. In the middle of it was something not unlike a summerhouse made of stone. Diana Ashley looked inquiringly at Haydon.

"'I call it The Idol House,' he said. 'It is the Idol House of Astarte.'

"He led the way up to it. Inside, on a rude ebony pillar, there reposed a curious little image representing a woman with crescent horns, seated on a lion.

"'Astarte of the Phoenicians,' said Haydon, 'the Goddess of the Moon.'

"'The Goddess of the Mooon,' cried Diana. 'Oh, do let us have a wild orgy tonight. Fancy dress. And we will come out here in the moonlight and celebrate the rites of Astarte.'

"I made a sudden movement and Elliot Haydon, Richard's cousin, turned quickly to me.

"'You don't like all this, do you, Padre?' he said.

"'No,' I said gravely. 'I don't.'

"He looked at me curiously. 'But it is only tomfoolery. Dick can't know that this really is a sacred grove. It is just a fancy of his; he likes to play with the idea. And anyway, if it were—'

"'If it were?'

"'Well—" he laughed uncomfortably. 'You don't believe in that sort of thing, do you? You, a parson.'

"'I am not sure that as a parson I ought not to believe in it.'

"'But that sort of thing is all finished and done with.'

"'I am not so sure,' I said musingly. 'I only know this: I am not as a rule a sensitive man to atmosphere, but ever since I entered this grove of trees I have felt a curious impression and sense of evil and menace all round me.'

"He glanced uneasily over his shoulder.

"'Yes,' he said, 'it is—it is queer, somehow. I know what you mean but I suppose it is only our imagination makes us feel like that. What do you say, Symonds?'

"The doctor was silent a minute or two before he replied. Then he said quietly:

"'I don't like it. I can't tell you why. But somehow or other, I don't like it.'

"At that moment Violet Mannering came across to me.

"'I hate this place,' she cried. 'I hate it. Do let's get out of it.'

"We moved away and the others followed us. Only Diana Ashley lingered. I turned my head over my shoulder and saw her standing in front of the Idol House gazing earnestly at the image within it.

"The day was an unusually hot and beautiful one and Diana Ashley's suggestion of a Fancy Dress party that evening was received with general favour. The usual laughing and whispering and frenzied secret sewing took place and when we all made our appearance for dinner there were the usual outcries of merriment. Rogers and his wife were Neolithic hut dwellers—explaining the sudden lack of hearth rugs. Richard Haydon called himself a Phoenician sailor, and his cousin was a Brigand Chief, Dr Symonds was a chef, Lady Mannering was a hospital nurse, and her daughter was a Circassian slave. I myself was arrayed somewhat too warmly as a monk. Diana Ashley came down last and was somewhat of a disappointment to all of us, being wrapped in a shapeless black domino.

"'The Unknown,' she declared airily. 'That is what I am. Now for goodness' sake let's go in to dinner.'

"After dinner we went outside. It was a lovely night, warm and soft, and the moon was rising.

"We wandered about and chatted and the time passed quickly enough. It must have been an hour later when we realized that Diana Ashley was not with us.

"'Surely she has not gone to bed,' said Richard Haydon.

"Violet Mannering shook her head.

"'Oh, no,' she said. 'I saw her going off in that direction about a quarter of an hour ago.' She pointed as she spoke towards the grove of trees that showed black and shadowy in the moonlight.

"'I wonder what she is up to,' said Richard Haydon, 'some devilment, I swear. Let's go and see.'

"We all trooped off together, somewhat curious as to what Miss Ashley had been up to. Yet I, for one, felt a curious reluctance to enter that dark foreboding belt of trees. Something stronger than myself seemed to be holding me back and urging me not to enter. I felt more definitely convinced than ever of the essential evilness of the spot. I think that some of the others experienced the same sensations that I did, though they would have been loath to admit it. The trees were so closely planted that the moonlight could not penetrate. There were a dozen soft sounds all round us, whisperings and sighings. The feeling was eerie in the extreme, and by common consent we all kept close together.

"Suddenly we came out into the open clearing in the middle of the grove and stood rooted to the spot in amazement, for there, on the threshold of the Idol House, stood a shimmering figure wrapped tightly round in diaphanous gauze and with two crescent horns rising from the dark masses of her hair.

"'My God!' said Richard Haydon, and the sweat sprang out on his brow.

"But Violet Mannering was sharper.

"'Why, it's Diana,' she exclaimed. 'What has she done to herself? Oh, she looks quite different somehow!'

"The figure in the doorway raised her hands. She took a step forward and chanted in a high sweet voice.

"'I am the Priestess of Astarte,' she crooned. 'Beware how you approach me, for I hold death in my hand.'

"'Don't do it, dear,' protested Lady Mannering. 'You give us the creeps, you really do.'

"Haydon sprang forward towards her.

"'My God, Diana!' he cried. 'You are wonderful.'

"My eyes were accustomed to the moonlight now and I could see more plainly. She did, indeed, as Violet had said, look quite different. Her face was more definitely Asian, and her eyes had something cruel in their gleam, and the strange smile on her lips was one that I had never seen there before.

"'Beware,' she cried warningly. 'Do not approach the Goddess. If anyone lays a hand on me it is death.'

"'You are wonderful, Diana,' cried Haydon, 'but do stop it. Somehow or other I—I don't like it.'

"He was moving towards her across the grass and she flung out a hand towards him.

"'Stop,' she cried. 'One step nearer and I will smite you with the magic of Astarte.'

"Richard Haydon laughed and quickened his pace, when all at once a curious thing happened. He hesitated for a moment, then seemed to stumble and fall headlong.

"He did not get up again, but lay where he had fallen prone on the ground.

"Suddenly Diana began to laugh hysterically. It was a strange horrible sound breaking the silence of the glade.

"With an oath Elliot sprang forward.

"'I can't stand this,' he cried, 'get up, Dick, get up, man.'

"But still Richard Haydon lay where he had fallen. Elliot Haydon reached his side, knelt by him and turned him gently over. He bent over him, peering in his face.

"Then he rose sharply to his feet and stood swaying a little.

"'Doctor,' he said. 'Doctor, for God's sake come. I—I think he is dead.'

"Symonds ran forward and Elliot rejoined us walking very slowly. He was looking down at his hands in a way I didn't understand.

"At that moment there was a wild scream from Diana.

"'I have killed him,' she cried. 'Oh, my God! I didn't mean to, but I have killed him.'

"And she fainted dead away, falling in a crumpled heap on the grass.

"There was a cry from Mrs Rogers.

"'Oh, do let us get away from this dreadful place,' she wailed, 'anything might happen to us here. Oh, it's awful!'

"Elliot got hold of me by the shoulder.

"'It can't be, man,' he murmured. 'I tell you it can't *be*. A man cannot be killed like that. It is—it's against Nature.'

"I tried to soothe him.

"'There is some explanation,' I said. 'Your cousin must have had some unsuspected weakness of the heart. The shock and excitement—'

"He interrupted me.

"'You don't understand,' he said. He held up his hands for me to see and I noticed a red stain on them.

"'Dick didn't die of shock, he was stabbed—stabbed to the heart, and *there is no weapon.*'

"I stared at him incredulously. At that moment Symonds rose from his examination of the body and came towards us. He was pale and shaking all over.

"'Are we all mad?' he said. 'What is this place—that things like this can happen in it?'

"'Then it is true,' I said.

"He nodded.

"'The wound is such as would be made by a long thin dagger, but—there is no dagger there.'

"We all looked at each other.

"'But it must be there,' cried Elliot Haydon. 'It must have dropped out. It must be on the ground somewhere. Let us look.'

"We peered about vainly on the ground. Violet Mannering said suddenly:

"'Diana had something in her hand. A kind of dagger. I saw it. I saw it glitter when she threatened him.'

"Elliot Haydon shook his head.

"'He never even got within three yards of her,' he objected.

"Lady Mannering was bending over the prostrate girl on the ground.

"'There is nothing in her hand now,' she announced, 'and I can't see anything on the ground. Are you sure you saw it, Violet? I didn't.'

"Dr Symonds came over to the girl.

"'We must get her to the house,' he said. 'Rogers, will you help?'

"Between us we carried the unconscious girl back to the house. Then we returned and fetched the body of Sir Richard."

Dr Pender broke off apologetically and looked round.

"One would know better nowadays," he said, "owing

to the prevalence of detective fiction. Every street boy knows that a body must be left where it is found. But in these days we had not the same knowledge, and accordingly we carried the body of Richard Haydon back to his bedroom in the square granite house and the butler was despatched on a bicycle in search of the police—a ride of some twelve miles.

"It was then that Elliot Haydon drew me aside.

"'Look here,' he said. 'I am going back to the grove. That weapon has got to be found.'

"'If there was a weapon,' I said doubtfully.

"He seized my arm and shook it fiercely. 'You have got that superstitious stuff into your head. You think his death was supernatural; well, I am going back to the grove to find out.'

"I was curiously averse to his doing so. I did my utmost to dissuade him, but without result. The mere idea of that thick circle of trees was abhorrent to me and I felt a strong premonition of further disaster. But Elliot was entirely pig-headed. He was, I think, scared himself, but would not admit it. He went off fully armed with determination to get to the bottom of the mystery.

"It was a very dreadful night, none of us could sleep, or attempt to do so. The police, when they arrived, were frankly incredulous of the whole thing. They evinced a strong desire to cross-examine Miss Ashley, but there they had to reckon with Dr Symonds, who opposed the idea vehemently. Miss Ashley had come out of her faint or trance and he had given her a long sleeping draught. She was on no account to be disturbed until the following day.

"It was not until about seven o'clock in the morning that anyone thought about Elliot Haydon, and then Symonds suddenly asked where he was. I explained what Elliot had done and Symonds's grave face grew a shade graver. 'I wish he hadn't. It is—it is foolhardy,' he said.

"'You don't think any harm can have happened to him?'

"'I hope not. I think, Padre, that you and I had better go and see.'

"I knew he was right, but it took all the courage in my command to nerve myself for the task. We set out together and entered once more that ill-fated grove of trees. We called him twice and got no reply. In a minute or two we came into the clearing, which looked pale and ghostly in the early morning light. Symonds clutched my arm and I uttered a muttered exclamation. Last night when we had seen it in the moonlight there had been the body of a man lying face downwards on the grass. Now in the early morning light the same sight met our eyes. Elliot Haydon was lying on the exact spot where his cousin had been.

"'My God!' said Symonds. '*It has got him too!*'

"We ran together over the grass. Elliot Haydon was unconscious but breathing feebly and this time there was no doubt of what had caused the tragedy. A long thin bronze weapon remained in the wound.

"'Got him through the shoulder, not through the heart. That is lucky,' commented the doctor. 'On my soul, I don't know what to think. At any rate he is not dead and he will be able to tell us what happened.'

"But that was just what Elliot Haydon was not able to do. His description was vague in the extreme. He had hunted about vainly for the dagger and at last giving up the search had taken up a stand near the Idol House. It was then that he became increasingly certain that someone was watching him from the belt of trees. He fought against this impression but was not able to shake it off. He described a cold strange wind that began to blow. It seemed to come not from the trees but from the interior of the Idol House. He turned round, peering inside it. He saw the small figure of the Goddess and he felt he was under an optical delusion. The figure seemed to grow larger and larger. Then he suddenly received something that felt like a blow between his temples which sent him reeling back, and as he fell he was conscious of a sharp burning pain in his left shoulder.

"The dagger was identified this time as being the identical one which had been dug up in the barrow on the hill, and which had been bought by Richard Haydon. Where he had kept it, in the house or in the Idol House in the grove, none seemed to know.

"The police were of the opinion, and always will be, that he was deliberately stabbed by Miss Ashley, but in view of our combined evidence that she was never within three yards of him, they could not hope to support the charge against her. So the thing has been and remains a mystery."

There was a silence.

"There doesn't seem anything to say," said Joyce Lemprière at length. "It is all so horrible—and uncanny. Have you no explanation for yourself, Dr Pender?"

The old man nodded. "Yes," he said. "I have an explanation—a kind of explanation, that is. Rather a curious one—but to my mind it still leaves certain factors unaccounted for."

"I have been to séances," said Joyce, "and you may say what you like, very queer things can happen. I suppose one can explain it by some kind of hypnotism. The girl really turned herself into a Priestess of Astarte, and I suppose somehow or other she must have stabbed him. Perhaps she threw the dagger that Miss Mannering saw in her hand."

"Or it might have been a javelin," suggested Raymond West. "After all, moonlight is not very strong. She might have had a kind of spear in her hand and stabbed him at a distance, and then I suppose mass hypnotism comes into account. I mean, you were all prepared to see him stricken down by supernatural means and so you saw it like that."

"I have seen many wonderful things done with weapons and knives at music halls," said Sir Henry. "I suppose it is possible that a man could have been concealed in the belt of trees, and that he might from there have thrown a knife or a dagger with sufficient accuracy—agreeing, of course, that he was a professional. I admit that that seems rather far-fetched, but it seems the only really feasible theory. You remember that the other man was distinctly under the impression that there was someone in the grove of trees watching him. As to Miss Mannering saying that Miss Ashley had a dagger in her hand and the others saying she hadn't, that doesn't surprise me. If you had had my experience you would know that five persons' account of the same thing will differ so widely as to be almost incredible."

Mr Petherick coughed.

"But in all these theories we seem to be overlooking one essential fact," he remarked. "What became of the weapon? Miss Ashley could hardly get rid of a javelin standing as she was in the middle of an open space; and if a hidden murderer had thrown a dagger, then the dagger would still have been in the wound when the man was turned over. We must, I think, discard all far-fetched theories and confine ourselves to sober fact."

"And where does sober fact lead us?"

"Well, one thing seems quite clear. No one was near the man when he was stricken down, so the only person who *could* have stabbed him was he himself. Suicide, in fact."

"But why on earth should he wish to commit suicide?" asked Raymond West incredulously.

The lawyer coughed again. "Ah, that is a question of theory once more," he said. "At the moment I am not concerned with theories. It seems to me, excluding the supernatural in which I do not for one moment believe, that that was the only way things could have happened. He stabbed himself, and as he fell his arms flew out, wrenching the dagger from the wound and flinging it far into the zone of the trees. That is, I think, although somewhat unlikely, a possible happening."

"I don't like to say, I am sure," said Miss Marple. "It all perplexes me very much indeed. But curious things do happen. At Lady Sharpley's garden party last year the man who was arranging the clock golf tripped over one of the numbers—quite unconscious he was—and didn't come round for about five minutes."

"Yes, dear Aunt," said Raymond gently, "but he wasn't stabbed, was he?"

"Of course not, dear," said Miss Marple. "That is what I am telling you. Of course there is only one way that poor Sir Richard could have been stabbed, but I do wish I knew what caused him to stumble in the first place. Of course, it might have been a tree root. He would be looking at the girl, of course, and when it is moonlight one does trip over things."

"You say that there is only one way that Sir Richard could have been stabbed, Miss Marple," said the clergyman, looking at her curiously.

"It is very sad and I don't like to think of it. He was a right-handed man, was he not? I mean to stab himself in the left shoulder he must have been. I was always so sorry for poor Jack Baynes in the War. He shot himself in the foot, you remember, after very severe fighting at Arras. He told me about it when I went to see him in hospital, and very ashamed of it he was. I don't expect this poor man, Elliot Haydon, profited much by his wicked crime."

"Elliot Haydon," cried Raymond. "You think he did it?"

"I don't see how anyone else could have done it," said Miss Marple, opening her eyes in gentle surprise. "I mean if, as Mr Petherick so wisely says, one looks at the facts and disregards all that atmosphere of heathen goddesses which I don't think is very nice. He went up to him first and turned him over, and of course to do that he would have to have had his back to them all, and being dressed as a brigand chief he would be sure to have a weapon of some kind in his belt. I remember dancing with a man dressed as a brigand chief when I was a young girl. He had five kinds of knives and daggers, and I can't tell you how awkward and uncomfortable it was for his partner."

All eyes were turned towards Dr Pender.

"I knew the truth," said he, "five years after that tragedy occurred. It came in the shape of a letter written to me by Elliot Haydon. He said in it that he fancied that I had always suspected him. He said it was a sudden temptation. He too loved Diana Ashley, but he was only a poor struggling barrister. With Richard out of the way and inheriting his title and estates, he saw a wonderful prospect opening up before him. The dagger had jerked out of his belt as he knelt down by his cousin, and almost before he had time to think he drove it in and returned it to his belt again. He stabbed himself later in order to divert suspicion. He wrote to me on the eve of starting on an expedition to the South Pole in case, as he said, he should never come back. I do not think that he meant to come back, and I know that, as Miss Marple has said, his crime profited him nothing. 'For five years,' he wrote, 'I have lived in Hell. I hope, at least, that I may expiate my crime by dying honourably.' "

There was a pause.

"And he did die honourably," said Sir Henry. "You have changed the names in your story, Dr Pender, but I think I recognize the man you mean."

"As I said," went on the old clergyman, "I do not think that explanation quite covers the facts. I still think there was an evil influence in that grove, an influence that directed Elliot Haydon's action. Even to this day I can never think without a shudder of The Idol House of Astarte."

The Rajah's Emerald

With a serious effort James Bond bent his attention once more on the little yellow book in his hand. On its outside the book bore the simple but pleasing legend, "Do you want your salary increased by £300 per annum?" Its price was one shilling. James had just finished reading two pages of crisp paragraphs instructing him to look his boss in the face, to cultivate a dynamic personality, and to radiate an atmosphere of efficiency. He had now arrived at a subtler matter, "There is a time for frankness, there is a time for discretion," the little yellow book informed him. "A strong man does not always blurt out *all* he knows." James let the little book close, and raising his head, gazed out over a blue expanse of ocean. A horrible suspicion assailed him, that he was *not* a strong man. A strong man would have been in command of the present situation, not a victim to it. For the sixtieth time that morning James rehearsed his wrongs.

This was his holiday. His holiday? Ha, ha! Sardonic laughter. Who had persuaded him to come to that fashionable seaside resort, Kimpton-on-Sea? Grace. Who had urged him into an expenditure of more than he could afford? Grace. And he had fallen in with the plan eagerly. She had got him here, and what was the result? Whilst he was staying in an obscure boarding-house about a mile and a half from the sea-front, Grace who should have been in a similar boarding-house (not the same one—the proprieties of James's circle were very strict) had flagrantly deserted him, and was staying at no less than the Esplanade Hotel upon the sea-front.

It seemed that she had friends there. Friends! Again James laughed sardonically. His mind went back over the last three years of his leisurely courtship of Grace. Extremely pleased she had been when he first singled her out for notice. That was before she had risen to heights of glory in the millinery salon at Messrs Bartles in the High Street. In those early days it had been James who gave himself airs, now alas! the boot was on the other leg. Grace was what is technically known as "earning good money." It had made her uppish. Yes, that was it, thoroughly uppish. A confused fragment out of a poetry book came back to James's mind, something about "thanking heaven fasting, for a good man's love." But there was nothing of that kind of thing observable about Grace. Well fed on an Esplanade Hotel breakfast, she was ignoring a good man's love utterly. She was indeed accepting the attentions of a poisonous idiot called Claud Sopworth, a man, James felt convinced, of no moral worth whatsoever.

James ground a heel into the the earth, and scowled darkly at the horizon. Kimpton-on-Sea. What had possessed him to come to such a place? It was pre-eminently a resort of the rich and fashionable, it possessed two large hotels, and several miles of picturesque bungalows belonging to fashionable actresses, rich Jews and those members of the English aristocracy who had married wealthy wives. The rent, furnished, of the smallest bungalow was twenty-five guineas a week. Imagination boggled at what the rent of the large ones might amount to. There was one of these palaces immediately behind

James's seat. It belonged to that famous sportsman Lord Edward Campion, and there were staying there at the moment a houseful of distinguished guests including the Rajah of Maraputna, whose wealth was fabulous. James had read all about him in the local weekly newspaper that morning; the extent of his Indian possessions, his palaces, his wonderful collection of jewels, with a special mention of one famous emerald which the papers declared enthusiastically was the size of a pigeon's egg. James, being town bred, was somewhat hazy about the size of a pigeon's egg, but the impression left on his mind was good.

"If I had an emerald like that," said James, scowling at the horizon again, "I'd show Grace."

The sentiment was vague, but the enunciation of it made James feel better. Laughing voices hailed him from behind, and he turned abruptly to confront Grace. With her was Clara Sopworth, Alice Sopworth, Dorothy Sopworth and—alas! Claud Sopworth. The girls were arm-in-arm and giggling.

"Why, you are quite a stranger," cried Grace archly.

"Yes," said James.

He could, he felt, have found a more telling retort. You cannot convey the impression of a dynamic personality by the use of the one word "yes." He looked with intense loathing at Claud Sopworth. Claud Sopworth was almost as beautifully dressed as the hero of a musical comedy. James longed passionately for the moment when an enthusiastic beach dog should plant wet, sandy forefeet on the unsullied whiteness of Claud's flannel trousers. He himself wore a serviceable pair of dark-grey flannel trousers which had seen better days.

"Isn't the air beautiful?" said Clara, sniffing it appreciatively. "Quite sets you up, doesn't it?"

She giggled.

"It's ozone," said Alice Sopworth. "It's as good as a tonic, you know." And she giggled also.

James thought:

"I should like to knock their silly heads together. What is the sense of laughing all the time? They are not saying anything funny."

The immaculate Claud murmured languidly:

"Shall we have a bathe, or is it too much of a fag?"

The idea of bathing was accepted shrilly. James fell into line with them. He even managed, with a certain amount of cunning, to draw Grace a little behind the others.

"Look here!" he complained, "I am hardly seeing anything of you."

"Well, I am sure we are all together now," said Grace, "and you can come and lunch with us at the hotel, at least—"

She looked dubiously at James's legs.

"What is the matter?" demanded James ferociously. "Not smart enough for you, I suppose?"

"I do think, dear, you might take a little more pains," said Grace. "Everyone is so fearfully smart here. Look at Claud Sopworth!"

"I have looked at him," said James grimly. "I have never seen a man who looked a more complete ass than he does."

Grace drew herself up.

"There is no need to criticize my friends, James, it's not manners. He's dressed just like any other gentleman at the hotel is dressed."

"Bah!" said James. "Do you know what I read the other day in 'Society Snippets?' Why, that the Duke of—the Duke of, I can't remember, but one duke, anyway, was the worst dressed man in England, there!"

"I dare say," said Grace, "but then, you see, he is a duke."

"Well?" demanded James. "What is wrong with my being a duke some day? At least, well, not perhaps a duke, but a peer."

He slapped the yellow book in his pocket, and recited to her a long list of peers of the realm who had started life much more obscurely than James Bond. Grace merely giggled.

"Don't be so soft, James," she said. "Fancy you Earl of Kimpton-on-Sea!"

James gazed at her in mingled rage and despair. The air of Kimpton-on-Sea had certainly gone to Grace's head.

The beach at Kimpton is a long, straight stretch of sand. A row of bathing-huts and boxes stretched evenly along it for about a mile and a half. The party had just stopped before a row of six huts all labelled imposingly, "For visitors to the Esplanade Hotel only."

"Here we are," said Grace brightly; "but I'm afraid you can't come in with us, James, you'll have to go along to the public tents over there. We'll meet you in the sea. So long!"

"So long!" said James, and he strode off in the direction indicated.

Twelve dilapidated tents stood solemnly confronting the ocean. An aged mariner guarded them, a roll of blue paper in his hand. He accepted a coin of the realm from James, tore him off a blue ticket from his roll, threw him over a towel, and jerked one thumb over his shoulder.

"Take your turn," he said huskily.

It was then that James awoke to the fact of competition. Others besides himself had conceived the idea of entering the sea. Not only was each tent occupied, but outside each tent was a determined-looking crowd of people glaring at each other. James attached himself to the smallest group and waited. The strings of the tent parted, and a beautiful young woman, sparsely clad, emerged on the scene settling her bathing-cap with the air of one who had the whole morning to waste. She strolled down to the water's edge, and sat down dreamily on the sands.

"That's no good," said James to himself, and attached himself forthwith to another group.

After waiting five minutes, sounds of activity were apparent in the second tent. With heavings and strainings, the flaps parted asunder and four children and a father and mother emerged. The tent being so small, it had something of the appearance of a conjuring trick. On the instant two women sprang forward each grasping one flap of the tent.

"Excuse me," said the first young woman, panting a little.

"Excuse *me*," said the other young woman, glaring.

"I would have you know I was here quite ten minutes before you were," said the first young woman rapidly.

"I have been here a good quarter of an hour, as anyone will tell you," said the second young woman defiantly.

"Now then, now then," said the aged mariner, drawing near.

Both young women spoke to him shrilly. When they had finished, he jerked his thumb at the second young woman, and said briefly:

"It's yours."

Then he departed, deaf to remonstrances. He neither knew nor cared which had been there first, but his decision, as they say in newspaper competitions, was final. The despairing James caught at his arm.

"Look here! I say!"

"Well, mister?"

"How long is it going to be before I get a tent?"

The aged mariner threw a dispassionate glance over the waiting throng. "Might be an hour, might be an hour and a half, I can't say."

At that moment James espied Grace and the Sopworth girls running lightly down the sands towards the sea.

"Damn!" said James to himself. "Oh, damn!"

He plucked once more at the aged mariner.

"Can't I get a tent anywhere else? What about one of these huts along here? They all seem empty."

"The huts," said the ancient mariner with dignity, "are private."

Having uttered this rebuke, he passed on. With a bitter feeling of having been tricked, James detached himself from the waiting groups, and strode savagely down the beach. It was the limit! It was the absolute, complete limit! He glared savagely at the trim bathing-boxes he passed. In that moment from being an Independent Liberal, he became a red-hot Socialist. Why should the rich have bathing-boxes and be able to bathe any minute they chose without waiting in a crowd? "This system of ours," said James vaguely, "is all *wrong*."

From the sea came the coquettish screams of the splashed. Grace's voice! And above her squeaks, the inane "Ha, ha, ha,' of Claud Sopworth.

"Damn!" said James, grinding his teeth, a thing which he had never before attempted, only read about in works of fiction.

He came to a stop, twirling his stick savagely, and turning his back firmly on the sea. Instead, he gazed with concentrated hatred upon Eagle's Nest, Buena Vista, and Mon Desir. It was the custom of the inhabitants of Kimpton-on-Sea to label their bathing-huts with fancy names. Eagle's Nest merely struck James as being silly, and Buena Vista was beyond his linguistic accomplishments. But his knowledge of French was sufficient to make him realize the appositeness of the third name.

And on that moment he saw that while the doors of the other bathing-huts were tightly closed, that of Mon Desir was ajar. James looked thoughtfully up and down the beach, this particular spot was mainly occupied by mothers of large families, busily engaged in superintending their offspring. It was only ten o'clock, too early as yet for the aristocracy of Kimpton-on-Sea to have come down to bathe.

"Eating quails and mushrooms in their beds as likely as not, brought to them on trays by powdered footmen, pah! Not one of them will be down here before twelve o'clock," thought James.

He looked again towards the sea. With the obedience of a well-trained "leitmotif," the shrill scream of Grace rose upon the air. It was followed by the "Ha, ha, ha," of Claud Sopworth.

"I will," said James between his teeth.

He pushed open the door of Mon Desir and entered. For the moment he had a fright, as he caught sight of sundry garments hanging from pegs, but he was quickly reassured. The hut was partitioned into two, on the right-hand side, a girl's yellow sweater, a battered panama hat and a pair of beach shoes were depending from a peg. On the left-hand side an old pair of grey flannel trousers, a pullover, and a sou'wester proclaimed the fact that the sexes were segregated. James hastily transferred himself to the gentlemen's part of the hut, and undressed rapidly. Three minutes later, he was in the sea puffing and snorting importantly, doing extremely short bursts of professional-looking swimming—head under the water, arms lashing the sea—that style.

"Oh, there you are!" cried Grace. "I was afraid you

wouldn't be in for ages with all that crowd of people waiting there."

"Really?" said James.

He thought with affectionate loyalty of the yellow book. "The strong man can on occasions be discreet." For the moment his temper was quite restored. He was able to say pleasantly but firmly to Claud Sopworth, who was teaching Grace the overarm stroke:

"No, no, old man, you have got it all wrong. *I'll* show her."

And such was the assurance of his tone, that Claud withdrew discomfited. The only pity of it was that his triumph was short-lived. The temperature of our English waters is not such as to induce bathers to remain in them for any length of time. Grace and the Sopworth girls were already displaying blue chins and chattering teeth. They raced up the beach, and James pursued his solitary way back to Mon Desir. As he towelled himself vigorously and slipped his shirt over his head, he was pleased with himself. He had, he felt, displayed a dynamic personality.

And then suddenly he stood still, frozen with terror. Girlish voices sounded from outside, and voices quite different from those of Grace and her friends. A moment later he had realized the truth, the rightful owners of Mon Desir were arriving. It is possible that if James had been fully dressed, he would have waited their advent in a dignified manner, and attempted an explanation. As it was he acted on panic. The windows of Mon Desir were modestly screened by dark green curtains. James flung himself on the door and held the knob in a desperate clutch. Hands tried ineffectually to turn it from outside.

"It's locked after all," said a girl's voice. "I thought Peg said it was open."

"No, Woggle said so."

"Woggle is the limit," said the other girl. "How perfectly foul, we shall have to go back for the key."

James heard their footsteps retreating. He drew a long, deep breath. In desperate haste he huddled on the rest of his garments. Two minutes later saw him strolling negligently down the beach with an almost aggressive air of innocence. Grace and the Sopworth girls joined him on the beach a quarter of an hour later. The rest of the morning passed agreeably in stone throwing, writing in the sand and light badinage. Then Claud glanced at his watch.

"Lunch-time," he observed. "We'd better be strolling back."

"I'm terribly hungry," said Alice Sopworth.

All the other girls said that they were terribly hungry too.

"Are you coming, James?" asked Grace.

Doubtless James was unduly touchy. He chose to take offence at her tone.

"Not if my clothes are not good enough for you," he said bitterly. "Perhaps, as you are so particular, I'd better not come."

That was Grace's cue for murmured protestations, but the seaside air had affected Grace unfavourably. She merely replied:

"Very well. Just as you like, see you this afternoon then."

James was left dumbfounded.

"Well!" he said, staring after the retreating group. "Well, of all the—"

He strolled moodily into the town. There were two cafés in Kimpton-on-Sea, they are both hot, noisy and overcrowded. It was the affair of the bathing-huts once more, James had to wait his turn. He had to wait longer than his turn, an unscrupulous matron who had just arrived forestalling him when a vacant seat did present itself. At last he was seated at a small table. Close to his left ear three raggedly bobbed maidens were making a determined hash of Italian opera. Fortunately James was not musical. He studied the bill of fare dispassionately, his hands thrust deep into his pockets. He thought to himself:

"Whatever I ask for it's sure to be 'off.' That's the kind of fellow I am."

His right hand, groping in the recesses of his pocket, touched an unfamiliar object. It felt like a pebble, a large round pebble.

"What on earth did I want to put a stone in my pocket for?" thought James.

His fingers closed round it. A waitress drifted up to him.

"Fried plaice and chipped potatoes, please," said James.

"Fried plaice is 'off,'" murmured the waitress, her eyes fixed dreamily on the ceiling.

"Then I'll have curried beef," said James.

"Curried beef is 'off.'"

"Is there anything on this beastly menu that isn't 'off?'" demanded James.

The waitress looked pained, and placed a pale-grey forefinger against haricot mutton. James resigned himself to the inevitable and ordered haricot mutton. His mind still seething with resentment against the ways of cafés, he drew his hand out of his pocket, the stone still in it. Unclosing his fingers, he looked absentmindedly at the object in his palm. Then with a shock all lesser matters passed from his mind, and he stared with all his eyes. The thing he held was not a pebble, it was—he could hardly doubt it—an emerald, an enormous green emerald. James stared at it horror-stricken. No, it couldn't be an emerald, it must be coloured glass. There couldn't be an emerald of that size, unless—printed words danced before James's eyes, "The Rajah of Maraputna—famous emerald the size of a pigeon's egg." Was it—could it be—*that* emerald at which he was now looking? The waitress returned with the haricot mutton, and James closed his fingers spasmodically. Hot and cold shivers chased themselves up and down his spine. He had the sense of being caught in a terrible dilemma. If this was the emerald—but was it? Could it be? He unclosed his fingers and peeped anxiously. James was no expert on precious stones, but the depth and the glow of the jewel convinced him this was the real thing. He put both elbows on the table and leaned forward staring with unseeing eyes at the haricot mutton slowly congealing on the dish in front of him. He had got to think this out. If this was the Rajah's emerald, what was he going to do about it? The word "police" flashed into his mind. If you found anything of value you took it to the police station. Upon this axiom had James been brought up.

Yes, but—how on earth had the emerald got into his trouser pocket? That was doubtless the question the police would ask. It was an awkward question, and it was moreover a question to which he had at the moment no answer. How had the emerald got into his trouser pocket? He looked despairingly down at his legs, and as he did so a misgiving shot through him. He looked more closely. One pair of old grey flannel trousers is very much like another pair of old grey flannel trousers, but all the same, James had an instinctive feeling that these were not his trousers after all. He sat back in his chair stunned with the force of the discovery. He saw now what had happened, in the hurry of getting out of the bathing-hut, he had taken the wrong trousers. He had hung his own, he remembered, on an adjacent peg to the old pair hanging there. Yes, that explained matters so far, he had taken the wrong trousers. But all the same, what on earth was an emerald worth hundreds and thousands of pounds doing there? The more he thought about it, the more curious it seemed. He could, of course, explain to the police—

It was awkward, no doubt about it, it was decidedly awkward. One would have to mention the fact that one had deliberately entered someone else's bathing-hut. It was not, of course, a serious offence, but it started him off wrong.

"Can I bring you anything else, sir?"

It was the waitress again. She was looking pointedly at the untouched haricot mutton. James hastily dumped some of it on his plate and asked for his bill. Having obtained it, he paid and went out. As he stood undecidedly in the street, a poster opposite caught his eye. The adjacent town of Harchester possessed an evening paper, and it was the contents bill of this paper that James was looking at. It announced a simple, sensational fact: "The Rajah's Emerald Stolen." "My God," said James faintly, and leaned against a pillar. Pulling himself together he fished out a penny and purchased a copy of the paper. He was not long in finding what he sought. Sensational items of local news were few and far between. Large headlines adorned the front page. "Sensational Burglary at Lord Edward Campion's. Theft of Famous Historical Emerald. Rajah of Maraputna's Terrible Loss." The facts were few and simple. Lord Edward Campion had entertained several friends the evening before. Wishing to show the stone to one of the ladies present, the Rajah had gone to fetch it and had found it missing. The police had been called in. So far no clue had been obtained.

James let the paper fall to the ground. It was still not clear to him how the emerald had come to be reposing in the pocket of an old pair of flannel trousers in a bathing-hut, but it was borne in upon him every minute that the police would certainly regard his own story as suspicious. What on earth was he to do? Here he was, standing in the principal street of Kimpton-on-Sea with stolen booty worth a king's ransom reposing idly in his pocket, whilst the entire police force of the district were busily searching for just that same booty. There were two courses open to him. Course number one, to go straight to the police station and tell his story—but it must be admitted that James funked that course badly. Course number two, somehow or other to get rid of the emerald. It occurred to him to do it up in a neat little parcel and post it back to the Rajah. Then he shook his head, he had read too many detective stories for that sort of thing. He knew how your super-sleuth could get busy with a magnifying glass and every kind of patent device. Any detective worth his salt would get busy on James's parcel and would in half an hour or so have discovered the sender's profession, age, habits and personal appearance. After that it would be a mere matter of hours before he was tracked down. It was then that a scheme of dazzling simplicity suggested itself to James.

It was the luncheon hour, the beach would be comparatively deserted, he would return to Mon Desir, hang up the trousers where he had found them, and regain his own garments. He started briskly towards the beach.

Nevertheless, his conscience pricked him slightly. The emerald *ought* to be returned to the Rajah. He conceived the idea that he might perhaps do a little detective work—once, that is, that he had regained his own trousers and replaced the others. In pursuance of this idea, he directed his steps towards the aged mariner, whom he rightly regarded as being an exhaustible source of Kimpton information.

"Excuse me!" said James politely; "but I belive a friend of mine has a hut on this beach, Mr Charles Lampton. It is called Mon Desir, I fancy."

The aged mariner was sitting very squarely in a chair, a pipe in his mouth, gazing out to sea. He shifted his pipe a little, and replied without removing his gaze from the horizon:

"Mon Desir belongs to his lordship, Lord Edward Campion, everyone knows that. I never heard of Mr Charles Lampton, he must be a newcomer."

"Thank you," said James, and withdrew.

The information staggered him. Surely the Rajah could not himself have slipped the stone into the pocket and forgotten it. James shook his head, the theory did not satisfy him, but evidently some member of the house-party must be the thief. The situation reminded James of some of his favourite works of fiction.

Nevertheless, his own purpose remained unaltered. All fell out easily enough. The beach was, as he hoped it would be, practically deserted. More fortunate still, the door of Mon Desir remained ajar. To slip in was the work of a moment, Edward was just lifting his own trousers from the hook, when a voice behind him made him spin round suddenly.

"So I have caught you, my man!" said the voice.

James stared open-mouthed. In the doorway of Mon Desir stood a stranger; a well-dressed man of about forty years of age, his face keen and hawk-like.

"So I have caught you!" the stranger repeated.

"Who—who are you?" stammered James.

"Detective-Inspector Merrilees from the Yard," said

the other crisply. "And I will trouble you to hand over that emerald."

"The—the emerald?"

James was seeking to gain time.

"That's what I said, didn't I?" said Inspector Merrilees.

He had a crisp, business-like enunciation. James tried to pull himself together.

"I don't know what you are talking about," he said with an assumption of dignity.

"Oh, yes, my lad, I think you do."

"The whole thing," said James, "is a mistake. I can explain it quite easily—" He paused.

A look of weariness had settled on the face of the other.

"They always say that," murmured the Scotland Yard man dryly. "I suppose you picked it up as you were strolling along the beach, eh? That is the sort of explanation."

It did indeed bear a resemblance to it, James recognized the fact, but still he tried to gain time.

"How do I know you are what you say you are?" he demanded weakly.

Merrilees flapped back his coat for a moment, showing a badge. Edward stared at him with eyes that popped out of his head.

"And now," said the other almost genially, "you see what you are up against! You are a novice—I can tell that. Your first job, isn't it?"

James nodded.

"I thought as much. Now, my boy, are you going to hand over that emerald, or have I got to search you?"

James found his voice.

"I—I haven't got it on me," he declared.

He was thinking desperately.

"Left it at your lodgings?" queried Merrilees.

James nodded.

"Very well, then," said the detective, "we will go there together."

He slipped his arm through James's.

"I am taking no chances of your getting away from me," he said gently. "We will go to your lodgings, and you will hand that stone over to me."

James spoke unsteadily.

"If I do, will you let me go?" he asked tremulously.

Merrilees appeared embarrassed.

"We know just how that stone was taken," he explained, "and about the lady involved, and, of course, as far as that goes—well, the Rajah wants it hushed up. You know what these Indian rulers are?"

James, who knew nothing whatsoever about Indian rulers, except for one *cause célèbre*, nodded his head with an appearance of eager comprehension.

"It will be most irregular, of course," said the detective; "but you *may* get off scot-free."

Again James nodded. They had walked the length of the Esplanade, and were now turning into the town. James intimated the direction, but the other man never relinquished his sharp grip on James's arm.

Suddenly James hesitated and half-spoke. Merrilees looked up sharply, and then laughed. They were just passing the police station, and he noticed James's agonized glances at it.

"I am giving you a chance first," he said good-humouredly.

It was at that moment that things began to happen. A loud bellow broke from James, he clutched the other's arm, and yelled at the top of his voice:

"Help! thief. Help! thief."

A crowd surrounded them in less than a minute. Merrilees was trying to wrench his arm from James's grasp.

"I charge this man," cried James. "I charge this man, he picked my pocket."

"What are you talking about, you fool?" cried the other.

A constable took charge of matters. Mr Merrilees and James were escorted into the police station. James reiterated his complaint.

"This man has just picked my pocket," he declared excitedly. "He has got my note-case in his right-hand pocket, there!"

"The man is mad," grumbled the other. "You can look for yourself, inspector, and see if he is telling the truth."

At a sign from the inspector, the constable slipped his hand deferentially into Merrilees's pocket. He drew something out and held it up with a gasp of astonishment.

"My God!" said the inspector, startled out of professional decorum. "It must be the Rajah's emerald."

Merrilees looked more incredulous than anyone else.

"This is monstrous," he spluttered; "monstrous. The man must have put it into my pocket himself as we were walking along together. It's a plant."

The forceful personality of Merrilees caused the inspector to waver. His suspicions swung round to James. He whispered something to the constable, and the latter went out.

"Now then, gentlemen," said the inspector, "let me have your statements please, one at a time."

"Certainly," said James. "I was walking along the beach, when I met this gentleman, and he pretended he was acquainted with me. I could not remember having met him before, but I was too polite to say so. We walked along together. I had my suspicions of him, and just when we got opposite the police station, I found his hand in my pocket. I held on to him and shouted for help."

The inspector transferred his glance to Merrilees.

"And now you, sir."

Merrilees seemed a little embarrassed.

"The story is very nearly right," he said slowly; "but not quite. It was not I who scraped acquaintance with him, but he who scraped acquaintance with me. Doubtless he was trying to get rid of the emerald, and slipped it into my pocket while we were talking."

The inspector stopped writing.

"Ah!" he said impartially. "Well, there will be a gentleman here in a minute who will help us to get to the bottom of the case."

Merrilees frowned.

"It is really impossible for me to wait," he murmured, pulling out his watch. "I have an appointment. Surely, inspector, you can't be so ridiculous as to suppose I'd steal the emerald and walk along with it in my pocket?"

"It is not likely, sir, I agree," the inspector replied. "But you will have to wait just a matter of five or ten minutes till we get this thing cleared up. Ah! here is his lordship."

A tall man of forty strode into the room. He was wearing a pair of dilapidated trousers and an old sweater.

"Now then, inspector, what is all this?" he said. "You have got hold of the emerald, you say? That's splendid, very smart work. Who are these people you have got here?"

His eyes ranged over James and came to rest on Merrilees. The forceful personality of the latter seemed to dwindle and shrink.

"Why—Jones!" exclaimed Lord Edward Campion.

"You recognize this man, Lord Edward?" asked the inspector sharply.

"Certainly I do," said Lord Edward dryly. "He is my valet, came to me a month ago. The fellow they sent down from London was on to him at once, but there was not a trace of the emerald anywhere among his belongings."

"He was carrying it in his coat pocket," the inspector declared. "This gentleman put us on to him." He indicated James.

In another minute James was being warmly congratulated and shaken by the hand.

"My dear fellow," said Lord Edward Campion. "So you suspected him all along, you say?"

"Yes," said James. "I had to trump up the story about my pocket being picked to get him into the police station."

"Well, it is splendid," said Lord Edward, "absolutely splendid. You must come back and lunch with us, that is if you haven't lunched. It is late, I know, getting on for two o'clock."

"No," said James; "I haven't lunched—but—"

"Not a word, not a word," said Lord Edward. "The Rajah, you know, will want to thank you for getting back his emerald for him. Not that I have quite got the hang of the story yet."

They were out of the police station by now, standing on the steps.

"As a matter of fact," said James, "I think I should like to tell you the true story."

He did so. His lordship was very much entertained.

"Best thing I ever heard in my life," he declared. "I see it all now. Jones must have hurried down to the bathing-hut as soon as he had pinched the thing, knowing that the police would make a thorough search of the house. That old pair of trousers I sometimes put on for going out fishing, nobody was likely to touch them, and he could recover the jewel at his leisure. Must have been a shock to him when he came today to find it gone. As soon as you appeared, he realized that you were the person who had removed the stone. I still don't quite see how you managed to see through that detective pose of his, though!"

"A strong man," thought James to himself, "knows when to be frank and when to be discreet."

He smiled deprecatingly whilst his fingers passed gently over the inside of his coat lapel feeling the small silver badge of that little-known club, the Merton Park Super Cycling Club. An astonishing coincidence that the man Jones should also be a member, but there it was!

"Hallo, James!"

He turned. Grace and the Sopworth girls were calling to him from the other side of the road. He turned to Lord Edward.

"Excuse me a moment?"

He crossed the road to them.

"We are going to the pictures," said Grace. "Thought you might like to come."

"I am sorry," said James. "I am just going back to lunch with Lord Edward Campion. Yes, that man over there in the comfortable old clothes. He wants me to meet the Rajah of Maraputna."

He raised his hat politely and rejoined Lord Edward.

The Oracle at Delphi

Mrs Willard J. Peters did not really care for Greece. And of Delphi she had, in her secret heart, no opinion at all.

Mrs Peters' spiritual homes were in Paris, London and the Riviera. She was a woman who enjoyed hotel life, but her idea of a hotel bedroom was a soft-pile carpet, a luxurious bed, a profusion of different arrangements of electric light, including a shaded bedside lamp, plenty of hot and cold water and a telephone beside the bed, by means of which you could order tea, meals, mineral waters, cocktails and speak to your friends.

In the hotel at Delphi there were none of these things. There was a marvellous view from the windows, the bed was clean and so was the whitewashed room. There was a chair, a wash-stand and a chest of drawers. Baths took place by arrangement and were occasionally disappointing as regarded hot water.

It would, she supposed, be nice to say that you had been to Delphi, and Mrs Peters had tried hard to take an interest in Ancient Greece, but she found it difficult. Their statuary seemed so unfinished; so lacking in heads and arms and legs. Secretly, she much preferred the handsome marble angel complete with wings which was erected on the late Mr Willard Peters' tomb.

But all these secret opinions she kept carefully to herself, for fear her son Willard should despise her. It was for Willard's sake that she was here, in this chilly and uncomfortable room, with a sulky maid and a disgusted chauffeur in the offing.

For Willard (until recently called Junior—a title which he hated) was Mrs Peters' eighteen-year-old son, and she worshipped him to distraction. It was Willard who had this strange passion for bygone art. It was Willard, thin, pale, spectacled and dyspeptic, who had dragged his adoring mother on this tour through Greece.

They had been to Olympia, which Mrs Peters thought a sad mess. She had enjoyed the Parthenon, but she considered Athens a hopeless city. And a visit to Corinth and Mycenae had been agony to both her and the chauffeur.

Delphi, Mrs Peters thought unhappily, was the last straw. Absolutely nothing to do but walk along the road and look at the ruins. Willard spent long hours on his knees deciphering Greek inscriptions, saying, "Mother, just listen to this! Isn't it splendid?" And then he would read out something that seemed to Mrs Peters the quintessence of dullness.

This morning Willard had started early to see some Byzantine mosaics. Mrs Peters, feeling instinctively that Byzantine mosaics would leave her cold (in the literal as well as the spiritual sense), had excused herself.

"I understand, Mother," Willard had said. "You want to be alone just to sit in the theatre or up in the stadium and look down over it and let it sink in."

"That's right, pet," said Mrs Peters.

"I knew this place would get you," said Willard exultantly and departed.

Now, with a sigh, Mrs Peters prepared to rise and breakfast.

She came into the dining-room to find it empty save for four people. A mother and daughter, dressed in what seemed to Mrs Peters a most peculiar style (not recognizing the peplum as such), who were discoursing on the art of self-expression in dancing; a plump, middle-aged gentleman who had rescued a suitcase for her when she got off the train and whose name was Thompson; and a newcomer, a middle-aged gentleman with a bald head who had arrived on the preceding evening.

This personage was the last left in the breakfast room, and Mrs Peters soon fell into conversation with him. She was a friendly woman and liked someone to talk to. Mr Thompson had been distinctly discouraging in manner (British reserve, Mrs Peters called it), and the mother and daughter had been very superior and highbrow, though the girl had got on rather well with Willard.

Mrs Peters found the newcomer a very pleasant person. He was informative without being highbrow. He told her several interesting, friendly little details about the Greeks, which made her feel much more as though they were real people and not just tiresome history out of a book.

Mrs Peters told her new friend all about Willard and what a clever boy he was, and how Culture might be said to be his middle name. There was something about this benevolent and bland personage which made him easy to talk to.

What he himself did and what his name was, Mrs Peters did not learn. Beyond the fact that he had been travelling and that he was having a complete rest from business (what business?), he was not communicative about himself.

Altogether, the day passed more quickly than might have been anticipated. The mother and daughter and Mr Thompson continued to be unsociable. They encountered the latter coming out of the museum, and he immediately turned in the opposite direction.

Mrs Peters' new friend looked after him with a little frown.

"Now I wonder who that fellow is!" he said.

Mrs Peters supplied him with the other's name, but could do no more.

"Thompson—Thompson. No, I don't think I've met him before and yet somehow or other his face seems familiar. But I can't place him."

In the afternoon Mrs Peters enjoyed a quiet nap in a shady spot. The book she took with her to read was not the excellent one on Grecian Art recommended to her by her son but was, on the contrary, entitled *The River Launch Mystery.* It had four murders in it, three abductions, and a large and varied gang of dangerous criminals. Mrs Peters found herself both invigorated and soothed by the perusal of it.

It was four o'clock when she returned to the hotel. Willard, she felt sure, would be back by this time. So far was she from any presentiment of evil that she almost forgot to open a note which the proprietor said had been left for her by a strange man during the afternoon.

It was an extremely dirty note. Idly she ripped it open. As she read the first few lines her face blanched and she put out a hand to steady herself. The handwriting was foreign but the language employed was English.

> *Lady* (it began),*—This to hand to inform you that your son is being held captive by us in place of great security. No harm shall happen to honoured young gentleman if you obey orders of yours truly. We demand for him ransom of ten thousand English pounds sterling. If you speak of this to hotel proprietor or police or any such person your son will be*

killed. This is given you to reflect. Tomorrow directions in way of paying money will be given. If not obeyed the honoured young gentleman's ears will be cut off and sent you. And following day if still not obeyed he will be killed. Again this is not idle threat. Let the Kyria reflect again—above all—be silent.

Demetrius the Black Browed

It were idle to describe the poor lady's state of mind. Preposterous and childishly worded as the demand was, it yet brought home to her a grim atmosphere of peril. Willard, her boy, her pet, her delicate, serious Willard.

She would go at once to the police; she would rouse the neighbourhood. But perhaps, if she did—she shivered.

Then, rousing herself, she went out of her room in search of the hotel proprietor—the sole person in the hotel who could speak English.

"It is getting late," she said. "My son has not returned yet."

The pleasant little man beamed at her. "True. Monsieur dismissed the mules. He wished to return on foot. He should have been here by now, but doubtless he has lingered on the way." He smiled happily.

"Tell me," said Mrs Peters abruptly, "have you any bad characters in the neighbourhood?"

Bad characters was a term not embraced by the little man's knowledge of English. Mrs Peters made her meaning plainer. She received in reply an assurance that all around Delphi were very good, very quiet people—all well disposed towards foreigners.

Words trembled on her lips, but she forced them back. That sinister threat tied her tongue. It might be the merest bluff. But suppose it wasn't? A friend of hers in America had had a child kidnapped, and on her informing the police, the child had been killed. Such things did happen.

She was nearly frantic. What was she to do? Ten thousand pounds—what was that?—between forty or fifty thousand dollars! What was that to her in comparison with Willard's safety? But how could she obtain such a sum? There were endless difficulties just now as regarded money and the drawing of cash. A letter of credit for a few hundred pounds was all she had with her.

Would the bandits understand this? Would they be reasonable? Would they *wait*?

When her maid came to her, she dismissed the girl fiercely. A bell sounded for dinner, and the poor lady was driven to the dining-room. She ate mechanically. She saw no one. The room might have been empty as far as she was concerned.

With the arrival of fruit, a note was placed before her. She winced, but the handwriting was entirely different from that which she had feared to see—a neat, clerkly English hand. She opened it without much interest, but she found its contents intriguing:

At Delphi you can no longer consult the oracle (so it ran), *but you can consult Mr Parker Pyne.*

Below that there was a cutting of an advertisement pinned to the paper, and at the bottom of the sheet a passport photograph was attached. It was the photograph of her bald-headed friend of the morning.

Mrs Peters read the printed cutting twice.

Are you happy? If not, consult Mr Parker Pyne.

Happy? Happy? Had anyone ever been so unhappy? It was like an answer to prayer.

Hastily she scribbled on a loose sheet of paper she happened to have in her bag:

Please help me. Will you meet me outside the hotel in ten minutes?

She enclosed it in an envelope and directed the waiter to take it to the gentleman at the table by the window. Ten minutes later, enveloped in a fur coat, for the night was chilly, Mrs Peters went out of the hotel and strolled slowly along the road to the ruins. Mr Parker Pyne was waiting for her.

"It's just the mercy of heaven you're here," said Mrs Peters breathlessly. "But how did you guess the terrible trouble I'm in. That's what I want to know."

"The human countenance, my dear madam," said Mr Parker Pyne gently. "I knew at once that *something* had happened, but what it is I am waiting for you to tell me."

Out it came in a flood. She handed him the letter, which he read by the light of his pocket torch.

"H'm," he said. "A remarkable document. A most remarkable document. It has certain points—"

But Mrs Peters was in no mood to listen to a discussion of the finer points of the letter. What was she to do about Willard? Her own dear, delicate Willard.

Mr Parker Pyne was soothing. He painted an attractive picture of Greek bandit life. They would be especially careful of their captive, since he represented a potential gold mine. Gradually he calmed her down.

"But what am I to *do*?" wailed Mrs Peters.

"Wait until tomorrow," said Mr Parker Pyne. "That is, unless you prefer to go straight to the police."

Mrs Peters interrupted him with a shriek of terror. Her darling Willard would be murdered out of hand!

"You think I'll get Willard back safe and sound?"

"There is no doubt of that," said Mr Parker Pyne soothingly. "The only question is whether you can get him back without paying ten thousand pounds."

"All I want is my boy."

"Yes, yes," said Mr Parker Pyne soothingly. "Who brought the letter, by the way?"

"A man the landlord didn't know. A stranger."

"Ah! There are possibilities there. The man who brings the letter tomorrow might be followed. What are you telling the people at the hotel about your son's absence?"

"I haven't thought."

"I wonder, now." Mr Parker Pyne reflected. "I think you might quite naturally express alarm and concern at his absence. A search party could be sent out."

"You don't think these fiends—?" She choked.

"No, no. So long as there is no word of the kidnapping or the ransom, they cannot turn nasty. After all, you can't be expected to take your son's disappearance with no fuss at all."

"Can I leave it all to you?"

"That is my business," said Mr Parker Pyne.

They started back towards the hotel again but almost ran into a burly figure.

"Who was that?" asked Mr Parker Pyne sharply.

"I think it was Mr Thompson."

"Oh!" said Mr Parker Pyne thoughtfully. "Thompson, was it? Thompson—h'm."

Mrs Peters felt as she went to bed that Mr Parker Pyne's idea about the letter was a good one. Whoever brought it *must* be in touch with the bandits. She felt consoled, and fell asleep much sooner than she could ever have believed possible.

When she was dressing on the following morning

she suddenly noticed something lying on the floor by the window. She picked it up—and her heart missed a beat. The same dirty, cheap envelope; the same hated characters. She tore it open.

Good-morning lady. Have you made reflections? Your son is well and unharmed—so far. But we must have the money. It may not be easy for you to get this sum, but it has been told us that you have with you a necklace of diamonds. Very fine stones. We will be satisfied with that, instead. Listen, this is what you must do. You, or anyone you choose to send must take this necklace and bring it to the Stadium. From there go up to where there is a tree by a big rock. Eyes will watch and see that only one person comes. Then your son will be exchanged for necklace. The time must be tomorrow six o'clock in the morning just after sunrise. If you put police on us afterwards we shoot your son as your car drives to station.

This is our last word, lady. If no necklace tomorrow morning your son's ears sent you. Next day he die.

With salutations, lady, Demetrius

Mrs Peters hurried to find Mr Parker Pyne. He read the letter attentively.

"Is this true," he asked, "about a diamond necklace?"

"Absolutely. A hundred thousand dollars my husband paid for it."

"Our well-informed thieves," murmured Mr Parker Pyne.

"What's that you say?"

"I was just considering certain aspects of the affair."

"My word, Mr Pyne, we haven't got time for aspects. I've got to get my boy back."

"But you are a woman of spirit, Mrs Peters. Do you enjoy being bullied and cheated out of ten thousand dollars? Do you enjoy giving up your diamonds meekly to a set of ruffians?"

"Well, of course, if you put it like that!" The woman of spirit in Mrs Peters wrestled with the mother. "How I'd like to get even with them—the cowardly brutes! The very minute I get my boy back, Mr Pyne, I shall set the whole police of the neighbourhood on them, and, if necessary, I shall hire an armoured car to take Willard and myself to the railway station!" Mrs Peters was flushed and vindictive.

"Ye—es," said Mr Parker Pyne. "You see, my dear madam, I'm afraid they will be prepared for that move on your part. They know that once Willard is restored to you nothing will keep you from setting the whole neighbourhood on the alert. Which leads one to suppose that they have prepared for that move."

"Well, what do you want to do?"

Mr Parker Pyne smiled. "I want to try a little plan of my own." He looked around the dining-room. It was empty and the doors at both ends were closed. "Mrs Peters, there is a man I know in Athens—a jeweller. He specializes in good artificial diamonds—first-class stuff." His voice dropped to a whisper. "I'll get him by telephone. He can get here this afternoon, bringing a good selection of stones with him."

"You mean?"

"He'll extract the real diamonds and replace them with paste replicas."

"Why, if that isn't the cutest thing I've ever heard of!" Mrs Peters gazed at him with admiration.

"Sh! Not so loud. Will you do something for me?"

"Surely."

"See that nobody comes within earshot of the telephone."

Mrs Peters nodded.

The telephone was in the manager's office. He vacated it obligingly, after having helped Mr Parker Pyne to obtain the number. When he emerged, he found Mrs Peters outside.

"I'm just waiting for Mr Parker Pyne," she said. "We're going for a walk."

"Oh, yes, madam."

Mr Thompson was also in the hall. He came towards them and engaged the manager in conversation.

Were there any villas to be let in Delphi? No? But surely there was one above the hotel?

"That belongs to a Greek gentleman, monsieur. He does not let it."

"And are there no other villas?"

"There is one belonging to an American lady. That is the other side of the village. It is shut up now. And there is one belonging to an English gentleman, an artist—that is on the cliff edge looking down to Itéa."

Mrs Peters broke in. Nature had given her a loud voice and she purposely made it louder. "Why," she said, "I'd just adore to have a villa here! So unspoilt and natural. I'm simply crazy about the place, aren't you, Mr Thompson? But of course you must be if you want a villa. Is it your first visit here? You don't say so."

She ran on determinedly till Mr Parker Pyne emerged from the office. He gave her just the faintest smile of approval.

Mr Thompson walked slowly down the steps and out into the road where he joined the highbrow mother and daughter, who seemed to be feeling the wind cold on their exposed arms.

All went well. The jeweller arrived just before dinner with a car full of other tourists. Mrs Peters took her necklace to his room. He grunted approval. Then he spoke in French.

"*Madame peut être tranquille. Je réussirai.*" He extracted some tools from his little bag and began work.

At eleven o'clock Mr Parker Pyne tapped on Mrs Peters' door. "Here you are!"

He handed her a little chamois bag. She glanced inside.

"My diamonds!"

"Hush! Here is the necklace with the paste replacing the diamonds. Pretty good, don't you think?"

"Simply wonderful."

"Aristopoulous is a clever fellow."

"You don't think they'll suspect?"

"How should they? They know you have the necklace with you. You hand it over. How can they suspect the trick?"

"Well, I think it's wonderful," Mrs Peters reiterated, handing the necklace back to him. "Will you take it to them? Or is that asking too much of you?"

"Certainly I will take it. Just give me the letter, so that I have the directions clear. Thank you. Now, good-night and *bon courage*. Your boy will be with you tomorrow for breakfast."

"Oh, if only that's true!"

"Now, don't worry. Leave everything in my hands."

Mrs Peters did not spend a good night. When she slept, she had terrible dreams. Dreams where armed bandits in armoured cars fired off a fusillade at Willard, who was running down the mountain in his pyjamas.

She was thankful to wake. At last came the first glimmer of dawn. Mrs Peters got up and dressed. She sat—waiting.

At seven o'clock there came a tap on the door. Her throat was so dry she could hardly speak.

"Come in," she said.

The door opened and Mr Thompson entered. She

stared at him. Words failed her. She had a sinister presentiment of disaster. And yet his voice when he spoke was completely natural and matter-of-fact. It was a rich, bland voice.

"Good-morning, Mrs Peters," he said.

"How dare you sir! How dare you—"

"You must excuse my unconventional visit at so early an hour," said Mr Thompson. "But you see, I have a matter of business to transact."

Mrs Peter leaned forward with accusing eyes. "So it was you who kidnapped my boy! It wasn't bandits at all!"

"It certainly wasn't bandits. Most unconvincingly done, that part of it, I thought. Inartistic, to say the least of it."

Mrs Peters was a woman of a single idea. "Where's my boy?" she demanded, with the eyes of an angry tigress.

"As a matter of fact," said Mr Thompson, "he's just outside the door."

"Willard!"

The door was flung open. Willard, sallow and spectacled and distinctly unshaven, was clasped to his mother's heart. Mr Thompson stood looking benignly on.

"All the same," said Mrs Peters, suddenly recovering herself and turning on him, "I'll have the law on you for this. Yes, I will."

"You've got it all wrong, Mother," said Willard. "This gentleman rescued me."

"Where were you?"

"In a house on the cliff point. Just a mile from here."

"And allow me, Mrs Peters," said Mr Thompson, "to restore your property."

He handed her a small packet loosely wrapped in tissue paper. The paper fell away and revealed the diamond necklace.

"You need not treasure that other little bag of stones, Mrs Peters," said Mr Thompson, smiling. "The real stones are still in the necklace. The chamois bag contains some excellent imitation stones. As your friend said, Aristopoulous is quite a genius."

"I just don't understand a word of all this," said Mrs Peters faintly.

"You must look at the case from my point of view," said Mr Thompson. "My attention was caught by the use of a certain name. I took the liberty of following you and your fat friend out of doors and I listened—I admit it frankly—to your exceedingly interesting conversation. I found it remarkably suggestive, so much so that I took the manager into my confidence. He took a note of the number to which your plausible friend telephoned and he also arranged that a waiter should listen to your conversation in the dining-room this morning.

"The whole scheme worked very clearly. You were being made the victim of a couple of clever jewel thieves. They know all about your diamond necklace; they follow you here; they kidnap your son, and write the rather comic 'bandit' letter, and they arrange that you shall confide in the chief instigator of the plot.

"After that, all is simple. The good gentleman hands you a bag of imitation diamonds and—clears out with his pal. This morning, when your son did not appear, you would be frantic. The absence of your friend would lead you to believe that he had been kidnapped too. I gather that they had arranged for someone to go to the villa tomorrow. That person would have discovered your son, and by the time you and he had put your heads together you might have got an inkling of the plot. But by that time the villains would have got an excellent start."

"And now?"

"Oh, now they are safely under lock and key. I arranged for that."

"The villain," said Mrs Peters, wrathfully remembering her own trustful confidences. "The oily, plausible villain."

"Not at all a nice fellow," agreed Mr Thompson.

"It beats me how you got on to it," said Willard admiringly. "Pretty smart of you."

The other shook his head deprecatingly. "No, no," he said. "When you are travelling incognito and hear your own name being taken in vain—"

Mrs Peters stared at him. "Who are you?" she demanded abruptly.

"*I am Mr Parker Pyne*," explained that gentleman.

The Adventure of the Sinister Stranger

"It's been a darned dull day," said Tommy, and yawned widely.

"Nearly tea time," said Tuppence and also yawned.

Business was not brisk in the International Detective Agency. The eagerly expected letter from the ham merchant had not arrived and *bona fide* cases were not forthcoming.

Albert, the office boy, entered with a sealed package which he laid on the table.

"The Mystery of the Sealed Packet," murmured Tommy. "Did it contain the fabulous pearls of the Russian Grand Duchess? Or was it an infernal machine destined to blow Blunt's Brilliant Detectives to pieces?"

"As a matter of fact," said Tuppence, tearing open the package. "It's my wedding present to Francis Haviland. Rather nice, isn't it?"

Tommy took a slender silver cigarette case from her outstretched hand, noted the inscription engraved in her own handwriting, "*Francis from Tuppence*," opened and shut the case, and nodded approvingly.

"You do throw your money about, Tuppence," he remarked. "I'll have one like it, only in gold, for my birthday next month. Fancy wasting a thing like that on Francis Haviland, who always was and always will be one of the most perfect asses God ever made!"

"You forget I used to drive him about during the war,

when he was a General. Ah! those were the good old days."

"They were," agreed Tommy. "Beautiful women used to come and squeeze my hand in hospital, I remember. But I don't send them all wedding presents. I don't believe the bride will care much for this gift of yours, Tuppence."

"It's nice and slim for the pocket, isn't it?" said Tuppence, disregarding his remarks.

Tommy slipped it into his own pocket.

"Just right," he said approvingly. "Hullo, here is Albert with the afternoon post. Very possibly the Duchess of Perthshire is commissioning us to find her prize Peke."

They sorted through the letters together. Suddenly Tommy gave vent to a prolonged whistle and held up one of them in his hand.

"A blue letter with a Russian stamp on it. Do you remember what the Chief said? We were to look out for letters like that."

"How exciting," said Tuppence. "Something has happened at last. Open it and see if the contents are up to schedule. A ham merchant, wasn't it? Half a minute. We shall want some milk for tea. They forgot to leave it this morning. I'll send Albert out for it."

She returned from the outer office, after despatching Albert on his errand, to find Tommy holding the blue sheet of paper in his hand.

"As we thought, Tuppence," he remarked. "Almost word for word what the Chief said."

Tuppence took the letter from him and read it.

It was couched in careful stilted English, and purported to be from one Gregor Feodorsky, who was anxious for news of his wife. The International Detective Agency was urged to spare no expense in doing their utmost to trace her. Feodorsky himself was unable to leave Russia at the moment owing to a crisis in the pork trade.

"I wonder what it really means," said Tuppence thoughtfully, smoothing out the sheet on the table in front of her.

"Code of some kind, I suppose," said Tommy. "That's not our business. Our business is to hand it over to the Chief as soon as possible. Better just verify it by soaking off the stamp and seeing if the number 16 is underneath."

"All right," said Tuppence. "But I should think—"

She stopped dead, and Tommy, surprised by her sudden pause, looked up to see a man's burly figure blocking the doorway.

The intruder was a man of commanding presence, squarely built, with a very round head and a powerful jaw. He might have been about forty-five years of age.

"I must beg your pardon," said the stranger, advancing into the room, hat in hand. "I found your outer office empty and this door open, so I ventured to intrude. This is Blunt's International Detective Agency, is it not?"

"Certainly it is."

"And you are, perhaps, Mr Blunt? Mr Theodore Blunt?"

"I am Mr Blunt. You wish to consult me? This is my secretary, Miss Robinson."

Tuppence inclined her head gracefully, but continued to scrutinise the stranger narrowly through her downcast eyelashes. She was wondering how long he had been standing in the doorway, and how much he had seen and heard. It did not escape her observation that even while he was talking to Tommy, his eyes kept coming back to the blue paper in her hand.

Tommy's voice, sharp with a warning note, recalled her to the needs of the moment.

"Miss Robinson, please, take notes. Now, sir, will you kindly state the matter on which you wish to have my advice?"

Tuppence reached for her pad and pencil.

The big man began in rather a harsh voice.

"My name is Bower. Dr Charles Bower. I live in Hampstead, where I have a practice. I have come to you, Mr Blunt, because several rather strange occurrences have happened lately."

"Yes, Dr Bower?"

"Twice in the course of the last week I have been summoned by telephone to an urgent case—in each case to find that the summons has been a fake. The first time I thought a practical joke had been played upon me, but on my return the second time I found that some of my private papers had been displaced and disarranged, and now I believe that the same thing had happened the first time. I made an exhaustive search and came to the conclusion that my whole desk had been thoroughly ransacked, and the various papers replaced hurriedly."

Dr Bower paused and gazed at Tommy.

"Well, Mr Blunt?"

"Well, Dr Bower," replied the young man, smiling.

"What do you think of it, eh?"

"Well, first I should like the facts. What do you keep in your desk?"

"My private papers."

"Exactly. Now, what do those private papers consist of? What value are they to the common thief—or any particular person?"

"To the common thief I cannot see that they would have any value at all, but my notes on certain obscure alkaloids would be of interest to anyone possessed of technical knowledge of the subject. I have been making a study of such matters for the last few years. These alkaloids are deadly and virulent poisons, and are in addition almost untraceable. They yield no known reactions."

"The secret of them would be worth money, then?"

"To unscrupulous persons, yes."

"And you suspect—whom?"

The doctor shrugged his massive shoulders.

"As far as I can tell, the house was not entered forcibly from the outside. That seems to point to some member of my household, and yet I cannot believe—" He broke off abruptly, then began again, his voice very grave.

"Mr Blunt, I must place myself in your hands unreservedly. I dare not go to the police in the matter. Of my three servants I am almost entirely sure. They have served me long and faithfully. Still, one never knows. Then I have living with me my two nephews, Bertram and Henry. Henry is a good boy—a very good boy—he has never caused me any anxiety, an excellent hard-working young fellow. Bertram, I regret to say, is of quite a different character—wild, extravagant, and persistently idle."

"I see," said Tommy thoughtfully. "You suspect your nephew Bertram of being mixed up in this business. Now I don't agree with you. I suspect the good boy—Henry."

"But why?"

"Tradition. Precedent." Tommy waved his hand airily. "In my experience, the suspicious characters are always innocent—and vice versa, my dear sir. Yes, decidedly, I suspect Henry."

"Excuse me, Mr Blunt," said Tuppence, interrupting in a deferential tone. "Did I understand Dr Bower to say that these notes on—er—obscure alkaloids—are kept in the desk with the other papers?"

"They are kept in the desk, my dear young lady, but in a secret drawer, the position of which is known only to myself. Hence they have so far defied the search."

"And what exactly do you want me to do, Dr Bower?" asked Tommy. "Do you anticipate that a further search will be made?"

"I do, Mr Blunt. I have every reason to believe so. This afternoon I received a telegram from a patient of mine whom I ordered to Bournemouth a few weeks ago. The telegram states that my patient is in a critical condition, and begs me to come down at once. Rendered suspicious by the events I have told you of, I myself despatched a telegram, prepaid, to the patient in question, and elicited the fact that he was in good health and had sent no summons to me of any kind. It occurred to me that if I pretended to have been taken in, and duly departed to Bournemouth, we should have a very good chance of finding the miscreants at work. They—or he—will doubtless wait until the household has retired to bed before commencing operations. I suggest that you should meet me outside my house at eleven o'clock this evening, and we will investigate the matter together."

"Hoping, in fact, to catch them in the act." Tommy drummed thoughtfully on the table with a paper-knife. "Your plan seems to me an excellent one, Dr Bower. I cannot see any hitch in it. Let me see, your address is—?"

"The Larches, Hangman's Lane—rather a lonely part, I am afraid. But we command magnificent views over the Heath."

"Quite so," said Tommy.

The visitor rose.

"Then I shall expect you tonight, Mr Blunt. Outside The Larches at—shall we say, five minutes to eleven—to be on the safe side?"

"Certainly. Five minutes to eleven. Good-afternoon, Dr Bower."

Tommy rose, pressed a buzzer on his desk, and Albert appeared to show the client out. The doctor walked with a decided limp, but his powerful physique was evident in spite of it.

"An ugly customer to tackle," murmured Tommy to himself. "Well, Tuppence, old girl, what do you think of it?"

"I'll tell you in one word," said Tuppence. "*Clubfoot!*"

"What?"

"I said Clubfoot! My study of the classics has not been in vain. Tommy, this thing's a plant. Obscure alkaloids indeed—I never heard a weaker story."

"Even I did not find it very convincing," admitted her husband.

"Did you see his eyes on the letter? Tommy, he's one of the gang. They've got wise to the fact that you're not the real Mr Blunt, and they're out for our blood."

"In that case," said Tommy, opening the side cupboard and surveying his rows of books with an affectionate eye, "our role is easy to select. We are the brothers Okewood! And I am Desmond," he added firmly.

Tuppence shrugged her shoulders.

"All right. Have it your own way. I'd as soon be Francis. Francis was much the more intelligent of the two. Desmond always gets into a mess, and Francis turns up as the gardener or something in the nick of time and saves the situation."

"Ah!" said Tommy, "but I shall be a super Desmond. When I arrive at the Larches—"

Tuppence interrupted him unceremoniously.

"You're not going to Hampstead tonight?"

"Why not?"

"Walk into a trap with your eyes shut!"

"No, my dear girl, walk into a trap with my eyes open. There's a lot of difference. I think our friend, Dr Bower, will get a little surprise."

"I don't like it," said Tuppence. "You know what happens when Desmond disobeys the Chief's orders and acts on his own. Our orders were quite clear. To send on the letters at once and to report immediately on anything that happened."

"You've not got it quite right," said Tommy. "We were to report immediately if any one came in and mentioned the number 16. Nobody has."

"That's a quibble," said Tuppence.

"It's no good. I've got a fancy for playing a lone hand. My dear old Tuppence, I shall be all right. I shall go armed to the teeth. The essence of the whole thing is that I shall be on my guard and they won't know it. The Chief will be patting me on the back for a good night's work."

"Well," said Tuppence. "I don't like it. That man's as strong as a gorilla."

"Ah!" said Tommy, "but think of my blue-nosed automatic."

The door of the outer office opened and Albert appeared. Closing the door behind him, he approached them with an envelope in his hand.

"A gentleman to see you," said Albert. "When I began the usual stunt of saying you were engaged with Scotland Yard, he told me he knew all about that. Said he came from Scotland Yard himself! And he wrote something on a card and stuck it up in this envelope."

Tommy took the envelope and opened it. As he read the card, a grin passed across his face.

"The gentleman was amusing himself at your expense by speaking the truth, Albert," he remarked. "Show him in."

He tossed the card to Tuppence. It bore the name Detective Inspector Dymchurch, and across it was scrawled in pencil—"A friend of Marriot's."

In another minute the Scotland Yard detective was entering the inner office. In appearance, Inspector Dymchurch was of the same type as Inspector Marriot, short and thick set, with shrewd eyes.

"Good-afternoon," said the detective breezily. "Marriot's away in South Wales, but before he went he asked me to keep an eye on you two, and on this place in general. Oh, bless you, sir," he went on, as Tommy seemed about to interrupt him, "*we* know all about it. It's not our department and we don't interfere. But somebody's got wise lately to the fact that all is not what it seems. You've had a gentleman here this afternoon. I don't know what he called himself, and I don't know what his real name is, but I know just a little about him. Enough to want to know more. Am I right in assuming that he made a date with you for some particular spot this evening?"

"Quite right."

"I thought as much. 16 Westerham Road, Finsbury Park—was that it?"

"You're wrong there," said Tommy with a smile. "Dead wrong. The Larches, Hampstead."

Dymchurch seemed honestly taken aback. Clearly he had not expected this.

"I don't understand it," he muttered. "It must be a new layout. The Larches, Hampstead, you said?"

"Yes. I'm to meet him there at eleven o'clock tonight."

"Don't you do it, sir."

"There!" burst from Tuppence.

Tommy flushed.

"If you think, Inspector—" he began heatedly.

But the Inspector raised a soothing hand.

"I'll tell you what I think, Mr Blunt. The place you want to be at eleven o'clock tonight is here in this office."

"What?" cried Tuppence, astonished.

"Here in this office. Never mind how I know—departments overlap sometimes—but you got one of those famous 'Blue' letters today. Old what's-his-name is after that. He lures you up to Hampstead, makes quite sure of your being out of the way, and steps in here at night when all the building is empty and quiet to have a good search round at his leisure."

"But why should he think the letter would be here? He'd know I should have it on me or else have passed it on."

"Begging your pardon, sir, that's just what he wouldn't know. He may have tumbled to the fact that you're not the original Mr Blunt, but he probably thinks that you're a *bona fide* gentleman who's bought the business. In that case, the letter would be all in the way of regular business and would be filed as such."

"I see," said Tuppence.

"And that's just what we've got to let him think. We'll catch him red-handed here tonight."

"So that's the plan, is it?"

"Yes. It's the chance of a lifetime. Now, let me see, what's the time? Six o'clock. What time do you usually leave here, sir?"

"About six."

"You must seem to leave the place as usual. Actually we'll sneak back to it as soon as possible. I don't believe they'll come here till about eleven, but of course they might. If you'll excuse me, I'll just go and take a look round outside and see if I can make out anyone watching the place."

Dymchurch departed, and Tommy began an argument with Tuppence.

It lasted some time and was heated and acrimonious. In the end Tuppence suddenly capitulated.

"All right," she said. "I give in. I'll go home and sit there like a good little girl whilst you tackle crooks and hobnob with detectives—but you wait, young man. I'll be even with you yet for keeping me out of the fun."

Dymchurch returned at that moment.

"Coast seems clear enough," he said. "But you can't tell. Better seem to leave in the usual manner. They won't go on watching the place once you've gone."

Tommy called Albert and gave him instructions to lock up.

Then the four of them made their way to the garage near by where the car was usually left. Tuppence drove and Albert sat beside her. Tommy and the detective sat behind.

Presently they were held up by a block in the traffic. Tuppence looked over her shoulder and nodded. Tommy and the detective opened the right hand door and stepped out into the middle of Oxford Street. In a minute or two Tuppence drove on.

"Better not go in just yet," said Dymchurch as he and Tommy hurried into Haleham Street. "You've got the key all right?"

Tommy nodded.

"Then what about a bite of dinner? It's early, but there's a little place here right opposite. We'll get a table by the window, so that we can watch the place all the time."

They had a very welcome little meal, in the manner the detective had suggested. Tommy found Inspector Dymchurch quite an entertaining companion. Most of his official work had lain amongst international spies, and he had tales to tell which astonished his simple listener.

They remained in the little restaurant until eight o'clock, when Dymchurch suggested a move.

"It's quite dark now, sir," he explained. "We shall be able to slip in without any one being the wiser."

It was, as he said, quite dark. They crossed the road, looked quickly up and down the deserted street, and slipped inside the entrance. Then they mounted the stairs, and Tommy inserted his key in the lock of the outer office.

Just as he did so, he heard, as he thought, Dymchurch whistle beside him.

"What are you whistling for?" he asked sharply.

"*I* didn't whistle," said Dymchurch, very much astonished. "I thought *you* did."

"Well, some one—" began Tommy.

He got no further. Strong arms seized him from behind, and before he could cry out, a pad of something sweet and sickly was pressed over his mouth and nose.

He struggled valiantly, but in vain. The chloroform did its work. His head began to whirl and the floor heaved up and down in front of him. Choking, he lost consciousness . . .

He came to himself painfully, but in full possession of his faculties. The chloroform had been only a whiff. They had kept him under long enough to force a gag into his mouth and ensure that he did not cry out.

When he came to himself, he was half-lying, half-sitting, propped against the wall in a corner of his own inner office. Two men were busily turning out the contents of the desk and ransacking the cupboards, and as they worked they cursed freely.

"Swelp me, guv'nor," said the taller of the two hoarsely, "we've turned the whole b—y place upside down and inside out. It's not there."

"It must be here," snarled the other. "It isn't on him. And there's no other place it can be."

As he spoke he turned, and to Tommy's utter amazement he saw that the last speaker was none other than Inspector Dymchurch. The latter grinned when he saw Tommy's astonished face.

"So our young friend is awake again," he said. "And a little surprised—yes, a little surprised. But it was so simple. We suspect that all is not as it should be with the International Detective Agency. I volunteer to find out if that is so, or not. If the new Mr Blunt is indeed a spy, he will be suspicious, so I send first my dear old friend, Carl Bauer. Carl is told to act suspiciously and pitch an improbable tale. He does so, and then I appear on the scene. I used the name of Inspector Marriot to gain confidence. The rest is easy."

He laughed.

Tommy was dying to say several things, but the gag in his mouth prevented him. Also, he was dying to *do* several things—mostly with his hands and feet—but alas, that too had been attended to. He was securely bound.

The thing that amazed him most was the astounding change in the man standing over him. As Inspector Dymchurch the fellow had been a typical Englishman. Now, no one could have mistaken him for a moment for anything but a well-educated foreigner who talked English perfectly without a trace of accent.

"Coggins, my good friend," said the erstwhile Inspector, addressing his rufflanly-looking associate, "take your life-preserver and stand by the prisoner. I am going to remove the gag. You understand, my dear Mr Blunt, do you not, that it would be criminally foolish on your part to cry out? But I am sure you do. For your age, you are quite an intelligent lad."

Very deftly he removed the gag and stepped back.

Tommy eased his stiff jaws, rolled his tongue round his mouth, swallowed twice—and said nothing at all.

"I congratulate you on your restraint," said the other. "You appreciate the position, I see. Have you nothing at all to say?"

"What I have to say will keep," said Tommy. "And it won't spoil by waiting."

"Ah! What I have to say will not keep. In plain English, Mr Blunt, where is that letter?"

"My dear fellow, I don't know," said Tommy cheerfully. "I haven't got it. But you know that as well as I do. I should go on looking about if I were you. I like to see you and friend Coggins playing hide-and-seek together."

The other's face darkened.

"You are pleased to be flippant, Mr Blunt. You see that square box over there. That is Coggins's little outfit. In it there is vitriol . . . yes, vitriol . . . and irons that can be heated in the fire, so that they are red hot and burn . . ."

Tommy shook his head sadly.

"An error in diagnosis," he murmured. "Tuppence and I labelled this adventure wrong. It's not a Clubfoot story. It's a Bull-dog Drummond, and you are the inimitable Carl Peterson."

"What is this nonsense you are talking," snarled the other.

"Ah!" said Tommy. "I see you are unacquainted with the classics. A pity."

"Ignorant fool! Will you do what we want or will you not? Shall I tell Coggins to get out his tools and begin?"

"Don't be so impatient," said Tommy. "Of course I'll do what you want, as soon as you tell me what it is. You don't suppose I want to be carved up like a filleted sole and fried on a gridiron? I loathe being hurt."

Dymchurch looked at him in contempt.

"Gott! What cowards are these English."

"Common sense, my dear fellow, merely common sense. Leave the vitriol alone and let us come down to brass tacks."

"I want the letter."

"I've already told you I haven't got it."

"We know that—we also know who must have it. The girl."

"Very possibly you're right," said Tommy. "She may have slipped it into her handbag when your pal Carl startled us."

"Oh, you do not deny. That is wise. Very good, you will write to this Tuppence, as you call her, bidding her bring the letter here immediately."

"I can't do that," began Tommy.

The other cut in before he had finished the sentence.

"Ah! You can't? Well, we shall soon see. Coggins!"

"Don't be in such a hurry," said Tommy. "And do wait for the end of the sentence. I was going to say that I can't do that unless you untie my arms. Hang it all, I'm not one of those freaks who can write with their noses or their elbows."

"You are willing to write, then?"

"Of course. Haven't I been telling you so all along? I'm all out to be pleasant and obliging. You won't do anything unkind to Tuppence, of course. I'm sure you won't. She's such a nice girl."

"We only want the letter," said Dymchurch, but there was a singularly unpleasant smile on his face.

At a nod from him the brutal Coggins knelt down and unfastened Tommy's arms. The latter swung them to and fro.

"That's better," he said cheerfully. "Will kind Coggins hand me my fountain pen? It's on the table, I think, with my other miscellaneous property."

Scowling, the man brought it to him, and provided a sheet of paper.

"Be careful what you say," Dymchurch said menacingly. "We leave it to you, but failure means—death—and slow death at that."

"In that case," said Tommy, "I will certainly do my best."

He reflected a minute or two, then began to scribble rapidly.

"How will this do?" he asked, handing over the completed epistle.

Dear Tuppence,

Can you come along at once and bring that blue letter with you?

We want to decode it here and now.

In haste,

Francis.

"Francis?" queried the bogus Inspector, with lifted eyebrows. "Was that the name she called you?"

"As you weren't at my christening," said Tommy, "I don't suppose you can know whether it's my name or not. But I think the cigarette case you took from my pocket is a pretty good proof that I'm speaking the truth."

The other stepped over to the table and took up the case, read "Francis from Tuppence' with a faint grin and laid it down again.

"I am glad to find you are behaving so sensibly," he said. "Coggins, give that note to Vassilly. He is on guard outside. Tell him to take it at once."

The next twenty minutes passed slowly, the ten minutes after that more slowly still. Dymchurch was striding up and down with a face that grew darker and darker. Once he turned menacingly on Tommy.

"If you have dared to double-cross us," he growled.

"If we'd had a pack of cards here, we might have had a game of picquet to pass the time," drawled Tommy. "Women always keep one waiting. I hope you're not going to be unkind to little Tuppence when she comes?"

"Oh, no," said Dymchurch. "We shall arrange for you to go to the same place—together."

"Will you, you swine," said Tommy under his breath.

Suddenly there was a stir in the outer office. A man whom Tommy had not yet seen poked his head in and growled something in Russian.

"Good," said Dymchurch. "She is coming—and coming alone."

For a moment a faint anxiety caught at Tommy's heart.

The next minute he heard Tuppence's voice.

"Oh! there you are, Inspector Dymchurch. I've brought the letter. Where is Francis?"

With the last words she came through the door, and Vassilly sprang on her from behind, clapping his hand over her mouth. Dymchurch tore the handbag from her grasp and turned over its contents in a frenzied search.

Suddenly he uttered an ejaculation of delight and held up a blue envelope with a Russian stamp on it. Coggins gave a hoarse shout.

And just in that minute of triumph the other door, the door into Tuppence's own office, opened noiselessly and Inspector Marriot and two men armed with revolvers stepped into the room, with the sharp command: "Hands up."

There was no fight. The others were taken at a hopeless disadvantage. Dymchurch's automatic lay on the table, and the two others were not armed.

"A very nice little haul," said Inspector Marriot with approval, as he snapped the last pair of handcuffs. "And we'll have more as time goes on, I hope."

White with rage, Dymchurch glared at Tuppence.

"You little devil," he snarled. "It was you put them on to us."

Tuppence laughed.

"It wasn't all my doing. I ought to have guessed, I admit, when you brought in the number sixteen this afternoon. But it was Tommy's note clinched matters. I rang up Inspector Marriot, got Albert to meet him with the duplicate key of the office, and came along myself with the empty blue envelope in my bag. The letter I forwarded according to my instructions as soon as I had parted with you two this afternoon."

But one word had caught the other's attention.

"*Tommy*?" he queried.

Tommy, who had just been released from his bonds, came towards them.

"Well done, brother Francis," he said to Tuppence, taking both her hands in his. And to Dymchurch: "As I told you, my dear fellow, you really ought to read the classics."

The Incredible Theft

As the butler handed round the soufflé, Lord Mayfield leaned confidentially towards his neighbour on the right, Lady Julia Carrington. Known as a perfect host, Lord Mayfield took trouble to live up to his reputation. Although unmarried, he was always charming to women.

Lady Julia Carrington was a woman of forty, tall, dark and vivacious. She was very thin, but still beautiful. Her hands and feet in particular were exquisite. Her manner was abrupt and restless, that of a woman who lived on her nerves.

About opposite to her at the round table sat her husband, Air Marshal Sir George Carrington. His career had begun in the Navy, and he still retained the bluff breeziness of the ex-Naval man. He was laughing and chaffing the beautiful Mrs Vanderlyn, who was sitting on the other side of her host.

Mrs Vanderlyn was an extremely good-looking blonde. Her voice held a soupçon of American accent, just enough to be pleasant without undue exaggeration.

On the other side of Sir George Carrington sat Mrs Macatta, M.P. Mrs Macatta was a great authority on Housing and Infant Welfare. She barked out short sentences rather than spoke them, and was generally of somewhat alarming aspect. It was perhaps natural that the Air Marshal would find his right-hand neighbour the pleasanter to talk to.

Mrs Macatta, who always talked shop wherever she was, barked out short spates of information on her special subjects to her left-hand neighbour, young Reggie Carrington.

Reggie Carrington was twenty-one, and completely uninterested in Housing, Infant Welfare, and indeed any political subject. He said at intervals, "How frightful!" and "I absolutely agree with you," and his mind was clearly elsewhere. Mr Carlile, Lord Mayfield's private secretary, sat between young Reggie and his mother. A pale young man with pince-nez and an air of intelligent reserve, he talked little, but was always ready to fling himself into any conversational breach. Noticing that Reggie Carrington was struggling with a yawn, he leaned forward and adroitly asked Mrs Macatta a question about her "Fitness for Children' scheme.

Round the table, moving silently in the subdued amber light, a butler and two footmen offered dishes and filled up wine-glasses. Lord Mayfield paid a very high salary to his chef, and was noted as a connoisseur of wines.

The table was a round one, but there was no mistaking who was the host. Where Lord Mayfield sat was so very decidedly the head of the table. A big man, square-shouldered, with thick silvery hair, a big straight nose and a slightly prominent chin. It was a face that lent itself easily to caricature. As Sir Charles McLaughlin, Lord Mayfield had combined a political career with being the head of a big engineering firm. He was himself a first-class engineer. His peerage had come a year ago, and at the same time he had been created first Minister of Armaments, a new ministry which had only just come into being.

The dessert had been placed on the table. The port had circulated once. Catching Mrs Vanderlyn's eye, Lady Julia rose. The three women left the room.

The port passed once more, and Lord Mayfield referred lightly to pheasants. The conversation for five minutes or so was sporting. Then Sir George said:

"Expect you'd like to join the others in the drawing-room, Reggie, my boy. Lord Mayfield won't mind."

The boy took the hint easily enough.

"Thanks, Lord Mayfield, I think I will."

Mr Carlile mumured:

"If you'll excuse me, Lord Mayfield—certain memoranda and other work to get through . . ."

Lord Mayfield nodded. The two young men left the room. The servants had retired some time before. The Minister for Armaments and the head of the Air Force were alone.

After a minute or two, Carrington said:

"Well—O.K.?"

"Absolutely! There's nothing to touch this new bomber in any country in Europe."

"Make rings round 'em, eh? That's what I thought."

"Supremacy of the air," said Lord Mayfield decisively.

Sir George Carrington gave a deep sigh.

"About time! You know, Charles, we've been through a ticklish spell. Lots of gunpowder everywhere all over Europe. And we weren't ready, damn it! We've had a narrow squeak. And we're not out of the wood yet, however much we hurry on construction."

Lord Mayfield murmured:

"Nevertheless, George, there are some advantages in starting late. A lot of the European stuff is out of date already—and they're perilously near bankruptcy."

"I don't believe that means anything," said Sir George gloomily. "One's always hearing this nation and that is bankrupt! But they carry on just the same. You know, finance is an absolute mystery to me."

Lord Mayfield's eyes twinkled a little. Sir George

Carrington was always so very much the old fashioned "bluff, honest old sea dog." There were people who said that it was a pose he deliberately adopted.

Changing the subject, Carrington said in a slightly over-casual manner:

"Attractive woman, Mrs Vanderlyn—eh?"

Lord Mayfield said:

"Are you wondering what she's doing here?"

His eyes were amused.

Carrington looked a little confused.

"Not at all—not at all."

"Oh, yes, you were! Don't be an old humbug, George. You were wondering, in a slightly dismayed fashion, whether I was the latest victim!"

Carrington said slowly:

"I'll admit that it *did* seem a trifle odd to me that she should be here—well, this particular weekend."

Lord Mayfield nodded.

"Where the carcass is, there are the vultures gathered together. We've got a very definite carcass, and Mrs Vanderlyn might be described as Vulture No. 1."

The Air Marshal said abruptly:

"Know anything about this Vanderlyn woman?"

Lord Mayfield clipped off the end of a cigar, lit it with precision and, throwing his head back, dropped out his words with careful deliberation.

"What do I know about Mrs Vanderlyn? I know that she's an American subject. I know that she's had three husbands, one Italian, one German and one Russian, and that in consequence she has made useful what I think are called 'contacts' in three countries. I know that she manages to buy very expensive clothes and live in a very luxurious manner, and that there is some slight uncertainty as to where the income comes from which permits her to do so."

With a grin, Sir George Carrington murmured:

"Your spies have not been inactive, Charles, I see."

"I know," Lord Mayfield continued, "that in addition to having a seductive type of beauty, Mrs Vanderlyn is also a very good listener, and that she can display a fascinating interest in what we call 'shop.' That is to say, a man can tell her all about his job and feel that he is being intensely interesting to the lady! Sundry young officers have gone a little too far in their zeal to be interesting, and their careers have suffered in consequence. They have told Mrs Vanderlyn a little more than they should have done. Nearly all the lady's friends are in the Services—but last winter she was hunting in a certain county near one of our largest armament firms, and she formed various friendships not at all sporting in character. To put it briefly, Mrs Vanderlyn is a very useful person to . . ." He described a circle in the air with his cigar. "Perhaps we had better not say to whom! We will just say to a European power—and perhaps to more than one European power."

Carrington drew a deep breath.

"You take a great load off my mind, Charles."

"You thought I had fallen for the siren? My dear George! Mrs Vanderlyn is just a little too obvious in her methods for a wary old bird like me. Besides, she is, as they say, not quite so young as she once was. Your young squadron leaders wouldn't notice that. But I am fifty-six, my boy. In another four years I shall probably be a nasty old man continually haunting the society of unwilling debutantes."

"I was a fool," said Carrington apologetically, "but it seemed a bit odd—"

"It seemed to you odd that she should be here, in a somewhat intimate family party just at the moment when you and I were to hold an unofficial conference over a discovery that will probably revolutionize the whole problem of air defence?"

Sir George Carrington nodded.

Lord Mayfield said, smiling:

"That's exactly it. That's the bait."

"The bait?"

"You see, George, to use the language of the movies, we've nothing actually 'on' the woman. And we want something! She's got away with rather more than she should in the past. But she's been careful—damnably careful. *We* know what she's been up to, but we've got no definite proof of it. We've got to tempt her with something big."

"Something big being the specification of the new bomber?"

"Exactly. It's got to be something big enough to induce her to take a risk—to come out into the open. And then—*we've got her!*"

Sir George grunted.

"Oh, well," he said. "I dare say it's all right. But suppose she won't take the risk?"

"That would be a pity," said Lord Mayfield. Then he added: "But I think she will . . ."

He rose.

"Shall we join the ladies in the drawing-room? We mustn't deprive your wife of her bridge."

Sir George grunted:

"Julia's a damned sight too fond of her bridge. Drops a packet over it. She can't afford to play as high as she does, and I've told her so. The trouble is, Julia's a born gambler."

Coming round the table to join his host, he said:

"Well, I hope your plan comes off, Charles."

In the drawing-room conversation had flagged more than once. Mrs Vanderlyn was usually at a disadvantage when left alone with members of her own sex. That charming sympathetic manner of hers, so much appreciated by members of the male sex, did not for some reason or other commend itself to women. Lady Julia was a woman whose manners were either very good or very bad. On this occasion she disliked Mrs Vanderlyn, and was bored by Mrs Macatta, and made no secret of her feelings. Conversation languished, and might have ceased altogether but for the latter.

Mrs Macatta was a woman of great earnestness of purpose. Mrs Vanderlyn she dismissed immediately as a useless and parasitic type. Lady Julia she tried to interest in a forthcoming charity entertainment which she was organizing. Lady Julia answered vaguely, stifled a yawn or two and retired into her own inner preoccupation. Why didn't Charles and George come? How tiresome men were. Her comments became even more perfunctory as she became absorbed in her own thoughts and worries.

The three women were sitting in silence when the men finally entered the room.

Lord Mayfield thought to himself:

"Julia looks ill tonight. What a mass of nerves the woman is."

Aloud he said:

"What about a rubber—eh?"

Lady Julia brightened at once. Bridge was as the breath of life to her.

Reggie Carrington entered the room at that minute, and a four was arranged. Lady Julia, Mrs Vanderlyn, Sir George and young Reggie sat down to the card-table. Lord Mayfield devoted himself to the task of entertaining Mrs Macatta.

When two rubbers had been played, Sir George looked ostentatiously at the clock on the mantelpiece.

"Hardly worth while beginning another," he remarked.

His wife looked annoyed.

"It's only a quarter to eleven. A short one."

"They never are, my dear," said Sir George good-temperedly. "Anyway, Charles and I have some work to do."

Mrs Vanderlyn murmured:

"How important that sounds! I suppose you clever men who are at the top of things never get a real rest."

"No forty-eight hour week for us," said Sir George.

Mrs Vanderlyn murmured:

"You know, I feel rather ashamed of myself as a raw American, but I do get so *thrilled* at meeting people who control the destinies of a country. I expect that seems a very crude point of view to you, Sir George."

"My dear Mrs Vanderlyn, I should never think of you as 'crude' or 'raw.'"

He smiled into her eyes. There was, perhaps, a hint of irony in the voice which she did not miss. Adroitly she turned to Reggie, smiling sweetly into his eyes.

"I'm sorry we're not continuing our partnership. That was a frightfully clever four no-trump call of yours."

Flushed and pleased, Reggie mumbled:

"Bit of a fluke that it came off."

"Oh, no, it was really a clever bit of deduction on your part. You'd deduced from the bidding exactly where the cards must be, and you played accordingly. I thought it was brilliant."

Lady Julia rose abruptly.

"The woman lays it on with a palette-knife," she thought disgustedly.

Then her eyes softened as they rested on her son. He believed it all. How pathetically young and pleased he looked. How incredibly naïve he was. No wonder he got into scrapes. He was too trusting. The truth of it was he had too sweet a nature. George didn't understand him in the least. Men were so unsympathetic in their judgements. They forgot that they had ever been young themselves. George was much too harsh with Reggie.

Mrs Macatta had risen. Goodnights were said.

The three women went out of the room. Lord Mayfield helped himself to a drink after giving one to Sir George, then he looked up as Mr Carlile appeared at the door.

"Get out the files and all the papers, will you, Carlile? Including the plans and the prints. The Air Marshal and I will be along shortly. We'll just take a turn outside first, eh, George? It's stopped raining."

Mr Carlile, turning to depart, murmured an apology as he almost collided with Mrs Vanderlyn.

She drifted towards them, murmuring:

"My book, I was reading it before dinner."

Reggie sprang forward and held up a book.

"Is this it? On the sofa?"

"Oh, yes. Thank you *so* much."

She smiled sweetly, said goodnight again and went out of the room.

Sir George had opened one of the french windows.

"Beautiful night now," he announced. "Good idea of yours to take a turn."

Reggie said:

"Well, goodnight, sir. I'll be toddling off to bed."

"Goodnight, my boy," said Lord Mayfield.

Reggie picked up a detective story which he had begun earlier in the evening and left the room.

Lord Mayfield and Sir George stepped out upon the terrace.

It was a beautiful night, with a clear sky studded with stars.

Sir George drew a deep breath.

"Phew, that woman uses a lot of scent," he remarked.

Lord Mayfield laughed.

"Anyway, it's not cheap scent. One of the most expensive brands on the market, I should say."

Sir George gave a grimace.

"I suppose one should be thankful for that."

"You should, indeed. I think a woman smothered in cheap scent is one of the greatest abominations known to mankind."

Sir George glanced up at the sky.

"Extraordinary the way it's cleared. I heard the rain beating down when we were at dinner."

The two men strolled gently along the terrace.

The terrace ran the whole length of the house. Below it the ground sloped gently away, permitting a magnificent view over the Sussex weald.

Sir George lit a cigar.

"About this metal alloy—" he began.

The talk became technical.

As they approached the far end of the terrace for the fifth time, Lord Mayfield said with a sigh:

"Oh, well, I suppose we'd better get down to it."

"Yes, good bit of work to get through."

The two men turned, and Lord Mayfield uttered a surprised ejaculation.

"Hallo! See that?"

"See what?" asked Sir George.

"Thought I saw someone slip across the terrace from my study window."

"Nonsense, old boy. I didn't see anything."

"Well, I did—or I thought I did."

"Your eyes are playing tricks on you. I was looking straight down the terrace, and I'd have seen anything there was to be seen. There's precious little *I* don't see—even if I do have to hold a newspaper at arm's length."

Lord Mayfield chuckled.

"I can put one over on you there, George. I read easily without glasses."

"But you can't always distinguish the fellow on the other side of the House. Or is that eyeglass of yours sheer intimidation?"

Laughing, the two men entered Lord Mayfield's study, the french window of which was open.

Mr Carlile was busy arranging some papers in a file by the safe.

He looked up as they entered.

"Ha, Carlile, everything ready?"

"Yes, Lord Mayfield, all the papers are on your desk."

The desk in question was a big important-looking writing-table of mahogany set across a corner by the window. Lord Mayfield went over to it, and began sorting through the various documents laid out.

"Lovely night now," said Sir George.

Mr Carlile agreed.

"Yes, indeed. Remarkable the way it's cleared up after the rain."

Putting away his file, Mr Carlile asked:

"Will you want me any more tonight, Lord Mayfield?"

"No, I don't think so, Carlile. I'll put all these away myself. We shall probably be late. You'd better turn in."

"Thank you. Goodnight, Lord Mayfield. Goodnight, Sir George."

"Goodnight, Carlile."

As the secretary was about to leave the room, Lord Mayfield said sharply:

"Just a minute, Carlile. You've forgotten the most important of the lot."

"I beg your pardon, Lord Mayfield."

"The actual plans of the bomber, man."

The secretary stared.

"They're right on the top, sir."

"They're nothing of the sort."

"But I've just put them there."

"Look for yourself, man."

With a bewildered expression, the young man came forward and joined Lord Mayfield at the desk.

Somewhat impatiently the Minister indicated the pile of papers. Carlile sorted through them, his expression of bewilderment growing.

"You see, they're not there."

The secretary stammered:

"But—but it's incredible. I laid them there not three minutes ago."

Lord Mayfield said good-humouredly:

"You must have made a mistake, they must be still in the safe."

"I don't see how—I *know* I put them there!"

Lord Mayfield brushed past him to the open safe. Sir George joined them. A very few minutes sufficed to show that the plans of the bomber were not there.

Dazed and unbelieving, the three men returned to the desk and once more turned over the papers.

"My God!" said Mayfield. "They're gone!"

Mr Carlile cried:

"But it's impossible!"

"Who's been in this room?" snapped out the Minister.

"No one. No one at all."

"Look here, Carlile, those plans haven't vanished into thin air. Someone has taken them. Has Mrs Vanderlyn been in here?"

"Mrs Vanderlyn? Oh, no, sir."

"I'll back that," said Carrington. He sniffed the air. "You'd soon smell if she had. That scent of hers."

"Nobody has been in here," insisted Carlile. "I can't understand it."

"Look here, Carlile," said Lord Mayfield. "Pull yourself together. We've got to get to the bottom of this. You're absolutely sure the plans were in the safe?"

"Absolutely."

"You actually saw them? You didn't just assume they were among the others?"

"No, no, Lord Mayfield. I saw them. I put them on top of the others on the desk."

"And since then, you say, nobody has been in the room. Have you been out of the room?"

"No—at least—yes."

"Ah!" cried Sir George. "Now we're getting at it!"

Lord Mayfield said sharply:

"What on earth—" when Carlile interrupted.

"In the normal course of events, Lord Mayfield, I should not, of course, have dreamt of leaving the room when important papers were lying about, but hearing a woman scream—"

"A woman scream?" ejaculated Lord Mayfield in a surprised voice.

"Yes, Lord Mayfield. It startled me more than I can say. I was just laying the papers on the desk when I heard it, and naturally I ran out into the hall."

"Who screamed?"

"Mrs Vanderlyn's French maid. She was standing half-way up the stairs, looking very white and upset and shaking all over. She said she had seen a ghost."

"Seen a ghost?"

"Yes, a tall woman dressed all in white who moved without a sound and floated in the air."

"What a ridiculous story!"

"Yes, Lord Mayfield, that is what I told her. I must say she seemed rather ashamed of herself. She went off upstairs and I came back in here."

"How long ago was this?"

"Just a minute or two before you and Sir George came in."

"And you were out of the room—how long?"

The secretary considered.

"Two minutes—at the most three."

"Long enough," groaned Lord Mayfield. Suddenly he clutched his friend's arm.

"George, that shadow I saw—slinking away from this window. That was it! As soon as Carlile left the room, he nipped in, seized the plans and made off."

"Dirty work," said Sir George.

Then he seized his friend by the arm.

"Look here, Charles, this is the devil of a business. What the hell are we going to do about it?"

"At any rate give it a trial, Charles."

It was half an hour later. The two men were in Lord Mayfield's study, and Sir George had been expending a considerable amount of persuasion to induce his friend to adopt a certain course.

Lord Mayfield, at first most unwilling, was gradually becoming less averse to the idea.

Sir George went on:

"Don't be so damned pig-headed, Charles."

Lord Mayfield said slowly:

"Why drag in a wretched foreigner we know nothing about?"

"But I happen to know a lot about him. The man's a marvel."

"Humph."

"Look here, Charles. It's a chance! Discretion is the essence of this business. If it leaks out—"

"*When* it leaks out is what you mean!"

"Not necessarily. This man, Hercule Poirot—"

"Will come down here and produce the plans like a conjurer taking rabbits out of his hat, I suppose?"

"He'll get at the truth. And the truth is what we want. Look here, Charles, I take all responsibility on myself."

Lord Mayfield said slowly:

"Oh, well, have it your own way, but I don't see what the fellow can do . . ."

Sir George picked up the phone.

"I'm going to get through to him—now."

"He'll be in bed."

"He can get up. Dash it all, Charles, you can't let that woman get away with it."

"Mrs Vanderlyn, you mean?"

"Yes. You don't doubt, do you, that she's at the bottom of this?"

"No, I don't. She's turned the tables on me with a vengeance. I don't like admitting, George, that a woman's been too clever for us. It goes against the grain. But it's true. We shan't be able to prove anything against her, and yet we both know that she's been the prime mover in the affair."

"Women are the devil," said Carrington with feeling.

"Nothing to connect her with it, damn it all! We may believe that she put the girl up to that screaming trick, and that the man lurking outside was her accomplice, but the devil of it is we can't prove it."

"Perhaps Hercule Poirot can."

Suddenly Lord Mayfield laughed.

"By the Lord, George, I thought you were too much of an old John Bull to put your trust in a Frenchman, however clever."

"He's not even a Frenchman, he's a Belgian," said Sir George in a rather shamefaced manner.

"Well, have your Belgian down. Let him try his wits

on this business. I'll bet he can't make more of it than we can."

Without replying, Sir George stretched a hand to the telephone.

Blinking a little, Hercule Poirot turned his head from one man to the other. Very delicately he smothered a yawn.

It was half-past two in the morning. He had been roused from sleep and rushed down through the darkness in a big Rolls-Royce. Now he had just finished hearing what the two men had to tell him.

"Those are the facts, M. Poirot," said Lord Mayfield.

He leaned back in his chair, and slowly fixed his monocle in one eye. Through it a shrewd, pale-blue eye watched Poirot attentively. Besides being shrewd the eye was definitely sceptical. Poirot cast a swift glance at Sir George Carrington.

That gentleman was leaning forward with an expression of almost childlike hopefulness on his face.

Poirot said slowly:

"I have the facts, yes. The maid screams, the secretary goes out, the nameless watcher comes in, the plans are there on top of the desk, he snatches them up and goes. The facts—they are all very convenient."

Something in the way he uttered the last phrase seemed to attract Lord Mayfield's attention. He sat up a little straighter, his monocle dropped. It was as though a new alertness came to him.

"I beg your pardon, M. Poirot?"

"I said, Lord Mayfield, that the facts were all very convenient—for the thief. By the way, you are sure it was a *man* you saw?"

Lord Mayfield shook his head.

"That I couldn't say. It was just a—shadow. In fact, I was almost doubtful if I had seen anyone."

Poirot transferred his gaze to the Air Marshal.

"And you, Sir George? Could you say if it was a man or a woman?"

"I didn't see anyone myself."

Poirot nodded thoughtfully. Then he skipped suddenly to his feet and went over to the writing-table.

"I can assure you that the plans are not there," said Lord Mayfield. "We have all three been through those papers half a dozen times."

"All three? You mean, your secretary also?"

"Yes, Carlile."

Poirot turned suddenly.

"Tell me, Lord Mayfield, which paper was on top when you went over to the desk?"

Mayfield frowned a little in the effort of remembrance.

"Let me see—yes, it was a rough memorandum of some sort of our air defence positions."

Deftly, Poirot nipped out a paper and brought it over.

"Is this the one, Lord Mayfield?"

Lord Mayfield took it and glanced over it.

"Yes, that's the one."

Poirot took it over to Carrington.

"Did you notice this paper on the desk?"

Sir George took it, held it away from him, then slipped on his pincenez.

"Yes, that's right. I looked through them too, with Carlile and Mayfield. This was on top."

Poirot nodded thoughtfully. He replaced the paper on the desk. Mayfield looked at him in a slightly puzzled manner.

"If there are any other questions—" he began.

"But yes, certainly there is a question. Carlile. Carlile is the question!"

Lord Mayfield's colour rose a little.

"Carlile, M. Poirot, is quite above suspicion! He has

been my confidential secretary for nine years. He has access to all my private papers, and I may point out to you that he could have made a copy of the plans and a tracing of the specifications quite easily without anyone being the wiser."

"I appreciate your point," said Poirot. "If he had been guilty there would be no need for him to stage a clumsy robbery."

"In any case," said Lord Mayfield, "I am sure of Carlile. I will guarantee him."

"Carlile," said Carrington gruffly, "is all right."

Poirot spread out his hands gracefully.

"And this Mrs Vanderlyn—she is all wrong?"

"She's a wrong 'un all right," said Sir George.

Lord Mayfield said in more measured tones:

"I think, M. Poirot, that there can be no doubt of Mrs Vanderlyn's—well—activities. The Foreign Office can give you more precious data as to that."

"And the maid, you take it, is in with her mistress?"

"Not a doubt of it," said Sir George.

"It seems to me a plausible assumption," said Lord Mayfield more cautiously.

There was a pause. Poirot sighed, and absent-mindedly rearranged one or two articles on a table at his right hand. Then he said:

"I take it that these papers represented money? That is, the stolen papers would be definitely worth a large sum in cash."

"If presented in a certain quarter—yes."

"Such as?"

Sir George mentioned the names of two European powers.

Poirot nodded.

"That fact would be known to anyone, I take it?"

"Mrs Vanderlyn would know it all right."

"I said to *anyone*?"

"I suppose so, yes."

"Anyone with a minimum of intelligence would appreciate the cash value of the plans?"

"Yes, but M. Poirot—" Lord Mayfield was looking rather uncomfortable.

Poirot held up a hand.

"I do what you call explore all the avenues."

Suddenly he rose again, stepped nimbly out of the window and with a flashlight examined the edge of the grass at the farther side of the terrace.

The two men watched him.

He came in again, sat down and said:

"Tell me, Lord Mayfield, this malefactor, this skulker in the shadows, you do not have him pursued?"

Lord Mayfield shrugged his shoulders.

"At the bottom of the garden he could make his way out to a main road. If he had a car waiting there, he would soon be out of reach—"

"But there are the police—the A.A. scouts—"

Sir George interrupted.

"You forget, M. Poirot. *We cannot risk publicity.* If it were to get out that these plans had been stolen, the result would be extremely unfavourable to the Party."

"Ah, yes," said Poirot. "One must remember *La Politique*. The great discretion must be observed. You send instead for me. Ah well, perhaps it is simpler."

"You are hopeful of success, M. Poirot?" Lord Mayfield sounded a trifle incredulous.

The little man shrugged his shoulders.

"Why not? One has only to reason—to reflect."

He paused a moment and then said:

"I would like now to speak to Mr Carlile."

"Certainly." Lord Mayfield rose. "I asked him to wait up. He will be somewhere at hand."

He went out of the room.

Poirot looked at Sir George.

"*Eh bien*," he said. "What about this man on the terrace?"

"My dear M. Poirot. Don't ask me! I didn't see him, and I can't describe him."

Poirot leaned forward.

"So you have already said. But it is a little different from that is it not?"

"What d'you mean?" asked Sir George abruptly.

"How shall I say it? Your disbelief, it is more profound."

Sir George started to speak, then stopped.

"But yes," said Poirot encouragingly. "Tell me. You are both at the end of the terrace. Lord Mayfield sees a shadow slip from the window and across the grass. Why do you not see that shadow?"

Carrington stared at him.

"You've hit it, M. Poirot. I've been worrying about that ever since. You see, I'd swear that no one did leave this window. I thought Mayfield had imagined it—branch of a tree waving—something of that kind. And then when we came in here and found there had been a robbery, it seemed as though Mayfield must have been right and I'd been wrong. And yet—"

Poirot smiled.

"And yet you still in your heart of hearts believe in the evidence (the negative evidence) of your own eyes?"

"You're right, M. Poirot, I do."

Poirot gave a sudden smile.

"How wise you are."

Sir George said sharply:

"There were no footprints on the grass edge?"

Poirot nodded.

"Exactly. Lord Mayfield, he fancies he sees a shadow.

Then there comes the robbery and he is sure—but sure! It is no longer a fancy—he actually *saw* the man. But that is not so. Me, I do not concern myself much with footprints and such things but for what it is worth we have that negative evidence. *There were no footprints on the grass.* It had rained heavily this evening. If a man had crossed the terrace to the grass this evening his footprints would have shown."

Sir George said, staring: "But then—but then—"

"It brings us back to the house. To the people in the house."

He broke off as the door opened and Lord Mayfield entered with Mr Carlile.

Though still looking very pale and worried, the secretary had regained a certain composure of manner. Adjusting his pince-nez he sat down and looked at Poirot inquiringly.

"How long had you been in this room when you heard the scream, monsieur?"

Carlile considered.

"Between five and ten minutes, I should say."

"And before that there had been no disturbance of any kind?"

"No."

"I understand that the house-party had been in one room for the greater part of the evening."

"Yes, the drawing-room."

Poirot consulted his notebook.

"Sir George Carrington and his wife. Mrs Macatta. Mrs Vanderlyn. Mr Reggie Carrington. Lord Mayfield and yourself. Is that right?"

"I myself was not in the drawing-room. I was working here the greater part of the evening."

Poirot turned to Lord Mayfield.

"Who went up to bed first?"

"Lady Julia Carrington, I think. As a matter of fact, the three ladies went out together."

"And then?"

"Mr Carlile came in and I told him to get out the papers as Sir George and I would be along in a minute."

"It was then that you decided to take a turn on the terrace?"

"It was."

"Was anything said in Mrs Vanderlyn's hearing as to your working in the study?"

"The matter was mentioned, yes."

"But she was not in the room when you instructed Mr Carlile to get out the papers?"

"No."

"Excuse me, Lord Mayfield," said Carlile. "Just after you had said that, I collided with her in the doorway. She had come back for a book."

"So you think she might have overheard?"

"I think it quite possible, yes."

"She came back for a book," mused Poirot. "Did you find her her book, Lord Mayfield?"

"Yes, Reggie gave it to her."

"Ah, yes, it is what you call the old gasp—no, pardon, the old wheeze—that—to come back for a book. It is often useful!"

"You think it was deliberate?"

Poirot shrugged his shoulders.

"And after that, you two gentlemen go out on the terrace. And Mrs Vanderlyn?"

"She went off with her book."

"And the young M. Reggie. He went to bed also?"

"Yes."

"And Mr Carlile he comes here and sometime between five and ten minutes later he heard a scream. Continue, M. Carlile. You heard a scream and you went out into the hall. Ah, perhaps it would be simplest if you reproduced exactly your actions."

Mr Carlile got up a little awkwardly.

"Here I scream," said Poirot helpfully. He opened his mouth and emitted a shrill bleat. Lord Mayfield turned his head away to hide a smile and Mr Carlile looked extremely uncomfortable.

"*Allez!* Forward! March!" cried Poirot. "It is your cue that I give you there."

Mr Carlile walked stiffly to the door, opened it and went out. Poirot followed him. The other two came behind.

"The door, did you close it after you or leave it open?"

"I can't really remember. I think I must have left it open."

"No matter. Proceed."

Still with extreme stiffness, Mr Carlile walked to the bottom of the staircase and stood there looking up.

Poirot said:

"The maid, you say, was on the stairs. Whereabouts?"

"About half-way up."

"And she was looking upset."

"Definitely so."

"*Eh bien*, me, I am the maid." Poirot ran nimbly up the stairs. "About here?"

"A step or two higher."

"Like this?"

Poirot struck an attitude.

"Well—er—not quite like that."

"How then?"

"Well, she had her hands to her head."

"Ah, her hands to her *head*. That is very interesting. Like this?" Poirot raised his arms, his hands rested on his head just above each ear.

"Yes that's it."

"Aha! And tell me, M. Carlile, she was a pretty girl—yes?"

"Really, I didn't notice."

Carlile's voice was repressive.

"Aha, you did not notice? But you are a young man. Does not a young man notice when a girl is pretty?"

"Really, M. Poirot, I can only repeat that *I* did not do so."

Carlile cast an agonized glance at his employer. Sir George Carrington gave a sudden chuckle.

"M. Poirot seems determined to make you out a dog, Carlile," he remarked.

"Me, I always notice when a girl is pretty," announced Poirot as he descended the stairs.

The silence with which Mr Carlile greeted this remark was somewhat pointed. Poirot went on:

"And it was then she told this tale of having seen a ghost?"

"Yes."

"Did you believe the story?"

"Well, hardly, M. Poirot!"

"I do not mean, do you believe in ghosts. I mean, did it strike you that the girl herself really thought she had seen something?"

"Oh, as to that, I couldn't say. She was certainly breathing fast and seemed upset."

"You did not see or hear anything of her mistress?"

"Yes, as a matter of fact I did. She came out of her room in the gallery above and called, 'Leonie.'"

"And then?"

"The girl ran up to her and I went back to the study."

"Whilst you were standing at the foot of the stairs here, could anyone have entered the study by the door you had left open?"

Carlile shook his head.

"Not without passing me. The study door is at the end of the passage, as you see."

Poirot nodded thoughtfully. Mr Carlile went on in his careful, precise voice.

"I may say that I am very thankful that Lord Mayfield actually saw the thief leaving the window. Otherwise I myself should be in a very unpleasant position."

"Nonsense, my dear Carlile," broke in Lord Mayfield impatiently. "No suspicion could possibly attach to you."

"It is very kind of you to say so, Lord Mayfield, but facts are facts, and I can quite see that it looks badly for me. In any case I hope that my belongings and myself may be searched."

"Nonsense, my dear fellow," said Mayfield.

Poirot murmured:

"You are serious in wishing that?"

"I should infinitely prefer it."

Poirot looked at him thoughtfully for a minute or two and murmured, "I see."

Then he asked:

"Where is Mrs Vanderlyn's room situated in regard to the study?"

"It is directly over it."

"With a window looking out over the terrace?"

"Yes."

Again Poirot nodded. Then he said:

"Let us go to the drawing-room."

Here he wandered round the room, examined the fastenings of the windows, glanced at the scorers on the bridge table and then finally addressed Lord Mayfield.

"This affair," he said, "is more complicated than it appears. But one thing is quite certain. The stolen plans have not left this house."

Lord Mayfield stared at him.

"But, my dear M. Poirot, the man I saw leaving the study—"

"There was no man."

"But I *saw* him—"

"With the greatest respect, Lord Mayfield, you imagined you saw him. The shadow cast by the branch of a tree deceived you. The fact that a robbery occurred naturally seemed a proof that what you had imagined was true."

"Really, M. Poirot, the evidence of my own eyes—"

"Back my eyes against yours any day, old boy," put in Sir George.

"You must permit me, Lord Mayfield, to be very definite on that point. *No one crossed the terrace to the grass.*"

Looking very pale and speaking stiffly, Mr Carlile said:

"In that case, if M. Poirot is correct, suspicion automatically attaches itself to me. I am the only person who could possibly have committed the robbery."

Lord Mayfield sprang up.

"Nonsense. Whatever M. Poirot thinks about it, I don't agree with him. I am convinced of your innocence, my dear Carlile. In fact, I'm willing to guarantee it."

Poirot murmured mildly:

"But I have not said that I suspect M. Carlile."

Carlile answered:

"No, but you've made it perfectly clear that no one else had a chance to commit the robbery."

"*Du tout! Du tout!*"

"But I have told you nobody passed me in the hall to get to the study door."

"I agree. But someone might have come in through the study *window.*"

"But that is just what you said did not happen?"

"I said that no one from *outside* could have come and

left without leaving marks on the grass. But it could have been managed from *inside* the house. Someone could have gone out from his room by one of these windows, slipped along the terrace, in at the study window, and back again in here."

Mr Carlile objected:

"But Lord Mayfield and Sir George Carrington were on the terrace."

"They were on the terrace, yes, but they were *en promenade.* Sir George Carrington's eyes may be of the most reliable"—Poirot made a little bow—"but he does not keep them in the back of his head! The study window is at the extreme left of the terrace, the windows of this room come next, but the terrace continues to the right past one, two, three, perhaps four rooms?"

"Dining-room, billiard-room, morning room and library," said Lord Mayfield.

"And you walked up and down the terrace, how many times?"

"At least five or six."

"You see, it is easy enough, the thief has only to watch for the right moment!"

Carlile said slowly:

"You mean that when I was in the hall, talking to the French girl, the thief was waiting in the drawing-room?"

"That is my suggestion. It is, of course, only a suggestion."

"It doesn't sound very probable to me," said Lord Mayfield. "Too risky."

The Air Marshal demurred.

"I don't agree with you, Charles. It's perfectly possible. Wonder I hadn't the wits to think of it for myself."

"So you see," said Poirot, "why I believe that the plans are still in the house. The problem now is to find them!"

Sir George snorted.

"That's simple enough. Search everybody."

Lord Mayfield made a movement of dissent, but Poirot spoke before he could.

"No, no, it is not so simple as that. The person who took those plans will anticipate that a search will be made and will make quite sure that they are not found amongst his or her belongings. They will have been hidden in neutral ground."

"Do you suggest that we've got to go playing hide and seek all over the bally house?"

Poirot smiled.

"No, no, we need not be so crude as that. We can arrive at the hiding-place (or alternatively at the identity of the guilty person) by reflection. That will simplify matters. In the morning I would like an interview with every person in the house. It would, I think, be unwise to seek those interviews now."

Lord Mayfield nodded.

"Cause too much comment," he said, "if we dragged everybody out of their beds at three in the morning. In any case you'll have to proceed with a good deal of camouflage, M. Poirot. This matter has got to be kept dark."

Poirot waved an airy hand.

"Leave it to Hercule Poirot. The lies I invent are always most delicate and most convincing. Tomorrow, then, I conduct my investigations. But tonight, I should like to begin by interviewing you, Sir George and you, Lord Mayfield."

He bowed to them both.

"You mean—alone?"

"That was my meaning."

Lord Mayfield raised his eyes slightly, then he said:

"Certainly. I'll leave you alone with Sir George. When you want me, you'll find me in my study. Come, Carlile."

He and the secretary went out, shutting the door behind them.

Sir George sat down, reaching mechanically for a cigarette. He turned a puzzled face to Poirot.

"You know," he said slowly. "I don't quite get this."

"That is very simply explained," said Poirot with a smile. "In two words, to be accurate. Mrs Vanderlyn!"

"Oh," said Carrington. "I think I see. Mrs Vanderlyn?"

"Precisely. It might be, you see, that it would not be very delicate to ask Lord Mayfield the question I want to ask. *Why* Mrs Vanderlyn? This lady, she is known to be a suspicious character. Why, then, should she be here? I say to myself there are three explanations. One, that Lord Mayfield has a *penchant* for the lady (and that is why I seek to talk to you alone. I do not wish to embarrass him). Two, that Mrs Vanderlyn is perhaps the dear friend of someone else in the house?"

"You can count me out!" said Sir George with a grin.

"Then, if neither of those cases is true, the question returns in redoubled force. *Why Mrs Vanderlyn?* And it seems to me I perceive a shadowy answer. There was a *reason*. Her presence at this particular juncture was definitely desired by Lord Mayfield for a special reason. Am I right?"

Sir George nodded.

"You're quite right," he said. "Mayfield is too old a bird to fall for her wiles. He wanted her here for quite another reason. It was like this."

He retailed the conversation that had taken place at the dinner-table. Poirot listened attentively.

"Ah," he said. "I comprehend now. Nevertheless, it seems that the lady has turned the tables on you both rather neatly!"

Sir George swore freely.

Poirot watched him with some slight amusement, then he said:

"You do not doubt that this theft is her doing—I mean, that she is responsible for it, whether or no she played an active part?"

Sir George stared.

"Of course not! There isn't any doubt of that. Why, who else would have any interest in stealing those plans?"

"Ah!" said Hercule Poirot. He leaned back and looked at the ceiling. "And yet, Sir George, we agreed, not a quarter of an hour ago, that these papers represented very definitely money. Not perhaps, in quite so obvious a form as banknotes, or gold, or jewellery, but nevertheless they were potential money. If there were anyone here who was hard up—"

The other interrupted him with a snort.

"Who isn't these days? I suppose I can say it without incriminating myself."

He smiled and Poirot smiled politely back at him and murmured:

"*Mais oui*, you can say what you like, for you, Sir George, have the one unimpeachable alibi in this affair."

"But I'm damned hard up myself!"

Poirot shook his head sadly.

"Yes, indeed, a man in your position has heavy living expenses. Then you have a young son at a most expensive age—"

Sir George groaned.

"Education's bad enough, then debts on top of it. Mind you, this lad's not a bad lad."

Poirot listened sympathetically. He heard a lot of the Air Marshal's accumulated grievances. The lack of grit and stamina in the younger generation, the fantastic way in which mothers spoilt their children and always took their side, the curse of gambling once it got hold of a woman, the folly of playing for higher stakes than you could afford. It was couched in general terms, Sir George did not allude directly to either his wife or his son, but his natural transparency made his generalizations very easy to see through.

He broke off suddenly.

"Sorry, mustn't take up your time with something that's right off the subject, especially at this hour of the night—or rather, morning."

He stifled a yawn.

"I suggest, Sir George, that you should go to bed. You have been most kind and helpful."

"Right, think I will turn in. You really think there is a chance of getting the plans back?"

Poirot shrugged his shoulders.

"I mean to try. I do not see why not."

"Well, I'll be off. Goodnight."

He left the room.

Poirot remained in his chair staring thoughtfully at the ceiling, then he took out a little notebook and turning to a clean page, he wrote:

> Mrs Vanderlyn?
> Lady Julia Carrington?
> Mrs Macatta?
> Reggie Carrington?
> Mr Carlile?

Underneath he wrote:

> Mrs Vanderlyn and Mr Reggie Carrington?
> Mrs Vanderlyn and Lady Julia?
> Mrs Vanderlyn and Mr Carlile?

He shook his head in a dissatisfied manner, murmuring:

"*C'est plus simple que ça.*"

Then he added a few short sentences.

Did Lord Mayfield see a "shadow?" If not, why did he say he did? Did Sir George see anything? He was positive he had seen nothing AFTER I examined flower-bed. Note: Lord Mayfield is near-sighted, can read without glasses but has to use a monocle to look across a room. Sir George is long-sighted. Therefore, from the far end of the terrace, his sight is more to be depended upon than Lord Mayfield's. Yet Lord Mayfield is very positive that he DID see something and is quite unshaken by his friend's denial.

Can anyone be quite as above suspicion as Mr Carlile appears to be? Lord Mayfield is very emphatic as to his innocence. Too much so. Why? Because he secretly suspects him and is ashamed of his suspicions? Or because he definitely suspects some other person? That is to say, some person OTHER than Mrs Vanderlyn?

He put the notebook away.

Then, getting up, he went along to the study.

Lord Mayfield was seated at his desk when Poirot entered the study. He swung round, laid down his pen, and looked up inquiringly.

"Well, M. Poirot, had your interview with Carrington?"

Poirot smiled and sat down.

"Yes, Lord Mayfield. He cleared up a point that had puzzled me."

"What was that?"

"The reason for Mrs Vanderlyn's presence here. You comprehend, I thought it possible—"

Mayfield was quick to realize the cause of Poirot's somewhat exaggerated embarrassment.

"You thought I had a weakness for the lady? Not at all. Far from it. Funnily enough, Carrington thought the same."

"Yes, he has told me of the conversation he held with you on the subject."

Lord Mayfield looked rather rueful.

"My little scheme didn't come off. Always annoying to have to admit that a woman has got the better of you."

"Ah, but she has not got the better of you *yet*, Lord Mayfield."

"You think we may yet win? Well, I'm glad to hear you say so. I'd like to think it was true."

He sighed.

"I feel I've acted like a complete fool—so pleased with my stratagem for entrapping the lady."

Hercule Poirot said, as he lit one of his tiny cigarettes:

"What *was* your stratagem exactly, Lord Mayfield?"

"Well," Lord Mayfield hesitated. "I hadn't exactly got down to details."

"You didn't discuss it with anyone?"

"No."

"Not even with Mr Carlile?"

"No."

Poirot smiled.

"You prefer to play a lone hand, Lord Mayfield."

"I have usually found it the best way," said the other a little grimly.

"Yes, you are wise. *Trust no one.* But you *did* mention the matter to Sir George Carrington?"

"Simply because I realized that the dear fellow was seriously perturbed about me."

Lord Mayfield smiled at the remembrance.

"He is an old friend of yours?"

"Yes. I have known him for over twenty years."

"And his wife?"

"I have known his wife also, of course."

"But (pardon me if I am impertinent) you are not on the same terms of intimacy with her?"

"I don't really see what my personal relationships to people has to do with the matter in hand, M. Poirot."

"But I think, Lord Mayfield, that they may have a good deal to do with it. You agreed, did you not, that my theory of someone in the drawing-room was a possible one?"

"Yes. In fact, I agree with you that that is what must have happened."

"We will not say 'must.' That is too self-confident a word. But if that theory of mine is true, who do you think the person in the drawing-room could have been?"

"Obviously Mrs Vanderlyn. She had been back there once for a book. She could have come back for another book, or a handbag, or a dropped handkerchief—one of a dozen feminine excuses. She arranges with her maid to scream and get Carlile away from the study. Then she slips in and out by the windows as you said."

"You forget it could not have been Mrs Vanderlyn. Carlile heard her call the maid from *upstairs* while he was talking to the girl."

Lord Mayfield bit his lip.

"True. I forgot that." He looked thoroughly annoyed.

"You see," said Poirot gently. "We progress. We have first the simple explanation of a thief who comes from *outside* and makes off with the booty. A very convenient theory as I said at the time, too convenient to be readily accepted. We have disposed of that. Then we come to the theory of the foreign agent, Mrs Vanderlyn, and that again seems to fit together beautifully up to a certain point. But now it looks as though that, too, was too easy—too convenient—to be accepted."

"You'd wash Mrs Vanderlyn out of it altogether?"

"It was not Mrs Vanderlyn in the drawing-room. It may have been an ally of Mrs Vanderlyn's who committed the theft, but it is just possible that it was committed by another person altogether. If so, we have to consider the question of motive."

"Isn't this rather far-fetched, M. Poirot?"

"I do not think so. Now what motives could there be? There is the motive of money. The papers may have been stolen with the object of turning them into cash. That is the simplest motive to consider. But the motive might possibly be something quite different."

"Such as—"

Poirot said slowly:

"It might have been done definitely with the idea of damaging someone."

"Who?"

"Possibly Mr Carlile. He would be the obvious suspect. But there might be more to it than that. The men who control the destiny of a country, Lord Mayfield, are particularly vulnerable to displays of popular feeling."

"Meaning that the theft was aimed at damaging *me*?"

Poirot nodded.

"I think I am correct in saying, Lord Mayfield, that about five years ago you passed through a somewhat trying time. You were suspected of friendship with a European Power at that time bitterly unpopular with the electorate of this country."

"Quite true, M. Poirot."

"A statesman in these days has a difficult task. He has to pursue the policy he deems advantageous to his country, but he has at the same time to recognize the force of popular feeling. Popular feeling is very often sentimental, muddle-headed, and eminently unsound, but it cannot be disregarded for all that."

"How well you express it! That is exactly the curse of a politician's life. He has to bow to the country's feeling, however dangerous and foolhardy he knows it to be."

"That was your dilemma, I think. There were rumours that you had concluded an agreement with the country in question. This country and the newspapers were up in arms about it. Fortunately the Prime Minister was able categorically to deny the story, and you repudiated it, though still making no secret of the way your sympathies lay."

"All this is quite true, M. Poirot, but why rake up past history?"

"Because I consider it possible that an enemy, disappointed in the way you surmounted that crisis, might endeavour to stage a further dilemma. You soon regained public confidence. Those particular circumstances have passed away, you are now, deservedly, one of the most popular figures in political life. You are spoken of freely as the next Prime Minister when Mr Hunberly retires."

"You think this is an attempt to discredit me? Nonsense!"

"*Tout de même*, Lord Mayfield, it would not look well if it were known that the plans of Britain's new bomber had been stolen during a weekend when a certain very charming lady had been your guest. Little hints in the newspapers as to your relationship with that lady would create a feeling of distrust in you."

"Such a thing could not really be taken seriously."

"My dear Lord Mayfield, you know perfectly well it could! It takes so little to undermine public confidence in a man."

"Yes, that's true," said Lord Mayfield. He looked suddenly very worried. "God! how desperately complicated this business is becoming. Do you really think—but it's impossible—impossible."

"You know of nobody who is—jealous of you?"

"Absurd!"

"At any rate you will admit that my questions about your personal relationships with the members of this house-party are not totally irrelevant."

"Oh, perhaps—perhaps. You asked me about Julia Carrington. There's really not very much to say. I've never taken to her very much, and I don't think she cares for me. She's one of these restless, nervy women, recklessly extravagant and mad about cards. She's old-fashioned enough, I think, to despise me as being a self-made man."

Poirot said:

"I looked you up in *Who's Who* before I came down. You were the head of a famous engineering firm and you are yourself a first-class engineer."

"There's certainly nothing I don't know about the practical side. I've worked my way up from the bottom."

Lord Mayfield spoke rather grimly.

"Oh la la!" cried Poirot. "I have been a fool—but a fool!"

The other stared at him.

"I beg your pardon, M. Poirot?"

"It is that a portion of the puzzle has become clear to me. Something I did not see before . . . But it all fits in. Yes—it fits in with beautiful precision."

Lord Mayfield looked at him in somewhat astonished inquiry.

But with a slight smile Poirot shook his head.

"No, no, not now. I must arrange my ideas a little more clearly."

He rose.

"Goodnight, Lord Mayfield. I think I know where those plans are."

Lord Mayfield cried out:

"You know? Then let us get hold of them at once!"

Poirot shook his head.

"No, no, that would not do. Precipitancy would be fatal. But leave it all to Hercule Poirot."

He went out of the room. Lord Mayfield raised his shoulders in contempt.

"Man's a mountebank," he muttered. Then, putting away his papers and turning out the lights, he, too, made his way up to bed.

"If there's been a burglary, why the devil doesn't old Mayfield send for the police?" demanded Reggie Carrington.

He pushed his chair slightly back from the breakfast table.

He was the last down. His host, Mrs Macatta and Sir George had finished their breakfasts some time before. His mother and Mrs Vanderlyn were breakfasting in bed.

Sir George, repeating his statement on the lines agreed upon between Lord Mayfield and Hercule Poirot, had a feeling that he was not managing it as well as he might have done.

"To send for a queer foreigner like this seems very odd to me," said Reggie. "What has been taken, Father?"

"I don't know exactly, my boy."

Reggie got up. He looked rather nervy and on edge this morning.

"Nothing—important? No—papers or anything like that?"

"To tell you the truth, Reggie, I can't tell you exactly."

"Very hush-hush, is it? I see."

Reggie ran up the stairs, paused for a moment halfway with a frown on his face, and then continued his ascent and tapped on his mother's door. Her voice bade him enter.

Lady Julia was sitting up in bed, scribbling figures on the back of an envelope.

"Good morning, darling." She looked up, then said sharply: "Reggie, is anything the matter?"

"Nothing much, but it seems there was a burglary last night."

"A burglary? What was taken?"

"Oh, I don't know. It's all very hush-hush. There's some odd kind of private-inquiry agent downstairs asking everybody questions."

"How extraordinary!"

"It's rather unpleasant," said Reggie slowly, "staying in a house when that kind of thing happens."

"What did happen exactly?"

"Don't know. It was some time after we all went to bed. Look out, Mother, you'll have that tray off."

He rescued the breakfast-tray and carried it to a table by the window.

"Was money taken?"

"I tell you I don't know."

Lady Julia said slowly:

"I suppose this inquiry man is asking everybody questions?"

"I suppose so."

"Where they were last night? All that kind of thing?"

"Probably. Well, I can't tell him much. I went straight up to bed and was asleep in next to no time."

Lady Julia did not answer.

"I say, Mother, I suppose you couldn't let me have a spot of cash. I'm absolutely broke."

"No, I couldn't," his mother replied decisively. "I've got the most frightful overdraft myself. I don't know what your father will say when he hears about it."

There was a tap at the door and Sir George entered.

"Ah, there you are, Reggie. Will you go down to the library? M. Hercule Poirot wants to see you."

Poirot had just concluded an interview with the redoubtable Mrs Macatta.

A few brief questions had elicited the information that Mrs Macatta had gone up to bed just before eleven, and had heard or seen nothing helpful.

Poirot slid gently from the topic of the burglary to more personal matters. He himself had a great admiration for Lord Mayfield. As a member of the general public he felt that Lord Mayfield was a truly great man. Of course, Mrs Macatta, being in the know, would have a far better means of estimating that than himself.

"Lord Mayfield has brains," allowed Mrs Macatta. "And he has carved his career out entirely for himself. He owes nothing to hereditary influence. He has a certain lack of vision, perhaps. In that I find all men sadly alike. They lack the breadth of a woman's imagination. Woman, M. Poirot, is going to be the great force in government in ten years' time."

Poirot said that he was sure of it.

He slid to the topic of Mrs Vanderlyn. Was it true, as he had heard hinted, that she and Lord Mayfield were very close friends?

"Not in the least. To tell you the truth I was very surprised to meet her here. Very surprised indeed."

Poirot invited Mrs Macatta's opinion of Mrs Vanderlyn—and got it.

"One of those absolutely *useless* women, M. Poirot. Women that make one despair of one's own sex! A parasite, first and last a parasite."

"Men admired her?"

"Men!" Mrs Macatta spoke the word with contempt. "Men are always taken in by those very obvious good looks. That boy, now, young Reggie Carrington, flushing up every time she spoke to him, absurdly flattered by being taken notice of by her. And the silly way she flattered him too. Praising his bridge—which actually was far from brilliant."

"He is not a good player?"

"He made all sorts of mistakes last night."

"Lady Julia is a good player, is she not?"

"Much *too* good in my opinion," said Mrs Macatta. "It's almost a profession with her. She plays morning, noon, and night."

"For high stakes?"

"Yes, indeed, much higher than I would care to play. Indeed I shouldn't consider it *right*."

"She makes a good deal of money at the game?" Mrs Macatta gave a loud and virtuous snort.

"She reckons on paying her debts that way. But she's been having a run of bad luck lately, so I've heard. She looked last night as though she had something on her mind. The evils of gambling, M. Poirot, are only slightly less than the evils caused by drink. If I had my way this country should be purified—"

Poirot was forced to listen to a somewhat lengthy discussion on the purification of England's morals. Then he closed the conversation adroitly and sent for Reggie Carrington.

He summed the young man up carefully as he entered the room, the weak mouth camouflaged by the rather charming smile, the indecisive chin, the eyes set far apart, the rather narrow head. He thought that he knew Reggie Carrington's type fairly well.

"Mr Reggie Carrington?"

"Yes. Anything I can do?"

"Just tell me what you can about last night?"

"Well, let me see, we played bridge—in the drawing-room. After that I went up to bed."

"That was at what time?"

"Just before eleven. I suppose the robbery took place after that?"

"Yes, after that. You did not hear or see anything?"

Reggie shook his head regretfully.

"I'm afraid not. I went straight to bed and I sleep pretty soundly."

"You went straight up from the drawing-room to your bedroom and remained there until the morning?"

"That's right."

"Curious," said Poirot.

Reggie said sharply:

"What do you mean, curious?"

"You did not, for instance, hear a scream?"

"No, I didn't."

"Ah, very curious."

"Look here, I don't know what you mean."

"You are, perhaps, slightly deaf?"

"Certainly not."

Poirot's lips moved. It was possible that he was repeating the word curious for the third time. Then he said:

"Well, thank you, Mr Carrington, that is all."

Reggie got up and stood rather irresolutely.

"You know," he said, "now you come to mention it, I believe I did hear something of the kind."

"Ah, you did hear something?"

"Yes, but you see, I was reading a book—a detective story as a matter of fact—and I—well, I didn't really quite take it in."

"Ah," said Poirot, "a most satisfying explanation."

His face was quite impassive.

Reggie still hesitated, then he turned and walked slowly to the door. There he paused and asked:

"I say, what was stolen?"

"Something of great value, Mr Carrington. That is all I am at liberty to say."

"Oh," said Reggie rather blankly.

He went out.

Poirot nodded his head.

"It fits," he murmured. "It fits very nicely."

He touched a bell and inquired courteously if Mrs Vanderlyn was up yet.

Mrs Vanderlyn swept into the room looking very handsome. She was wearing an artfully-cut russet sports-suit that showed up the warm lights of her hair. She swept to a chair and smiled in a dazzling fashion at the little man in front of her.

For a moment something showed through the smile. It might have been triumph, it might almost have been mockery. It was gone almost immediately, but it had been there. Poirot found the suggestion of it interesting.

"Burglars? Last night? But how dreadful! Why no, I never heard a *thing*. What about the police? Can't they *do* anything?"

Again, just for a moment, the mockery showed in her eyes.

Hercule Poirot thought:

"It is very clear that *you* are not afraid of the police, my lady. You know very well that they are not going to be called in."

And from that followed—what?

He said soberly:

"You comprehend, madame, it is an affair of the most discreet."

"Why, naturally, M.—Poirot—isn't it?—I shouldn't dream of breathing a word. I'm much too great an admirer of dear Lord Mayfield's to do anything to cause him the least little bit of worry."

She crossed her knees. A highly-polished slipper of brown leather dangled on the tip of her silk-shod foot.

She smiled, a warm, compelling smile of perfect health and deep satisfaction.

"Do tell me if there's anything at all I can do?"

"I thank you, madame. You played bridge in the drawing-room last night?"

"Yes."

"I understand that then all the ladies went up to bed?"

"That is right."

"But someone came back to fetch a book. That was you, was it not, Mrs Vanderlyn?"

"I was the first one to come back—yes."

"What do you mean—the *first* one?" said Poirot sharply.

"I came back right away," explained Mrs Vanderlyn. "Then I went up and rang for my maid. She was a long time in coming. I rang again. Then I went out on the landing. I heard her voice and I called her. After she had brushed my hair I sent her away, she was in a nervous, upset state and tangled the brush in my hair once or twice. It was then, just as I sent her away, that I saw Lady Julia coming up the stairs. She told me she had been down again for a book, too. Curious, wasn't it?"

Mrs Vanderlyn smiled as she finished, a wide, rather feline smile. Hercule Poirot thought to himself that Mrs Vanderlyn did not like Lady Julia Carrington.

"As you say, madame. Tell me, did you hear your maid scream?"

"Why, yes, I did hear something of that kind."

"Did you ask her about it?"

"Yes. She told me she thought she had seen a floating figure in white—such nonsense!"

"What was Lady Julia wearing last night?"

"Oh, you think perhaps—Yes, I see. She *was* wearing a white evening-dress. Of course, that explains it. She must have caught sight of her in the darkness just as a white figure. These girls are so superstitious."

"Your maid has been with you a long time, madame?"

"Oh, no." Mrs Vanderlyn opened her eyes rather wide. "Only about five months."

"I should like to see her presently, if you do not mind, madame."

Mrs Vanderlyn raised her eyebrows.

"Oh, certainly," she said rather coldly.

"I should like, you understand, to question her."

"Oh, yes."

Again a flicker of amusement.

Poirot rose and bowed.

"Madame," he said. "You have my complete admiration."

Mrs Vanderlyn for once seemed a trifle taken aback.

"Oh, M. Poirot, how nice of you, but why?"

"You are, madame, so perfectly armoured, so completely sure of yourself."

Mrs Vanderlyn laughed a little uncertainly.

"Now I wonder," she said, "if I am to take that as a compliment?"

Poirot said:

"It is, perhaps, a warning—not to treat life with arrogance."

Mrs Vanderlyn laughed with more assurance. She got up and held out a hand.

"Dear M. Poirot, I do wish you all success. Thank you for all the charming things you have said to me."

She went out. Poirot murmured to himself:

"You wish me success, do you? Ah, but you are very sure I am not going to meet with success! Yes, you are very sure indeed. That, it annoys me very much."

With a certain petulance, he pulled the bell and asked that Mademoiselle Leonie might be sent to him.

His eyes roamed over her appreciatively as she stood hesitating in the doorway, demure in her black dress with her neatly-parted black waves of hair and her modestly-dropped eyelids. He nodded slow approval.

"Come in, Mademoiselle Leonie," he said. "Do not be afraid."

She came in and stood demurely before him.

"Do you know," said Poirot with a sudden change of tone, "that I find you very good to look at."

Leonie responded promptly. She flashed him a glance out of the corner of her eyes and murmured softly:

"Monsieur is very kind."

"Figure to yourself," said Poirot. "I demand of M. Carlile whether you are or not good-looking and he replies that he does not know!"

Leonie cocked her chin up contemptuously.

"That image!"

"That describes him very well."

"I do not believe he has ever looked at a girl in his life, that one."

"Probably not. A pity. He has missed a lot. But there are others in this house who are more appreciative, is it not so?"

"Really, I do not know what monsieur means."

"Oh, yes, Mademoiselle Leonie, you know very well. A pretty history that you recount last night about a ghost that you have seen. As soon as I hear that you are standing there with your hands to your head, I know very well that there is no question of ghosts. If a girl is frightened she clasps her heart, or she raises her hands to her mouth to stifle a cry, but if her hands are on her hair it means something very different. *It means that her hair has been ruffled and that she is hastily getting it into shape again!* Now then, mademoiselle, let us have the truth. Why did you scream on the stairs?"

"But monsieur it is true, I saw a tall figure all in white—"

"Mademoiselle, do not insult my intelligence. That story, it may have been good enough for M. Carlile, but it is not good enough for Hercule Poirot. The truth is that you had just been kissed, is it not so? And I will make a guess that it was M. Reggie Carrington who kissed you."

Leonie twinkled an unabashed eye at him.

"*Eh bien*," she demanded, "after all, what is a kiss?"

"What, indeed?" said Poirot gallantly.

"You see, the young gentleman he came up behind me and caught me round the waist—and so naturally he startled me and I screamed. If I had known—well, then naturally I would not have screamed."

"Naturally," agreed Poirot.

"But he came upon me like a cat. Then the study door opened and out came M. le secrétaire and the young gentleman slipped away upstairs and there I was looking like a fool. Naturally I had to say something—especially to—" she broke into French, "*un jeune homme comme ça, tellement comme il faut!*"

"So you invent a ghost?"

"Indeed, monsieur, it was all I could think of. A tall figure all in white, that floated. It is ridiculous but what else could I do?"

"Nothing. So now, all is explained. I had my suspicions from the first."

Leonie shot him a provocative glance.

"Monsieur is very clever, and very sympathetic."

"And since I am not going to make you any embarrassments over the affair you will do something for me in return?"

"Most willingly, monsieur."

"How much do you know of your mistress's affairs?"

The girl shrugged her shoulders.

"Not very much, monsieur. I have my ideas, of course."

"And those ideas?"

"Well, it does not escape me that the friends of madame are always soldiers or sailors or airmen. And then there are other friends—foreign gentlemen who come to see her very quietly sometimes. Madame is very handsome, though I do not think she will be so much longer. The young men, they find her very attractive. Sometimes I think, they say too much. But it is only my idea, that. Madame does not confide in me."

"What you would have me to understand is that madame plays a lone hand?"

"That is right, monsieur."

"In other words, you cannot help me."

"I fear not, monsieur. I would do if I could."

"Tell me, your mistress is in a good mood today?"

"Decidedly, monsieur."

"Something has happened to please her?"

"She has been in good spirits ever since she came here."

"Well, Leonie, you should know."

The girl answered confidently:

"Yes, monsieur. I could not be mistaken there. I know all madame's moods. She is in high spirits."

"Positively triumphant?"

"That is exactly the word, monsieur."

Poirot nodded gloomily.

"I find that—a little hard to bear. Yet I perceive that it is inevitable. Thank you, mademoiselle, that is all."

Leonie threw him a coquettish glance.

"Thank you, monsieur. If I meet monsieur on the stairs, be well assured that I shall not scream."

"My child," said Poirot with dignity. "I am of advanced years. What have I to do with such frivolities?"

But with a little twitter of laughter, Leonie took herself off.

Poirot paced slowly up and down the room. His face became grave and anxious.

"And now," he said at last, "for Lady Julia. What will she say, I wonder?"

Lady Julia came into the room with a quiet air of assurance. She bent her head graciously, accepted the chair that Poirot drew forward and spoke in a low, well-bred voice.

"Lord Mayfield says that you wish to ask me some questions."

"Yes, madame. It is about last night."

"About last night, yes?"

"What happened after you had finished your game of bridge?"

"My husband thought it was too late to begin another. I went up to bed."

"And then?"

"I went to sleep."

"That is all?"

"Yes. I'm afraid I can't tell you anything of much interest. When did this"—she hesitated—"burglary occur?"

"Very soon after you went upstairs."

"I see. And what exactly was taken?"

"Some private papers, madame."

"Important papers?"

"Very important."

She frowned a little and then said:

"They were—valuable?"

"Yes, madame, they were worth a good deal of money."

"I see."

There was a pause, and then Poirot said:

"What about your book, madame?"

"My book?" She raised bewildered eyes to him.

"Yes, I understand Mrs Vanderlyn to say that some time after you three ladies had retired you went down again to fetch a book."

"Yes, of course, so I did."

"So that, as a matter of fact, you did *not* go straight to bed when you went upstairs? You returned to the drawing-room?"

"Yes, that is true. I had forgotten."

"While you were in the drawing-room, did you hear someone scream?"

"No—yes—I don't think so."

"Surely, madame. You could not have failed to hear it in the drawing-room."

Lady Julia flung her head back and said firmly:

"I heard nothing."

Poirot raised his eyebrows, but did not reply.

The silence grew uncomfortable. Lady Julia asked abruptly:

"What is being done?"

"Being done? I do not understand you, madame."

"I mean about the robbery. Surely the police must be doing something."

Poirot shook his head.

"The police have not been called in. I am in charge."

She stared at him, her restless haggard face sharpened and tense. Her eyes, dark and searching, sought to pierce his impassivity.

They fell at last—defeated.

"You cannot tell me what is being done?"

"I can only assure you, madame, that I am leaving no stone unturned."

"To catch the thief—or to—recover the papers?"

"The recovery of the papers is the main thing, madame."

Her manner changed. It became bored, listless.

"Yes," she said indifferently. "I suppose it is."

There was another pause.

"Is there anything else, M. Poirot?"

"No, madame. I will not detain you further."

"Thank you."

He opened the door for her. She passed out without glancing at him.

Poirot went back to the fireplace and carefully rearranged the ornaments on the mantelpiece. He was still at it when Lord Mayfield came in through the window.

"Well?" said the latter.

"Very well, I think. Events are shaping themselves as they should."

Lord Mayfield said, staring at him:

"You are pleased."

"No, I am not pleased. But I am content."

"Really, M. Poirot, I cannot make you out."

"I am not such a charlatan as you think."

"I never said—"

"No, but you *thought*! No matter. I am not offended. It is sometimes necessary for me to adopt a certain pose."

Lord Mayfield looked at him doubtfully with a certain amount of distrust. Hercule Poirot was a man he did not understand. He wanted to despise him, but something warned him that this ridiculous little man was not so futile as he appeared. Charles McLaughlin had always been able to recognize capability when he saw it.

"Well," he said, "we are in your hands. What do you advise next?"

"Can you get rid of your guests?"

"I think it might be arranged . . . I could explain that I have to go to London over this affair. They will then probably offer to leave."

"Very good. Try and arrange it like that."

Lord Mayfield hesitated.

"You don't think—?"

"I am quite sure that that would be the wise course to take."

Lord Mayfield shrugged his shoulders.

"Well, if you say so."

He went out.

The guests left after lunch. Mrs Vanderlyn and Mrs Macatta went by train, the Carringtons had their car. Poirot was standing in the hall as Mrs Vanderlyn bade her host a charming farewell.

"So terribly sorry for you having this bother and anxiety. I do hope it will turn out all right for you. I shan't breathe a word of anything."

She pressed his hand and went out to where the Rolls was waiting to take her to the station. Mrs Macatta was already inside. Her adieu had been curt and unsympathetic.

Suddenly Leonie, who had been getting in front with the chauffeur, came running back into the hall.

"The dressing-case of madame, it is not in the car," she exclaimed.

There was a hurried search. At last Lord Mayfield discovered it where it had been put down in the shadow of an old oak chest. Leonie uttered a glad little cry as she seized the elegant affair of green morocco, and hurried out with it.

Then Mrs Vanderlyn leaned out of the car.

"Lord Mayfield, Lord Mayfield." She handed him a letter. "Would you mind putting this in your post-bag? If I keep it meaning to post it in town, I'm sure to forget. Letters just stay in my bag for days."

Sir George Carrington was fidgeting with his watch, opening and shutting it. He was a maniac for punctuality.

"They're cutting it fine," he murmured. "Very fine. Unless they're careful, they'll miss the train—"

His wife said irritably:

"Oh, don't fuss, George. After all, it's their train, not ours!"

He looked at her reproachfully.

The Rolls drove off.

Reggie drew up at the front door in the Carringtons' Morris.

"All ready, Father," he said.

The servants began bringing out the Carringtons' luggage. Reggie supervised its disposal in the dickey.

Poirot moved out of the front door, watching the proceedings.

Suddenly he felt a hand on his arm. Lady Julia's voice spoke in an agitated whisper.

"M. Poirot. I must speak to you—at once."

He yielded to her insistent hand. She drew him into a small morning-room and closed the door. She came close to him.

"Is it true what you said—that the discovery of the papers is what matters most to Lord Mayfield?"

Poirot looked at her curiously.

"It is quite true, madame."

"If—if those papers were returned to you, would you undertake that they should be given back to Mayfield, and no questions asked?"

"I am not sure that I understand you."

"You must! I am sure that you do! I am suggesting that the—the thief should remain anonymous if the papers are returned."

Poirot asked:

"How soon would that be, madame?"

"Definitely within twelve hours."

"You can promise that?"

"I can promise it."

As he did not answer, she repeated urgently:

"Will you guarantee that there will be no publicity?"

He answered then—very gravely:

"Yes, madame, I will guarantee that."

"Then everything can be arranged."

She passed abruptly from the room. A moment later Poirot heard the car drive away.

He crossed the hall and went along the passage to the study. Lord Mayfield was there. He looked up as Poirot entered.

"Well?" he said.

Poirot spread out his hands.

"The case is ended, Lord Mayfield."

"What?"

Poirot repeated word for word the scene between himself and Lady Julia.

Lord Mayfield looked at him with a stupefied expression.

"But what does it mean? I don't understand."

"It is very clear, is it not? Lady Julia knows who stole the plans."

"You don't mean she took them herself?"

"Certainly not. Lady Julia may be a gambler. She is not a thief. But if she offers to return the plans, it means that they were taken by her husband or her son. Now Sir George Carrington was out on the terrace with you. That leaves us the son. I think I can reconstruct the happenings of last night fairly accurately. Lady Julia went to her son's room last night and found it empty. She came downstairs to look for him, but did not find him. This morning she hears of the theft, and she also hears that her son declares that he went straight to his room *and never left it*. That, she knows, is not true. And she knows something else about her son. She knows that he is weak, that he is desperately hard-up for money. She has observed his infatuation for Mrs Vanderlyn. The whole thing is clear to her. Mrs Vanderlyn has persuaded Reggie to steal the plans. But she determines to play her part also. She will tackle Reggie, get hold of the papers and return them."

"But the whole thing is quite impossible," cried Lord Mayfield.

"Yes, it is impossible, but Lady Julia does not know that. She does not know what I, Hercule Poirot, know, that young Reggie Carrington was not stealing papers last night, but instead was philandering with Mrs Vanderlyn's French maid."

"The whole thing is a mare's nest!"

"Exactly."

"And the case is not ended at all!"

"Yes, it is ended. *I, Hercule Poirot, know the truth*. You do not believe me? You did not believe me yesterday when I said I knew where the plans were. But I did know. They were very close at hand."

"Where?"

"They were in your pocket, my lord."

There was a pause, then Lord Mayfield said:

"Do you really know what you are saying, M. Poirot?"

"Yes, I know. I know that I am speaking to a very clever man. From the first it worried me that you, who were admittedly short-sighted, should be so positive about the figure you had seen leaving the window. You wanted that solution—the convenient solution—to be accepted. Why? Later, one by one, I eliminated everyone else. Mrs Vanderlyn was upstairs, Sir George was with you on the terrace, Reggie Carrington was with the French girl on the stairs, Mrs Macatta was blamelessly in her bedroom. (It is next to the housekeeper's room, and Mrs Macatta snores!) Lady Julia clearly believed her son guilty. So there remained only two possibilities. Either Carlile did not put the papers on the desk but into his own pocket (and that is not reasonable, because, as you pointed out, he could have taken a tracing of them), or else—or else the plans were there when you walked over to the desk, and the only place they could have gone was into *your* pocket. In that case everything was clear. Your insistence on the figure you had seen, your insistence on Carlile's innocence, your disinclination to have me summoned.

"One thing did puzzle me—the motive. You were, I was convinced, an honest man, a man of integrity. That showed in your anxiety that no innocent person should be suspected. It was also obvious that the theft of the plans might easily affect your career unfavourably. Why, then, this wholly unreasonable theft? And at last the answer came to me. The crisis in your career, some years ago, the assurances given to the world by the Prime Minister that you had had no negotiations with the power in question. Suppose that that was not strictly true, that there remained some record—a letter, perhaps—showing that in actual fact you *had* done what you had publicly denied. Such a denial was necessary in the interests of public policy. But it is doubtful if the man in the street would see it that way. It might mean that at the moment when supreme power might be given into your hands, some stupid echo from the past would undo everything.

"I suspect that that letter has been preserved in the hands of a certain government, that that government offered to trade with you—the letter in exchange for the plans of the new bomber. Some men would have refused. You—did not! You agreed. Mrs Vanderlyn was the agent in the matter. She came here by arrangement to make the exchange. You gave yourself away when you admitted that you had formed no definite stratagem for entrapping her. That admission made your reason for inviting her here incredibly weak.

"You arranged the robbery. Pretended to see the thief on the terrace—thereby clearing Carlile of suspicion. Even if he had not left the room, the desk was so near the window that a thief might have taken the plans while Carlile was busy at the safe with his back turned. You walked over to the desk, took the plans and kept them on your own person until the moment when, by prearranged plan, you slipped them into Mrs Vanderlyn's dressing-case. In return she handed you the fatal letter disguised as an unposted letter of her own."

Poirot stopped.

Lord Mayfield said:

"Your knowledge is very complete, M. Poirot. You must think me an unutterable skunk."

Poirot made a quick gesture.

"No, no, Lord Mayfield. I think, as I said, that you are a very clever man. It came to me suddenly as we talked here last night. You are a first-class engineer. There will be, I think, some subtle alterations in the specifications of that bomber, alterations done so skilfully that it will be difficult to grasp why the machine is not the success it ought to be. A certain foreign power will find the type a failure . . . It will be a disappointment to them, I am sure . . ."

Again there was a silence—then Lord Mayfield said:

"You are much too clever, M. Poirot. I will only ask you to believe one thing. I have faith in myself. I believe that I am the man to guide England through the days of crisis that I see coming. If I did not honestly believe that I am needed by my country to steer the ship of state, I would not have done what I have done—made the best of both worlds—saved myself from disaster by a clever trick."

"My lord," said Poirot, "if you could not make the best of both worlds, you could not be a politician!"

BIBLIOGRAPHY

Agatha Christie's short stories typically appeared first in magazines and then in her short story books, which tended to be different collections in the UK and the US. This list attempts to catalogue the first publication of each, and gives alternative story titles when used.

Summer in the Pyrenees

Excerpted from *An Autobiography* (1977).

The Blood-Stained Pavement

First published in the UK in *Royal Magazine* No. 353, March 1928, and in the US as "Drip! Drip!" in *Detective Story Magazine*, 23 June 1928. Reprinted in *The Thirteen Problems* (UK, 1932) and *The Tuesday Night Club* (US, 1933).

The Double Clue

First published in the UK in *The Sketch* No. 1610, 5 December 1923, and in the US in *Blue Book Magazine* Vol. 41, No. 4, August 1925. Reprinted in *Poirot's Early Cases* (UK, 1974) and *Double Sin* (US, 1961).

Death on the Nile

First published in the UK in *Nash's Pall Mall* Vol. 91, No. 482, July 1933, and in the US in *Cosmopolitan*, April 1933. Reprinted in *Parker Pyne Investigates* (UK, 1934) and *Mr Parker Pyne, Detective* (US, 1934).

Harlequin's Lane

First published in the UK in *Storyteller* No. 241, May 1927, and in the US in *The Magic of Mr Quin* No. 5, May 1927. Reprinted in *The Mysterious Mr Quin* (1930).

The Adventure of the Italian Nobleman

First published in the UK in *The Sketch* No. 1604, 24 October 1923, and in the US as "The Italian Nobleman' in *Blue Book Magazine* Vol. 40, No. 2, December 1924. Reprinted in *Poirot Investigates* (UK, 1924; US, 1925).

Jane in Search of a Job

First published in the UK in *Grand Magazine* No. 234, August 1924. Reprinted in *The Listerdale Mystery* (UK, 1934) and *The Golden Ball* (US, 1971).

The Disappearance of Mr Davenheim

First published in the UK in *The Sketch* No. 1574, 28 March 1923, and in the US as "Mr Davenby Disappears' in *Blue Book Magazine* Vol. 38, No. 2, December 1923. Reprinted in *Poirot Investigates* (UK, 1924; US, 1925).

The Idol House of Astarte

First published in the UK in *Royal Magazine* No. 351, January 1928, and in the US as "The Solving Six and the Evil Hour' in *Detective Story Magazine*, 9 June 1928. Reprinted in *The Thirteen Problems* (UK, 1932) and *The Tuesday Night Club* (US, 1933).

The Rajah's Emerald

First published in the UK in *Red Magazine*, 30 July 1926. Reprinted in *The Listerdale Mystery* (UK, 1934) and *The Golden Ball* (US, 1971).

The Oracle at Delphi

First published in the UK in *Nash's Pall Mall* Vol. 91, No. 482, July 1933, and in the US in *Cosmopolitan*, April 1933. Reprinted in *Parker Pyne Investigates* (UK, 1934) and *Mr Parker Pyne, Detective* (US, 1934).

The Adventure of the Sinister Stranger

First published in the UK in *The Sketch* No. 1656, 22 October 1924. Reprinted in *Partners in Crime* (1929).

The Incredible Theft

First published in the UK as "The Submarine Plans," 1923, and later expanded in the *Daily Express*, 6–12 April 1937. Reprinted as *Murder in the Mews* (UK, 1937) and *Dead Man's Mirror* (US, 1937).